MOUNTAIN SHADOWS

NICOLE GARDNER

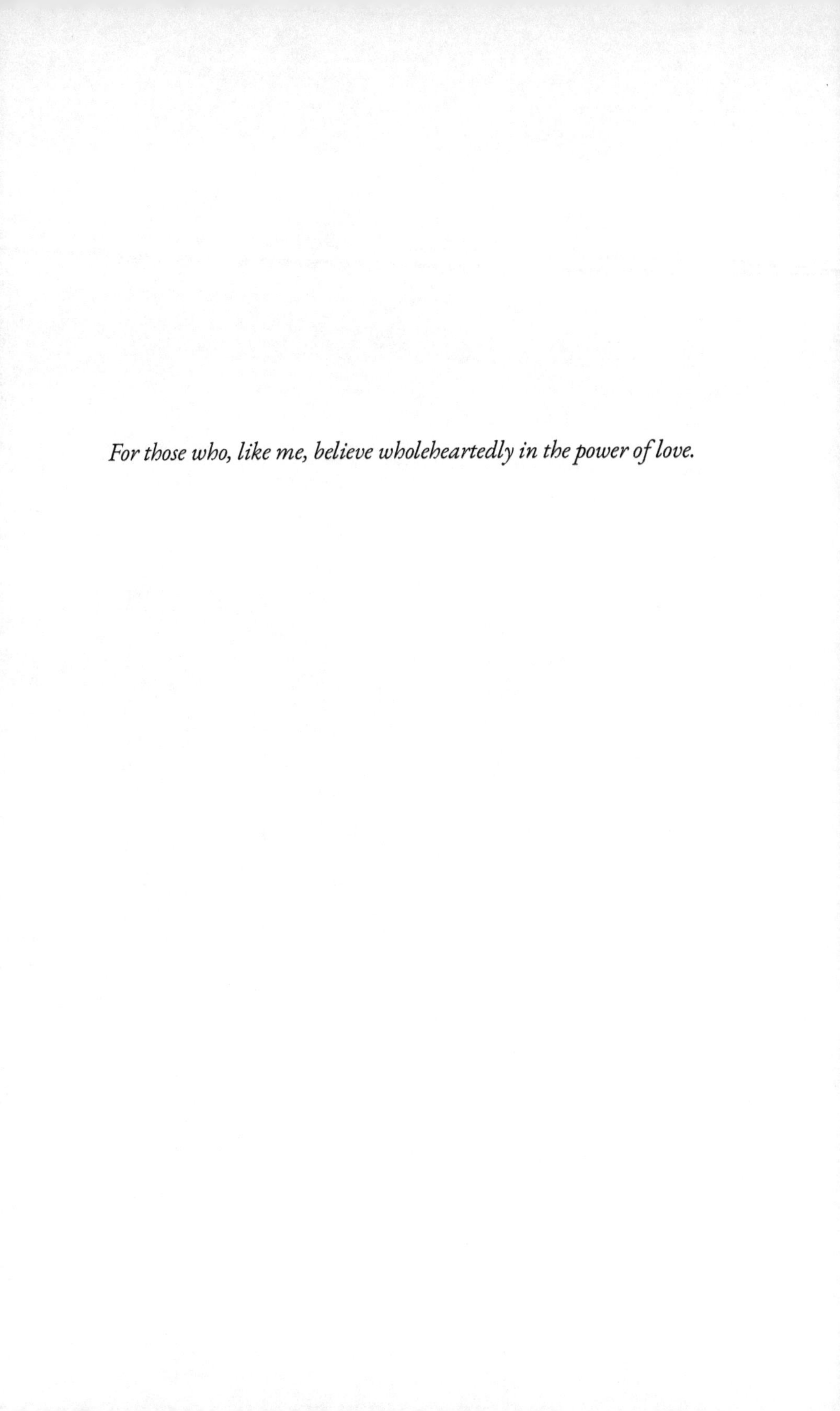

For those who, like me, believe wholeheartedly in the power of love.

Chapter One

Janet

I glanced at the clock on my dashboard as I parked my car on the street in front of a run-down little house in Rosemary Mountain. Seventeen minutes late. As if I weren't already nervous enough about today.

I turned my eyes toward the little house and let out a groan. This was just like Daphne, rushing into something instead of taking time to do it properly. We should have been meeting in Asheville, at one of the adorable bridal boutiques I had found online. But no, Daphne insisted this new friend of hers could make her dress. My jaw clenched, just thinking of it. My only daughter, wearing a homemade wedding dress! I leaned my head back and tried to channel some inner patience, reminding myself that it was her day, not mine. If she wanted a homemade wedding dress, then—but no. It would never do.

I would just have to talk some sense into her.

Eighteen minutes late now. I grabbed my handbag and stepped out of the car, wishing I had worn something other than my trademark stilettos. Rosemary Mountain wasn't made for shoes like this. I winced as I attempted to navigate the gravel driveway; then I gave up and traded the driveway for the grass, wincing again as I felt my heels sink into the dirt with each step.

These shoes would never be the same again.

I made it up to the doorway, hesitating briefly before knocking. This appeared to be the right place. Daphne's car was in the driveway, along with Fiona's antique truck. But I couldn't imagine that whoever lived *here* knew anything about sewing a wedding gown.

I was calculating the odds of being able to get a proper gown delivered and altered at such short notice when the door flew open, revealing a young woman in a crop top and pencil pants, with a mess of brown hair piled high on her head. Her whole face lit up when she saw me.

"You must be Janet! Come on in. We've been waiting for you!"

I plastered a fake smile on my face. "You must be Willa. The, um, *dressmaker.*"

"That's right," she said. Her eyes sparkled.

"Nice to meet you."

She just grinned. "Uh, huh," she said, opening the door wider for me to come inside.

I stepped into the doorway and surveyed the little house. It was clean at least. Even cute, in its own way, if you were into that Bohemian-type thing. *Shabby chic,* they used to call it. She had style, but it was a far cry from a bridal boutique in Asheville.

I should have made some calls before coming in, even if it would have pushed back my arrival time and made me later than I already was.

"Mom! You're here!" Daphne waved from the kitchen, where she was busy pinning her hair up in a twist. She quickly stuck the last two pins in the back and came to me.

My heart dropped as I watched her altered walk.

I hugged her tightly, then pulled back, my hands still on her shoulders. "Daphne, you're still limping," I said quietly, hoping the others didn't hear. "I thought you said you had fully recovered."

"I'm fine," she said, waving it off. "It's getting better every day. I'll be back to normal in no time."

"Yes, but we could put this off," I whispered as I glanced at Fiona and Willa chatting in the kitchen. I realized Abby, Daphne's best friend from college, was there too. I hadn't realized she was driving in so soon.

"Emerson won't mind," I continued. "A few more weeks and you'll be completely recovered. Plus, that will give us more time to prepare…" *And find a proper gown.*

"No," Daphne said, shaking her head. Her face was set in a firm line, one I recognized.

I sighed, knowing I wouldn't win this one, but I still had to try. "What's the rush?" I asked. "It's only been three months since he proposed, for goodness' sakes! Normal engagements last a year at least, maybe even two. Why not stretch it out, really enjoy it, and plan something more formal? Unless…" I turned my gaze down to her thin waist, wondering if there was something I didn't know.

She shook her head and gave me an amused smile. "No, Mom, we're not rushing because of anything like that." Her face turned serious. "If there's one thing I've learned over the past year, it's that none of us are guaranteed tomorrow. Life is short. Sometimes shorter than you can ever imagine. We were lucky enough to find each other, luckier still to survive everything we went through. We don't want to wait. We want to live the rest of our lives as husband and wife, and we're not putting it off for a year."

"Daphne," I said, lowering my voice even more, as I glanced to make sure Willa was still occupied in the kitchen. "A limping bride *and* a homemade dress? What will people think?"

Daphne just laughed again. "Yes, a limping bride. It's barely noticeable though, and if I don't care, why do you? Besides, I think you'll be surprised by the dress."

My face flushed with embarrassment, as she hadn't bothered to lower her voice. Willa looked up and exchanged amused smiles with Daphne.

"That's right, Janet," Willa called from the kitchen, her voice full of laughter. "In fact, you may just decide to let me make your own wedding gown someday!"

"I'm sure you do beautiful work," I said tightly, plastering another fake smile on my face. "But as I have no intention of ever marrying again, I can assure you you'll never be making a wedding gown for me."

"Don't be so quick to say never," Daphne said, her eyes twinkling. "You might change your mind after you see Greg in a tux. I'm going to get changed so you can see the magic Willa works." She threw me a wink, then linked arms with Willa and headed down the hallway.

Greg Morrison in a tux.

I blinked quickly, feeling pure embarrassment as I wondered if Daphne had recognized my long-held attraction to Greg, the county sheriff. The same sheriff who had *arrested* her after basically accusing her of murder. That alone had to make him off-limits. Didn't it?

Even though common sense told me he was off-limits, he had fascinated me from the moment we met. The man was pure muscle, with a strong jawline and gorgeous salt and pepper in his hair. Beyond that, he was kind and considerate, and he obviously cared about the people he served. He had all the confidence of a man in his position, and he carried himself with a quiet authority that was extremely attractive. He didn't even bother wearing a uniform. Everyone knew him and respected him without it.

I had only ever seen him in his standard flannel and jeans, the outfit that seemed to be the uniform of most men who lived out here in what barely counted as civilization.

But Greg—Sheriff Morrison—in a tux?

The thought made my mouth go dry.

I must have stood there picturing it for longer than I'd realized, because the next thing I was aware of was Fiona, Daphne's elderly neighbor, chuckling.

"Oh, I'd say you've got it bad," she said, elbowing me.

I stiffened. "I don't know what you're talking about."

"Sure you don't." She just smiled and wrapped an arm around my waist.

I relaxed slightly until I heard the bedroom door open. I stiffened again, preparing myself to see Daphne's "wedding dress," wondering how to talk her into letting me find something more suitable. I would have to be smart about it. Daphne was stubborn, and if I wasn't careful, I would push her to wear the homemade dress out of pure hardheadedness. God certainly knew what he was doing when he gave her red hair.

"Relax," Fiona whispered as the girls headed our way, still too far down the hallway for me to see. "Oftentimes, things work out differently than we expect."

"I find the opposite to be true," I replied.

"Well, we'll see."

I could hear the grin in her voice.

When Daphne came around the corner, I gasped, speechless for once.

The dress had spaghetti straps with a ruched top that fell into the most graceful sheath I had ever seen. The cut was precise, highlighting Daphne's slim figure to perfection, and the flared train was the perfect length for a simple wedding. Had I not known what Daphne had paid Willa, I would have assumed the dress to be very expensive.

I stepped forward, dropping down to inspect the train of the dress more closely.

"This is hand-stitched," I said, looking up with a frown.

"That's right," Willa said, barely containing her smile.

"Hand-stitched silk," I repeated. "Excellent quality silk, at that. The stitching..." I looked again for any error, any sign that this was anything less than a custom-made designer gown.

I couldn't find a single flaw.

"Are you surprised?" Daphne asked, fighting a grin of her own.

I stood up, lost for words. "It's marvelous," I said, shaking my head in disbelief. "I'll admit when I'm wrong, and, well, I was very wrong. Willa, this dress is remarkable. Why are you not designing in a big city? I could help you make connections, if you need. With these skills, you could go anywhere. New York, Los Angeles. Paris, even. You could make a fortune!"

A flicker of annoyance crossed her face before she shrugged. "I like it here," she said in a tone that suggested the topic wasn't up for conversation. "Now, let's talk about your next surprise."

"My next surprise?"

Daphne grabbed my hand. "I had Willa make you a dress too."

"But I already have—" I started to protest. Then I stopped. If whatever Willa had designed for me was anything close to the level of beauty she had made for Daphne, I couldn't resist.

"Come on," Willa said, grabbing my arm. "I was able to get it close from pictures and from the clothes Daphne stole from you and sent to me for measurements"—she and Daphne exchanged grins—"but I need you to try it on so I can finish it to perfection."

"We're cutting it close, aren't we?" I asked, worried. "The wedding is tomorrow."

"I planned for that," she said, giving me a little tug. "Come on. Let's go make you gorgeous."

Chapter Two

Greg

"You look terrible," I announced, shaking my head as Emerson emerged from the changing room wearing his tux.

His face fell. "Really?"

I cracked up. "Of course not. You look fine. Not that I've ever figured out what Daphne sees in you in the first place." I was just teasing him, of course.

Truth was, Emerson was a good man. I was proud of him—and frankly relieved to see him finally happy. Daphne was the best thing to ever happen to him. They were a good match, and I had no doubt they would have a happy marriage.

If part of me envied his happiness, I pushed that down. Today was about him, not me.

"You look pretty good yourself," he said, grinning as I squirmed in my tux.

When he and Daphne had said they were having a rustic, outdoor wedding, I had felt relief, thinking that meant a casual dress code. But no, Daphne's idea of rustic was pretty far removed from my own. As the best man, I had to wear a tux too. I hadn't been in one since my own wedding over two decades ago. Considering how that had turned out, I was pretty sure tuxedos were bad luck.

If I had my way about it, I would never wear one again once this wedding hoopla was over and done with. Give me blue jeans any day of the week. I needed something I could actually move in. I had never understood the fascination with dress clothes.

"That's me," I said dryly, adjusting my bow tie in the mirror. "I'm a regular Hollywood star now."

"I'm sure Janet will think so." Emerson shot me an amused glance in the mirror.

I grinned back. "Maybe she will." It wasn't the first time I had thought about finally getting to see her again. I had been looking forward to it since she'd last left town, after a lengthy visit that had given us several opportunities to see each other in social situations. Every single one had sent me home smiling. Janet Sullivan was one gorgeous, interesting woman. She was elegant and sophisticated.

The type of woman who probably dated men who wore tuxedos on the regular, I realized with a frown.

Janet was exactly the kind of woman I normally stayed as far from as possible, but there was something different about her. The first time I met her, I was arresting her daughter. Instead of causing a bunch of drama about the whole thing, Janet acted with extraordinary strength and grace. She listened quietly to everything I had to say. It was clear she loved her daughter and would go to bat for her, but she could also listen to reason.

She had impressed me from the start.

And unless I had been imagining it—which was entirely possible, considering what a long dry spell I had been going through—the sparks between us were mutual. I hadn't missed the way she blushed every time I came around or how her breathing would speed up when I touched her.

I hadn't yet made a move to test my theory. For one thing, she was way out of my league. For another, I had zero interest in a long-distance relationship. But Daphne had mentioned to me and Emerson both that she was expecting an announcement soon that Janet had decided to move to Rosemary Mountain. Daphne had "seen" Janet moving with her second sight or whatever she liked to call it. She was overjoyed and could hardly wait to hear the good news.

If it was true that Janet was relocating to the mountain, well then, I might get to test out my theory after all. I wondered if it would hurt my friendship with Emerson for me to marry his wife's mom. Boy, that would be the source of some hillbilly jokes for sure.

"What are you grinning about over there?" Emerson asked, breaking my train of thought.

I grinned at him. "Oh, I'm just over here thinking about your future wife's mom."

He punched me on the shoulder, but not hard enough to hurt.

"Seriously, man," I said, losing the grin. "You know I'm not going to start anything long distance. That's stressful enough on a couple. You add in the strain of my job and it's just a recipe for disaster. But, assuming Daphne's right about Janet moving, would you—I mean, how would you feel..." I cleared my throat awkwardly, not sure how to ask.

Emerson's grin was easy. "Man, I think it would be awesome."

"Really?"

"Really. First off, Janet is Daphne's stepmother, and she's only forty-two. You're what, forty-five?"

I nodded, confirming.

"See?" he asked like that solved everything. "It's not weird like...like you'd all of a sudden feel like my stepdad and start bossing me around or something." He grinned again. "We'll still be buddies. Besides, I think Janet's lonely and needs someone in her life. Someone solid, like you."

"Thanks, man." My heart swelled with gratitude. Emerson didn't give compliments often, and I appreciated hearing his vote of confidence. I was something of a mentor to him, given our age difference, but I had a hell of a lot of respect for him. It was a good friendship, one that meant the world to me.

"Besides," he continued, "she'd be good for you too."

"You think? How so?" I asked, fiddling with my bowtie in the mirror. The damn thing was going to drive me crazy.

He grinned. "Just trust me."

· · ·

After picking up our tuxes, Emerson and I headed to O'Malley's for lunch. I wasn't an emotional man, but I couldn't help feeling something as we slid into our normal booth. Emerson had changed dramatically since he had come to Rosemary Mountain a couple of years ago—in a good way. We had connected immediately, both being outsiders so to speak. But it was more than that. We understood each other. We were both veterans, and we had both experienced loss. We were brothers in that way. Today, helping him get ready to marry his bride, well, I couldn't help but feel proud of him.

I also worried that something was going to go wrong and ruin things for him. But I tried to keep that out of my mind.

"Last day as a single man," I commented, wanting to tease him a bit and lighten my own mood. "You sure I don't need to have a getaway car ready for you tomorrow?"

I joked, knowing there wasn't anything in the world that could stop Emerson from marrying Daphne. Once he had decided she was the one, he had practically married her in his heart, then just waited around for her to catch up.

He grinned. "Nah. But I may need you to come up with some fake emergency so we can get out of the reception and on to the honeymoon early."

"Done." I tried to smile, but Emerson didn't buy it. We were both always tuned into people's moods, their expressions—the kind of hyper-vigilance that comes from needing it to stay alive.

"What is it?" he asked, his face turning serious.

"Nothing," I said, shaking my head. I didn't want to worry him, especially not on his wedding weekend.

But he wasn't the kind of guy to let things drop. He waited for the waitress to place mugs of ale in front of us—our usual order, one so habitual she hadn't bothered to ask us what we wanted before bringing them over—then leaned forward and asked again.

I sighed and took a swallow of my drink before answering. "Maybe nothing," I said. "Just one of those feelings in my gut."

Emerson studied me. "What are you not telling me?"

I ran my hands over my face, feeling tired already. I was tired of thinking about it all, tired of trying to figure it all out.

Tired of looking over my shoulder all the time.

I shook my head. "It's your wedding weekend. You don't need to hear my problems."

"Knock it off and tell me what's wrong."

"Like I said. Maybe nothing." I shook my head again, this time irritated as hell by the whole thing. "There's just been little things happening," I said when I realized he wasn't going to give up.

"Like what?"

"At first, I thought I was just imagining things. Some files were moved on my desk, but they weren't important and I thought, well, maybe I just didn't remember where I had placed them. Next day, I had a flat tire. But again, those things happen. Day after that, I went to the gym to get in a workout. Pretty sure my locker had been tampered with. Nothing was missing, but the lock was scratched, like someone had picked it or tried to. It felt like someone was messing with me. I don't know," I said, shaking my head. It all sounded stupid as I said it out loud. "Maybe I'm just being paranoid."

Emerson's face wrinkled in concern. "You're not a paranoid guy."

"Yeah, but we all get itchy sometimes." I gave him a pointed look. I knew he knew what I meant. That veteran hypervigilance thing again. We all carried it to some degree, and some of us carried more than others.

He nodded in agreement. "Yeah, we do. But I don't think this is what that is. You're super conscientious. If you think someone is messing with your stuff, I would listen to your gut."

"Yeah, well..." I cleared my throat awkwardly. I hadn't planned on telling him any of this, but I changed my mind. "There was a note on my truck this morning."

His eyebrows shot up. "A note?"

I nodded and took another long drink, trying to keep the anger off of my face even though I was mad as hell about the whole thing. "Yeah. It said 'I own this town now, and that means I own you. Keep your eyes open, because I'm about to prove it.'"

Emerson's eyes widened. "Well, that's a clear threat."

"Yeah." The phrasing was also too familiar for comfort. "If it escalates, I may need to call in the state investigators."

His eyes widened again. "Is it that serious, you think?"

I shrugged, not wanting to tell him how concerned I really was. "Hopefully not. But with everything that went down a few months ago..." I trailed off, knowing he knew exactly what I was talking about.

For years, someone had hidden in plain sight in Rosemary Mountain, running the town under the alias "Mr. Boddy." Taking him down had meant taking down an entire organization, corruption at all levels—including within my own office. One of my own jail workers had even helped murder a potential witness while she was in custody. Between myself and the TBI, we hoped we had cleared out everyone who had been involved.

But there was a part of me that still didn't fully trust everyone who worked underneath me, especially with the little things happening in my office.

The other issue I was struggling with was the timing of the note being left on my truck the day before Emerson's wedding. The whole takedown had been instigated by Emerson's future wife and her "sight." Had she not doggedly pursued the truth, desperate to solve her birth mother's murder, that organization would almost certainly still be intact —making her a serious target for anyone looking to make a statement.

Emerson gave me a hard look, realizing what I was saying. "You think it may be connected?"

"I don't know, man. But the language in the note bothers me. It's just too similar."

It was Emerson's time to take a long drink. "Nothing's happened on our end. No threats, no disturbances. Daphne would know."

"Right. But she stirred up a lot, and there may still be angry people. Plus, Daphne's a key witness in Luke Kistler's trial. And with the timing of the note coinciding with your wedding..." I couldn't finish the sentence.

"You think we should be concerned?"

"I don't know," I said. "It was just a thought I had, mulling it over. If someone wants to make a statement of power, an event is the place to do it, and the whole town knows I'll be there. I feel better knowing you guys haven't noticed anything weird. But just so you know, I'll be packing at the wedding, just in case. Jackson will too. We're going to keep our eyes peeled for trouble." Jackson—Deputy Ford—was the only one in my office I trusted completely.

Emerson nodded. "You've got me, too. Plus, my brother, Alex, will be there, and my buddy Cole. You'll meet him tonight. We served together. He did some time in special forces. You can trust him. We can all be carrying too."

I nodded, a bit of relief flooding my chest. Five solid guys was something I could work with.

Chapter Three

Janet

I changed outfits three times before settling back on the one I had picked for the rehearsal dinner in the first place. I just wanted to look my best for the pictures. It had nothing to do with the fact that Greg Morrison was going to be there.

He certainly wasn't the reason I redid my French twist three times, either.

For the life of me, I didn't understand why I went weak at the knees every time I saw the man. He wasn't my type. Oh yes, he had movie-star good looks. Those piercing gray eyes, that sharp chin, that body that obviously put in long hours at the gym... I nearly dropped my curling iron just thinking about it. But the man lived in jeans and flannel. Jeans that looked remarkably good on him, I had to admit. But still. *Jeans and flannel.*

I had never dated a man who wore jeans. No, my type of man wore suits or golf attire. Although, considering how well those relationships had worked out, maybe it was time to rethink my policy.

Greg was definitely a different kind of man, and it wasn't just the clothes he wore. There was an innate goodness in him I could sense.

I shook my head, bringing myself back to reality. There was no use thinking about a relationship with Greg Morrison, now or in the future. My future plans were already in motion, and they didn't involve a relationship at all, much less one with a flannel-wearing Rosemary Mountain man who probably expected his woman to stay home and "mind the house."

I had already fallen for a man like that, and I had spent nearly a decade of my life trapped in a loveless marriage. Loveless on his side, anyway. I could only wish I hadn't loved Lonnie. It would have been less painful.

No, I would never make that kind of mistake again.

I would just have to get over this silly little crush on Greg.

I drove to the rehearsal alone, as Daphne had left early to take care of some last-minute wedding details. It was my first time to see the wedding venue. I hadn't known what to expect when Daphne told me they were planning a simple outdoor wedding. But I had to admit, the spot they had chosen was quite pretty. The sign said it was a wildlife reserve, which made me a bit nervous. A wedding, surrounded by mountain wildlife? Would raccoons crash the reception?

Still, as I walked down the stone pathway, following the white wooden arrows leading to the wedding site, I was surprised to feel somewhat enchanted. The path was lit with twinkle lights as it wound through the woods, opening to a clearing where they had already begun setting up for tomorrow. It was rustic, for sure—a pergola covered in flowers, with wooden chairs set up for the guests. But here, surrounded by the forest and the lights, well, it was beautiful. Magical. Perfect for Daphne.

"You made it!" Daphne said, spotting me. She came straight over and gave me a hug.

"Hey, Janet," Emerson said, catching up with his bride-to-be. He put his arm around her and pulled her close. She looked up at him, in pure adoration, mirroring the love in his eyes.

My heart ached with joy for them, and with a familiar longing. Emerson looked at Daphne in a way nobody had ever looked at me. I had fallen hard for Daphne's father. He had swept me off my feet in a whirlwind romance, making me feel like the luckiest girl in the world. But the truth was, he had never felt anything for me like what I had felt for him. He had never stopped loving Eileen, the young bride who had died when Daphne was a toddler. He only wanted me because he was suddenly alone and needed a nanny and housekeeper. His heart was always Eileen's.

I was just too stupid to realize it until after I had walked down the aisle. Worse, I had been stupid enough to hang around for years, thinking if I proved myself to be a wonderful wife he would finally fall in love with me.

Stupid, stupid, stupid.

But Emerson was head-over-heels in love with Daphne. I had no doubt about that. I could see it in his eyes, in his words, and in the way he treated her. Theirs would be a happy marriage. I was so grateful and so happy for them both.

They would have the kind of love I had always wanted.

The rehearsal started almost immediately. I floated through my part of it in a haze, caught up in sad memories from my own wedding. I jumped when Fiona drew me out of my thoughts, poking me in the ribs from where she was seated next to me, as Daphne's honorary grandmother.

"This is supposed to be a happy occasion," Fiona whispered, poking me again. "Why the long face?"

"Oh, I'm sorry," I said, glancing at her. "I didn't mean to look morose. I'm very happy for them. Truly." I fixed a smile on my face, feeling mortified that I had allowed my own gloom to show. I would never want Daphne or Emerson to see me as anything less than over-joyed for them.

"Oh, I know you're happy for them," Fiona said, refusing to drop the point. "But maybe you have a bit of your own heartache?"

I opened my mouth to protest but stopped. Something about Fiona made a person want to open up to her.

I sighed, then leaned over to whisper. "Sorry. Just thoughts of my own marriage. I know you were friends with Lonnie, and Daphne's told me how much you loved Eileen. I don't mean to speak negatively about either of them. But, well, my marriage wasn't a happy one, and all of this has brought a lot of those memories back. I'm genuinely overjoyed for Daphne and Emerson though. He loves her. That's all I could ask for."

Fiona patted my hand. "Daphne's told me a little of how things were between you and Lonnie," she whispered back. "I can't say I'm surprised, knowing how crazy he was over Eileen. But I'm real sorry you went through that. It was wrong of him to marry you when he didn't love you, without you at least knowing the truth of what you were signing up for. A life without love is a hard thing."

I looked over at Fiona. "Were you ever married?"

She nodded slowly as a look of grief passed over her.

"Were you happy?" The question was rude, I knew, and it was unlike me to ask. I wasn't entirely sure why I did. Maybe I was looking for assurance that a woman really could be happy in marriage, that Daphne really did have a chance. I hadn't personally known many—if any—women who were truly happily married.

Or maybe I was just looking for someone to commiserate with.

"I was very happy," she said softly, that look of grief growing stronger.

I immediately felt terrible for having asked. "I'm sorry," I said, not knowing what else I could say. I wouldn't pry anymore, no matter how much I wanted to ask what had happened.

She just squeezed my hand and turned her focus back toward Daphne and Emerson at the front, who were obviously in their own little world as they walked through the rehearsal, both appearing completely ready to commit their lives to each other. They were lucky to have found one another, and I was so happy for my daughter.

Even if I felt more alone than ever.

THE REHEARSAL DINNER WAS HELD AT A CUTE LITTLE BISTRO, in a private back room reserved for our party. I had to admit the whole thing was more elegant than I would have expected for a small town like Rosemary Mountain. They even had an open bar set up, with champagne, a small wine selection, and a few curated cocktails. I headed straight for the bar and ordered a Chardonnay.

"I'd love to never see the bottom of this glass tonight," I told the bartender, slipping him a twenty. I was tired of feeling sorry for myself and wanted to loosen up and celebrate my daughter's happiness.

"Easy there," said a familiar voice with a low chuckle, sending shivers up my spine before I even turned to look at him.

Not that I hadn't already seen him standing beside Emerson at the altar, practicing the part of best man. I had barely been able to keep my eyes off of him up there.

He leaned in close. "I wouldn't want to have to take you in for public drunkenness."

"Sheriff Morrison," I said, turning to him, grateful to already feel a little bit of a buzz from the Chardonnay.

"Call me Greg," he said with a smile that let me know he had just been teasing me.

My heart raced as he leaned closer, giving me a whiff of the citrus and spice notes in his cologne. He was still in his customary jeans and boots, paired with a casual white button-down—apparently his version of dressing up for an elegant dinner—but there was something so very appealing about him despite it. Maybe even because of it, though I hated to admit it. He was just so very *masculine.* So rugged. So strong looking.

Or maybe this Chardonnay had already gone straight to my head.

"Are you not drinking anything, Sheriff—I mean, Greg?" My cheeks flamed as I suddenly felt shy saying his first name, as if it were somehow too intimate. That was silly though. Daphne and Emerson called him Greg all the time, and it wasn't as if this was our first time chatting in a social situation.

He shook his head. "Not tonight."

There was something behind his words, just the smallest touch of worry. I wondered about it. Was that the norm for someone in law enforcement? His smile was relaxed, but his eyes weren't. They were alert, completely present and aware of everything happening around him.

I shook myself, realizing I was standing there studying the man's eyes, practically gazing at him like a lovesick puppy.

"Well," I said, stepping away slightly, needing to put some distance between our bodies, "we should probably find our seats. I think they're getting ready to begin."

I began to walk away, but he followed me to the table, where the place cards showed we were seated beside each other.

"Looks like we're dinner buddies," he said in an easy tone as he pulled my chair out for me.

I stared at the chair for a moment before taking my seat. When was the last time someone had done that for me? Quite a while, I'd say. It just wasn't done anymore in my circles. But there was something honestly lovely about that bit of chivalry.

I looked up and caught Daphne giving me a mischievous smile. She looked at Greg and raised her eyebrows, making me blush again. So this was a setup.

I wasn't sure whether to scold her or thank her.

CHAPTER FOUR

Greg

I SAT DOWN NEXT TO JANET, WANTING THE CHANCE TO GET to know her a little better, but my brain wouldn't cooperate. It was infuriating. I was seated next to the most beautiful woman in the room, eating a fabulous meal, and celebrating the happiness of my best friend in the world. It should have been a perfect night.

But that little feeling in my gut just wouldn't let go.

I found myself scanning the corners of the room, looking for anyone acting suspicious, not that I should have had to worry about that here. We had a private room and these people were all close friends and family to Daphne and Emerson. None of them should have been involved in whatever was going on, but there was always an outside chance. Worse, the restaurant was open to the public. Since gossip was practically the number-one pastime in Rosemary Mountain, the whole town knew exactly where I was. If someone wanted to get to me and cause problems, well, this would be the place to do it.

Which was why I couldn't let myself relax, no matter how much I wanted to.

It annoyed me to death, because I wanted nothing more than to put my entire focus and attention on Janet Sullivan. From the minute she had walked down the pathway to the rehearsal, looking like a damn vision in that little red dress that hugged her in all the right places, I had wanted to be next to her.

Here I was, finally sitting beside her—something I could thank Emerson for, I was sure—and I couldn't think of anything to say because my entire body was tense, just waiting for trouble.

"How long have you lived in Rosemary Mountain?" she asked, turning toward me.

I allowed myself one quick look at her eyes—gorgeous hazel eyes, the kind of eyes a man could get lost in, if he had the luxury—before turning back to watch the doorway. A man I didn't recognize had just passed by, and it had all my internal alarms ringing.

"Oh, a couple of years now," I said, keeping my tone easy. I knew I should ask her a follow-up question, keep the conversation going, but I was busy wondering why that man felt so familiar. There was something about the way he walked. It reminded me of someone, but I couldn't think who. I started mentally going through my files, trying to remember if it matched anyone in my office.

"Have you always been in law enforcement?" Janet asked, interrupting my mental flow.

I glanced back at her. She brought her glass of wine to her lips and took a sip, looking at me expectantly. Between the man still taking up my thoughts and the distraction of those eyes gazing at me, I had to shake myself to remember what she had asked me in the first place.

"In a manner of speaking," I finally answered, returning my eyes to the doorway. "I served in the military. MP—military police. Became a sheriff's deputy when I got out." I paused as part of my brain yelled at me to ask her a damn question already. The other part of my brain was still sorting through files, trying to remember who that man reminded me of. I wasn't going to be able to focus completely until I remembered. "Um. What do you do?" I finally asked her.

This time, she was the one who hesitated. I took my eyes off the door and looked at her, wondering why she looked so unsure.

"I'm a buyer for Jessica Blair," she finally answered.

I frowned because I had no idea what that meant. And because she was sending signals that she wasn't being entirely truthful.

"Someone pays you to buy stuff for them?" I asked.

Janet laughed. "Not someone. Jessica Blair is a brand, a fashion retailer with stores across America. You haven't heard of it?"

I grinned until movement from the doorway caught my eye again. "I can't say that I have. Of course, fashion's not really my thing."

"I can see that," she said.

She started explaining about the store and what exactly she did there. I was trying to pay attention to what she was saying, but it was hard to focus. The same man had now passed by the doorway to our party three times, like he was trying to get a look inside. I still didn't recognize him, but he definitely reminded me of someone, and it was driving me crazy that I couldn't place who. He wasn't dressed like the waitstaff, and he wasn't one of the restaurant owners—I knew them personally.

It was probably nothing. Probably just a curious passerby. The town was full of summer hikers and family vacationers looking to get away from the cities. It was possible this guy was a repeat visitor and that was why he seemed familiar. Odds were, it was nothing. But I wasn't taking any chances.

"Will you excuse me for a moment?" I asked, interrupting Janet's monologue about her work.

She seemed surprised but said of course. I stepped away from the table and headed straight for the door to see exactly what this guy was up to.

Chapter Five

Janet

My jaw dropped when Greg got up and walked away, blowing me off like I was boring him to death. I had thought the attraction between us was mutual, but apparently, I was mistaken. He had looked for the first opportunity to escape.

Truthfully, the whole thing had reminded me of one too many conversations with Lonnie after our hasty marriage—nights spent at the dinner table with me attempting to make conversation, trying so hard to connect, while he obviously couldn't care less. His thoughts were always elsewhere, his attention always focused on something else. Never on me. I wasn't interesting enough for him.

Apparently, Greg felt the same way. Two very different men, yet their reaction to me was the same.

The rejection stung, but it was for the best. I didn't need to lose sight of my future.

The rehearsal dinner soon got going, with toasts and stories from friends. Greg returned to his seat, but I purposefully ignored him, choosing to angle my chair away and talk with Fiona instead. Her eyes twinkled a bit, as if she knew exactly what I was doing. Which, to be honest, she probably did. Sometimes I thought the woman was half witch. Her sharp eyes seemed to notice everything, and I had no doubt she noticed how deliberate I was to not even look Greg's way again.

I was glad Daphne had Fiona looking after her. It made it easier to move on with my own life. Not that I really had the right to worry about Daphne anyway. No matter how much things had improved between us, I knew I would never be her real mother, and I could never make up for the misunderstandings and years of strain between us. I wouldn't overstep now and try to claim a role that wasn't mine to claim, but I was grateful for what we had—and grateful for the woman who looked out for her in my absence.

"I'm glad Daphne has you," I told Fiona, suddenly.

"Well, that's a lovely thing to hear," she said. "I'm glad she has you, too."

I gave her a little smile. "Thank you. That's nice of you to say, especially knowing how much you loved her mother. I appreciate you accepting me."

Fiona frowned, peering at me intently. "What's that look for?"

"What look?"

"The sadness on your face. Honey, you've been moping around all night, and I'm starting to think it's not just about your own sad marriage. What's going on? You can tell old Fiona your problems." Her face was kind as she welcomed me to unburden myself.

I hesitated, then decided to trust her. I would have to tell Daphne the truth soon anyway. I was just waiting for her to get back from her honeymoon, so as not to overshadow the wedding.

"I–I got an incredible job offer."

Fiona smiled. "Well, that sounds like a good thing. Congratulations! But if it's an incredible offer, why do you look so sad about it?"

"I'm not sad," I insisted. "I'm overjoyed. It's everything I've ever wanted, really. But...it's in Paris."

"Oh, I see," Fiona said quietly. "Paris is a long ways away."

"Yes, it is." I hesitated again. "It will be fine. Daphne's always been so independent, and I was never really much of a mother to her anyway. It's not like she needs me, especially now. She'll be just fine here, with Emerson, and you…" I trailed off, turning my eyes to the only daughter I would ever have. She was the only good thing to come out of my marriage.

"You're at least partly right about that," Fiona agreed, nodding. "She's independent, and if this job really makes you happy, she'll be just fine. She'll celebrate with you and be proud of you. But the question I have is: Will *you* be happy?"

"Me?" I asked, surprised. "Of course. I just told you it's an amazing opportunity. Paris is incredible, and to have the chance to actually live there is a dream come true. I've outgrown my old job, and being in the heart of the fashion world is everything I could ever dream of. It will be an adjustment, of course, but really, it's everything I've ever wanted."

Fiona nodded again. "It sounds like it. Maybe I'm overstepping, but I just think if this is what you really want, you'd sound more excited about it. You know, have a smile on your face instead of looking like you're heading to a funeral."

"I'm thrilled," I said, knowing the words sounded hollow. I *was* happy though. It was just too much Chardonnay combined with too many old ghosts and the sting of Greg's disinterest getting me down. I straightened my shoulders and took a breath. "I'm thrilled about it," I repeated, forcing some happiness into my voice. "I can't wait to move there and get started."

Fiona nodded, her eyes reflecting entirely too much sympathy for the good news I had just shared. "Maybe you're right," she agreed. "Maybe this is an incredible opportunity. And maybe you're right that Daphne doesn't really need you. I don't know if that's true, though. I think she needs a mother more than you realize, especially as she steps into this new role as a wife and maybe, God willing, becomes a mother herself someday. But maybe you're right and she'll be fine without you. Tell me though, will you really be fine without *her*? Is the job really so great that you want to give up your family and move alone to a foreign country? Take it from someone who did it too many years ago to count. Starting over in a new country, alone, isn't always easy. Sometimes it's the right choice, but that doesn't make it any easier."

I stared at her for a moment, not sure what to say.

She reached over and patted my hand. "Rhetorical question," she said. "You don't have to answer."

"Work's the only thing I've ever really been good at," I whispered over the lump in my throat, confessing my failures. I had failed as a wife, failed as a mother, failed as a woman—work was the only place I had ever succeeded. "And it's my dream job."

She stared at me for a moment, with eyes that seemed to see right through to my soul. "Well then, congratulations, my dear," she said finally. "Getting your dream job is something to celebrate for sure." She clinked her wine glass to mine and gave me a kind smile.

I smiled back, but I knew it didn't quite reach my eyes. It didn't matter though. Daphne had blossomed after moving to Rosemary Mountain—away from me. That stung too, but it was true. She didn't need me, and frankly, she was thriving without me interfering in her life. But without her, there wasn't anything left for me in Little Rock. I had known that for a long time. I had reached the peak of my job there and was ready for a new challenge. If I was being honest, I was ready for a new life. I was tired of a city that only reminded me of my many failures. My work was the one place I succeeded, and it had rewarded me with this chance of starting over somewhere fresh.

Starting over had worked for Daphne. I had to believe it would work for me too.

Chapter Six

Greg

When the party wound down and I felt sure any threat had passed, I excused myself and headed out to the parking lot, glad to make an early night of it. I didn't like to brood, but I wasn't happy at all with how the evening had gone.

Janet barely spoke to me after I excused myself to go after the man I saw spying on our party. I apologized for my sudden departure and tried to strike up conversation again, but she just talked to Fiona all through dinner. Then she spent the rest of the evening chatting with Emerson's parents. Anytime I tried to approach her, she seemed to flit off and immediately strike up a conversation with someone else.

The upside to that was it left me free to keep my eyes open. But all I wanted to keep my eyes on was her.

Worse, I hadn't even found the guy who had distracted me during our conversation.

As I got close to my truck, I spotted something out of place. I could see the note on the window before I even got there, a piece of paper with a single sentence typed in large letters.

Are your eyes open? If not, they will be.

I GRABBED AN EVIDENCE BAG FROM MY TRUCK AND carefully put the note inside. I would send it off for fingerprinting, but I knew odds were it was clean.

"Hey, Jackson," I called out as I spotted him coming out of the restaurant. "Come over here."

He jogged over to me. "Another one?" His face was grim.

"Yep. You see anything suspicious tonight?"

"Not a thing."

"There was a man who passed by our doorway three times," I told him. "But when I got up to go check him out, he had mysteriously disappeared."

"Hmmm." Jackson frowned. "Description?"

"Tall and thin. Probably six feet. One hundred eighty pounds tops. Greasy black hair. No distinguishing features. Probably late thirties or early forties. Skulked around like he had something to hide."

"Got it. I'll ask around."

I glanced up at the building. "What are the odds they have security cameras covering this parking lot?"

"They should. I'll find out."

"Do that, and let me know. You think there's any way Daphne and Emerson would reschedule their wedding?"

Jackson grinned. "Emerson would be happy to elope, if you ask me. He wants to get married as soon as possible, and I don't think he cares how. But I don't think you'll talk Daphne into changing anything at this point."

I sighed. "Not even if I tell her about the threats?"

Jackson just gave me a look. "Since when has that kind of thing ever stopped her?"

"Redheaded women," I mumbled under my breath. "Well, look, I already told Emerson about the other one. I'm going to tell him about this one too and encourage him to make other plans. I can't make them do anything, but maybe he'll put his foot down and tell Daphne how it's going to be."

Jackson just leaned his head back and let out a roar of laughter. "Right. Sure. That's how that will work."

WE HEADED BACK INTO THE BISTRO, WHERE DAPHNE, Emerson, Janet, and Emerson's brother Alex were still talking, apparently trying to figure out some issue with the seating for the next day. Janet looked over at me, then immediately looked away. I knew I had screwed that up. My head was all kinds of messed up tonight, and I couldn't imagine how I had come across. But hopefully she would understand once she heard what was going on.

Emerson frowned when he looked up and saw me and Jackson, realizing immediately something was wrong.

"What is it?" he asked, crossing to me. Alex followed on his heels.

I held out the evidence bag. "Another note on my truck. Any way I could talk you two into eloping?"

By this point, the ladies had walked over to us as well. Daphne looked at Emerson and he immediately handed her the bag. She held it and closed her eyes.

Instant discomfort crept up my neck as I realized Daphne was trying to "see" something. I had all the respect in the world for Emerson, and I knew he believed wholeheartedly in Daphne's "sight," but I still wasn't sure what to think of the whole thing.

She handed the bag back a moment later with a shrug. "I'm not getting anything," she said.

I wasn't sure if I was disappointed or relieved.

"So about that elopement idea," I repeated.

"You can't be serious," Janet said before either of them could reply. "You want them to cancel their wedding and elope because of a silly little note on *your* truck?"

"I may very well be overreacting," I said, annoyed to have to defend myself, "but after everything that's happened the last few months, maybe we shouldn't take any chances. And this isn't the first note. Like I told Emerson earlier, there's been some weird stuff going on for a few days, and now this makes the second note. Warnings. I don't like it. If this has anything to do with the work we've been doing here, then it may not just be me this guy's after." I looked directly at Janet, forcing her to meet my eyes. "He may have Daphne in his sights too."

Janet flinched but said nothing.

"What do you think? Do we have to cancel our plans?" Daphne asked, looking up at Emerson with eyes full of disappointment.

"I'm not sure," he replied. "What's your gut saying?"

"My gut's saying this is bad news," I interjected.

"He didn't ask about your gut," Janet said. She turned to Daphne, essentially putting herself in between me and the couple. "Daphne. I'll admit, I thought you were rushing things. But it's obvious how much care and love has gone into this wedding. Everything is already set up, and so many people have driven in from out of state. It seems like a shame to cancel it now because of something that may not even involve you. But if you think that's best, then that's what we'll do. Everyone will understand. I just don't want you to be pressured into it because of Sheriff Morrison."

I winced at that. She was already back to calling me by my title again.

"What do *you* think, Daphne?" Janet asked, putting a hand on Daphne's shoulder. "Do you think something bad is going to happen, or do you think it's safe to go forward? What do *you* want? Don't worry about anyone else."

Daphne bit her lip and looked back at Emerson like they were having some sort of silent meeting, communicating only through their eyes. After a minute, they both nodded and turned back toward me.

"We're going forward with the wedding," Emerson said. "We'll all keep an eye out, but Daphne doesn't feel anything bad coming. It seems this is directed specifically toward you. No offense," he said, grinning.

"None taken." I scowled at Janet.

Daphne had surprised me by actually entertaining the idea of eloping. Maybe she had learned a thing or two after all. I felt certain I could have convinced them both to cancel this thing if Janet hadn't intervened.

"Alright," I said, back in business mode. "But I want to have a meeting between those of us who are going to be carrying tomorrow. Let's make sure we're all on the same page and know what we're looking for. I want a plan in place in case anything goes wrong. Emerson, is it alright with you if we head to your house and talk this out? I want the four of us, plus your ex-special forces friend, to be prepared." I looked at him, then at Alex.

Emerson nodded. Alex looked a little uneasy, but he nodded too. I turned on my heels and headed back to my truck, trying very hard to focus on my plan for tomorrow.

Unfortunately, my mind kept returning to a certain woman in a fine red dress, wondering what it would feel like to dance with her at the wedding.

Chapter Seven

Janet

THE SUN WAS ALREADY SHINING THROUGH THE WINDOWS
when I woke, bathing Daphne's guest bedroom in a warm glow. I
stretched underneath the quilt, allowing myself a few quiet moments
before jumping into the bustle of the day. I felt exhausted already, my
sleep having been disrupted too many times by dreams of a certain
gray-eyed man.

That would never do.

I finally sat up and forced myself out of bed, knowing if I wanted to
get in my morning workout, there wasn't time to lounge around. Today
was a big day—Daphne's wedding day. I could hardly believe it, yet here
we were. While Daphne had taken care of nearly all the arrangements
herself, leaving me very little to do other than get dressed and show up, I
knew weddings were always long, stressful events.

And that was without the additional stress of Sheriff Morrison's
concerns about the notes on his truck.

I slipped out of my silk pajamas, folded them neatly, and tucked
them away inside my suitcase, exchanging them for a matching yoga set.
Cardio would have to be skipped out here—Daphne was downright

insane for jogging on this mountain road. Gravel roads, winding curves, and wildlife everywhere? *No, thank you.* But I had prepared in advance and brought my yoga mat and resistance bands. I would make myself a cup of tea, then hit the mat.

Daphne was already in the kitchen, sipping coffee, when I made it downstairs. She looked radiant, practically glowing with happiness. My heart swelled with joy, knowing she was exactly where she was meant to be. She might have only been a stepdaughter, and our relationship had withstood a thousand trials—including our personalities, opposites in so many ways—but I loved her more than I could ever put into words. I was so proud of her and so grateful to know she was happy and whole.

"A yoga mat?" she asked, an eyebrow raised, before taking another sip of her coffee. The girl was practically addicted. I made a mental note to talk to her, again, about how too much caffeine could cause premature aging and wrinkles.

"Yes," I answered, moving to the stove to turn on the teakettle. I smiled when I opened Daphne's pantry, seeing she had stocked several boxes of Darjeeling along with the dried fruit I liked to snack on when I had a sweet tooth.

"I didn't take you for the yoga type," she commented. "That must be new."

"Oh, I don't do yoga," I said, dismissing it. "I tried the classes at the gym a few times, but it's annoyingly slow. Besides, the teacher was one of those hippie types who only wears natural deodorant. Not a pleasant experience at a gym, let me tell you. But Pilates is a different story. Faster moves, more intensity, with a great focus on the core. Plus, it's easy to pack a mat and some bands, and I can do it anywhere." *Like in Paris, where there's not a gym on every corner.*

"Gotcha," she said, rising from the table. "I'm meeting Abby for breakfast in half an hour. Want to join us?"

I felt torn. On one hand, I wanted to soak up as much time with Daphne as I possibly could. She'd leave for her honeymoon tonight, and I would fly to Paris shortly after she returned. But I also knew I wouldn't have another chance to work out today if I skipped it this morning, and I always felt "off" if I abandoned my routine.

"You go ahead," I finally said, deciding. "Enjoy catching up with your friend. I'll meet up with you both in a bit. I think I'll have break-fast here."

"Okay." She glanced at her watch. "Don't forget, we have manicure appointments at ten. Want to meet us there?"

"Perfect," I said, making a mental note.

After my workout and shower, I packed up what I would need for the day and headed out to meet the girls. Willa had my dress—a dream dress, one that made me feel practically giddy when I thought about wearing it—but I would do my own hair and makeup. Daphne had made appointments for those things with a local hair and makeup artist, but this was still Rosemary Mountain. It was probably some girl who had watched a few videos online and had built a makeup kit with items you could get at the local drugstore. No, thank you.

I also didn't need a manicure, as I had already taken care of that in Little Rock. I would compromise though and get a pedicure with the girls to be part of the experience. After all, I had brought a pair of closed-toed heels, just in case the salon wasn't up to par.

The day flew by, as I had known it would. Manicures for the girls and a surprisingly good pedicure for me, followed by a bridal luncheon, then hair and makeup. Daphne and Abby might have exchanged amused looks over my insisting on doing my own, but neither of them said anything. I had to admit though, Daphne's hair and makeup both looked so beautiful that I almost regretted doing mine myself.

Finally, it was the moment I had been waiting for all day—time for the dresses. As excited as I was for my own, I was even more excited to see Daphne in her gown again and to finally see the full picture of her as a bride. Fiona and I waited eagerly in Willa's living room, while Willa and Abby helped Daphne dress. When Daphne walked down the hall-way, I flashed back to memories of her as a little girl, playing dress-up in my clothes. My eyes filled with tears before I could stop them.

"You look absolutely stunning," I said, embracing her. "I am so, so happy for you."

"I'm happy too," she said, beaming.

There was so much more I wanted to say about how, if I had it to do all over again, I never would have let Lonnie dismiss me from her life so quickly. How I regretted having been so hard on her and criticizing her so much as she grew up. How proud I was of the woman she had become, and how, in many ways, I wanted to be more like her. How grateful I was to have a place in her life now, and…

How much I would miss her.

But, while we were surrounded by people, with the photographer eagerly snapping pictures, it wasn't the time or place for a conversation like that. So I simply hugged her again and held everything else in my heart, hoping she somehow knew.

We left early for the wildlife refuge. Daphne and Emerson had planned a "first look," where they would see each other privately and get most of the wedding photos out of the way before the ceremony began. I still preferred the old tradition of waiting until the ceremony, but that's how I had done it and look how my marriage had turned out. So, for once, I stopped myself from saying anything critical and simply let them do things their way. Besides, Daphne had told me that was the way to get the very best wedding photos. She would know, being a photographer herself and having worked in the wedding industry as a photo editor. Considering how lovely this quickly-put-together event was turning out to be, I had to admit she must have known what she was talking about when it came to weddings.

So far, the day had been a whirlwind of joy and laughter. But when the photographer whisked Daphne away for the private first look, I felt a keen sense of loss. This whole trip had been a rollercoaster of emotion, the highest highs as I rejoiced for her happiness, and the lowest lows as I realized how utterly alone in the world I really was.

But Paris was waiting for me. I held that in my heart, hoping I might find there what Daphne had found here. Not that I was looking for love or a husband. Goodness. I would never make that mistake again. But she had more than that. She had found a community, a place in this world that brought out the very best in her.

Yes, Paris was waiting for me. Paris was exactly what I needed.

Chapter Eight

Greg

I sent Emerson away for his private photographs with Daphne and fidgeted awkwardly with the bowtie I just couldn't seem to get right. I felt stiff and uncomfortable in this damn tux, as well as entirely too old to be playing the part of best man. Not that I had minded before today. But everything felt wrong now. I was still on edge, wondering if tonight would be the night the guy making threats would make his move. He could come after me. I didn't care. I knew how to handle myself. But I didn't want anything going down at an event full of civilians—hell, full of my friends.

Cole and Alex were both steady guys though. After getting to know them a bit at Emerson's the night before, I was glad to have them there. Between them, Jackson, Emerson, and myself, we had a formidable crew watching out for everyone. If anyone did try anything, they'd have a fight on their hands.

I stepped away from our group, letting the guys know I was going to check out a few of the side trails just to make sure nobody was watching and waiting for us. I knew Jackson had already checked out the ceremony spot before we arrived, and Cole and Alex were both keeping an eye on the parking lot while we waited for guests to arrive. Thus far, there had been zero signs of anything to worry about. But there were an awful lot of places to hide in the woods around here, and I knew I'd feel better if I had at least checked out the areas surrounding the pathway and ceremony.

I started methodically walking the pathway, looking for signs of disturbance in the surrounding woods, and checking the few side trails that branched off of it and led to other parts of the reserve. The first few checked out fine, but when I turned down the last one, my heart nearly stopped.

Janet Sullivan.

The woman was a damn vision, standing there alone on the trail like she was the subject in one of those fancy museum paintings. She was wearing a slip of a dress, silky dark-blue fabric that covered only one shoulder and swooped down, leaving the other arm completely bare. The hem stopped short of her knees, shimmering as she moved, showing off a killer pair of legs. Her dark hair was swept back, and all I could think about was tracing kisses up that bare arm.

I shook myself, bringing myself back to earth, and cleared my throat to alert her to my presence.

When she heard me, she looked up sharply. She put a finger to her lips, telling me to be quiet. I frowned, suddenly wondering if something was wrong.

I moved silently toward her as she held up a hand, warning me again to be quiet. When I got to her, I saw what she saw. Not danger, not someone lurking in the woods—it was just a young fawn curled up in the grass beside the path, looking up at her with the same curiosity she held for him.

"Isn't it beautiful?" she said breathlessly, apparently in awe of the little guy.

I let out a breath, suddenly feeling more relaxed than I had all day. "He's cute alright," I agreed.

I looked down at her, letting my gaze drift once more, until she looked up at me. Then I was just lost—lost in those hazel eyes. They sparkled tonight, reminding me of the way the rising sun sparkled on the lake in those early morning hours when the rest of the world was asleep. It was damn beautiful. Just like her.

"What are you doing out here by yourself?" I asked her when I came back to my senses. "I'd prefer everyone stay together in a group, just in case someone shows up to cause trouble."

"Oh. Right," she said absently, returning her gaze to the fawn, who was still just watching us. Here in the reserve, animals were more relaxed around humans than out in the wild, like they knew we couldn't touch them here. "Of course," she said. "I'm sorry. I just needed a minute to myself."

I frowned again, hearing the sadness in her voice. "Is everything okay?" I asked, tugging at that ridiculous bowtie. The stupid thing was choking me, and I couldn't make it look right to save my life.

She looked up at me, and this time, she was the one to frown. She reached for my bowtie, grazing my fingers with her own as she pushed my hands out of the way. My mouth went suddenly dry as she came close to me and untied it in one smooth motion. She adjusted it and tied it, then smoothed it down and put her hands on my chest for just the briefest moment before yanking them away.

"Better?" she asked.

I swallowed hard. "Yes. Thank you." I felt better and worse all at the same time, and it had nothing to do with the bowtie.

She straightened and cleared her throat. "Well, I do apologize for slipping away, Sheriff Morrison. I can see how that would make your job more difficult, considering your concern about a potential threat. I'll return to the wedding party." She nodded once, dismissing me, and started to walk back up to the main path.

"Hey, wait," I said. I wanted to reach out and pull her back to me, but I shoved my hands inside my pockets instead.

She turned and gave me an impatient look.

"Are you okay?" I asked. "It just seemed like you were, I dunno, sad."

Something flashed in her eyes, almost like my just asking her about it had brought another wave of sadness. My chest tightened. I didn't know Janet all that well, but even in the worst of times, I hadn't seen this kind of emotion in her. Something was definitely not okay, and all of a sudden, it felt like my life's mission was to find out what it was and make it better. I had always seen so much grace and strength in her, whatever the situation. Seeing that strength falter made me want to pull her into my arms and protect her from whatever was hurting her.

But she just nodded. "Weddings are emotional events, Sheriff. That's all. Thank you for your concern."

With that, she turned her back to me and walked away.

DESPITE MY MISGIVINGS, THE WEDDING WENT OFF WITHOUT a hitch. I kept my eyes open the entire time, but there was no sign of the mystery man from last night, no notes left on vehicles, and not a thing went wrong.

Which was good, considering how distracted I was.

As I stood beside Emerson while he pledged his life to his bride, I could barely take my eyes off of Janet. She never looked my way. In fact, she seemed to be downright avoiding looking at me, which made me feel all kinds of terrible. But her beauty captivated me, and I couldn't look away if I tried.

She had her mask back up—I could see that much. But watching her the way I did, I could see glimpses of what was beneath it. There was still a hell of a lot of emotion there, and I got the feeling it wasn't all about Daphne's wedding.

And damn if it wasn't driving me crazy to see her struggling with something when I wasn't able to do a thing about it.

AFTER THE CEREMONY, WE ALL WENT BACK TO THE SAME restaurant where the rehearsal dinner had been held for a small reception. My guard went back up, considering the events from the night before. I was once again grateful for our group of guys watching everything. We had all agreed to skip the alcohol, minus Emerson's champagne toast with Daphne, and were essentially acting as security for our own event. Alex might not have had training in anything like that, but he was steady, and I observed him paying close attention all night.

All I knew of Cole's background was that he was ex-special forces, but that was enough. I could plainly see from how he carried himself that he was well equipped for the job. Hell, I wouldn't want to go up against him. I had a feeling he was lethal, and I was glad he was on our side.

Because despite the safety we enjoyed during the ceremony, my gut was telling me we weren't in the clear just yet.

Chapter Nine

Janet

THE WEDDING WAS, IN A WORD, PERFECT. MY HEART FELT SO full while I watched Emerson lead Daphne out onto the dance floor for their first dance as husband and wife. I had worried she wouldn't be able to dance after the accident that had injured her leg so badly. But she was right. Her limp was barely noticeable, and Emerson was holding her so tightly he practically carried her through the dance anyway. It was the perfect picture of love, two souls who were obviously overjoyed to simply be together. Even if I had never had such a thing in my own life, I was beyond grateful to witness my daughter experiencing it.

I had noticed, of course, how ridiculously good Greg looked standing beside Emerson. I had tried not to. I had forced myself to keep my eyes on Daphne and Emerson, promising not to spend a single minute thinking about another Rosemary Mountain man.

But it turned out to be difficult to think of anything else.

When I had turned to see him on the trail, I had been shocked. Not just by how sophisticated and, frankly, sexy he looked in that gray tuxedo that perfectly matched the piercing storm-cloud color of his eyes, but also by the look on his face. He was staring at me like I was the only thing he wanted to see.

But that was ridiculous. He barely knew me, and if last night was any indication, he didn't really care to. I was just swept up in the romance of the day and was losing my head—again—for a man who hadn't even found me interesting enough to converse with the night before. I was wearing a stunning dress that was cut to perfection, that was all. He might have liked the picture, but he wasn't interested in the person, and I needed to remember that.

I KEPT MYSELF BUSY AND SURROUNDED BY PEOPLE, CHATTING the night away with Fiona and Emerson's parents. I avoided eye contact with Greg and prepared myself to turn him down if he asked me to dance—all while trying to ignore how disappointed I would be if he didn't.

Despite the mental preparation, it still caught me off guard when he approached me. Emerson's parents had left me to join the couples on the dance floor, and Fiona was grinning her way through a dance with Emerson's brother, Alex. I was looking for someone else to talk to when I became suddenly aware of Greg next to me, standing so close it sent a thrill up my spine, even as I cursed myself for it.

"May I have the pleasure of this dance?" he asked, leaning in close with that low voice.

I looked up and saw his eyes, and all my prepared speeches went out the window. "I'm not sure that's a good idea," I said.

"It's a wedding, Janet. Everyone's dancing. How could it possibly be a bad idea?" He gestured to the floor, which was, indeed, filled with couples swaying to the music.

"Do you even know how to dance?" I blurted out.

He was obviously taken aback. He stared at me for a moment, then cleared his throat. "I mostly know how to two-step, but this song calls for a waltz, now doesn't it?"

"Yes," I said, my face flushing at just how awkward I felt around him, how I seemed to always do or say the wrong thing.

"Is that a yes, it calls for a waltz, or yes, I can have this dance?"

"Um. Yes. Yes, I guess we can dance." My mind felt fuzzy, and not just from the champagne. I couldn't seem to think straight with him standing this close to me, making me feel all sorts of things I shouldn't feel. Not for him. Not in Rosemary Mountain.

He smiled before he led me out to the dance floor, slipped a hand around my waist, and held up his other hand in a traditional ballroom posture. I raised an eyebrow but placed my hand in his. He easily fell into rhythm and began leading me around the floor in what was a surprisingly good waltz. Here, at least, I relaxed a bit, falling into the familiar dance like it was an anchor in a stormy sea.

"Well, aren't you full of surprises," I murmured.

"What? You're surprised a mountain man like me knows anything about how to dance with a woman?" He frowned, then sent me spinning before pulling me back into him, more closely than was strictly proper in a waltz.

"Well, yes," I admitted, once again struggling to think straight with my body pressed up against his. "You have to admit, that doesn't seem like a skill you'd utilize often in a place like Rosemary Mountain. Or in your profession."

He chuckled and looked straight into my eyes. "You'd be surprised. Folks around here like to celebrate. We have lots of old-fashioned community dances. But"—he surprised me, dipping me, then pulling me back into his arms—"I also had a mother who insisted on cotillion classes. And I remember a thing or two."

"I'm impressed," I said, breathless. And I was. This was certainly not what I had expected from Greg Morrison.

He looked like a movie star in a tux, and he was leading me around the dance floor with as much skill as anyone I had ever danced with before. The feel of his hand on my back, the thrill when our bodies connected, the way he was looking deep into my eyes like the room had faded away and all he could see was me...

I blushed as I looked over and saw Daphne and Emerson grinning at us both. It snapped me back to reality, knowing they were rooting for something that could never—would never—happen.

"Ah, well," I said, stopping suddenly. "Thank you for the dance, Sheriff Morrison."

"Didn't I tell you to call me Greg?" He frowned.

"Yes, well, that feels rather disrespectful considering your position. And speaking of your position, I know you need to keep an eye on things tonight. My friends seem to have finished dancing. So I think I'll rejoin them." I knew I was babbling. But I couldn't help myself. I felt breathless, confused, and all I knew was that I needed to get far away from this man who was making me feel things I absolutely couldn't feel —and making my kids think things they didn't need to think.

"Janet—" he began, but I had already slipped away.

I went straight to the bar, downed a champagne flute, then disappeared into the ladies' room to get my bearings.

I STARED AT MYSELF IN THE BATHROOM MIRROR, MY CHEEKS pink both from the dance and from the embarrassment of getting so caught up in a fantasy about a man I already knew I didn't have a future with. As if I needed another reminder, my cell phone buzzed in my wristlet as a call came in from the assistant who was handling my move to Paris.

I took the call, grateful for a chance to get my head back in the game, to refocus on what was really important. The job of my dreams was waiting for me. Tonight was likely the last time I would see Sheriff Morrison, at least in a social capacity. After tonight, I could hole up at Daphne's house while I dog-sat for them. The pantry was stocked. There was no need to even go into town. Once Daphne and Emerson came back from their honeymoon, I could give them the news about the upcoming move and put to rest any false notions about a match between me and Greg. After that, I would be on a plane to Paris, starting my new life. It was time to squash all of this nonsense.

"I promise you," I said, whispering to myself in the mirror. "I won't let you down again."

Chapter Ten

Greg

After all my nerves about the threats, I had to admit maybe I had been overreacting. We sent Daphne and Emerson off in fine fashion, with a parade of sparklers. The entire wedding, start to finish, had been drama free. I was glad for it. They deserved a peaceful celebration after everything they had been through.

Now that it was over, all I wanted was to get out of this tux. Go home, grab a beer. Maybe nurse my wounds for a bit.

Janet had made it clear she wasn't interested. Oh, she was attracted to me. She couldn't hide that, no matter how hard she tried. But in the end, all she saw me as was a lowly sheriff in a mountain town. Not good enough for her—that was clear enough. I had to admit I had felt attracted to her elegance and sophistication. I had thought she was different though—the kind of elegance that doesn't have anything to prove. But now? Well, now, I knew the truth. There wasn't anything different about her after all. She was a snob through and through, and I would never be good enough for her.

Been there, done that.

I was about halfway home when my cell phone rang. I looked at it and frowned. *Emerson.* He shouldn't have been calling me, not now. Not when he and Daphne were supposed to be en route to their honeymoon.

"What is it?" I answered, not wasting time on greetings.

"Another threat," he said. "Only this time, it was left for us."

"Is everyone okay?"

"Yeah," he answered. "Everyone's okay. Just another warning."

"Where are you?" I asked.

"Daphne's cottage."

"I'm on my way."

I immediately pulled a U-turn and called Jackson to meet me there. This guy was playing games with us again.

But I wasn't going to let him win.

EMERSON WAS WAITING FOR ME AT THE DOOR WHEN I PULLED up to Daphne's cottage. This wasn't the first time I had been here on official business, and frankly I was tired of my friends getting caught up in this mess. I had signed up for that kind of thing, and I could handle it. But I was downright angry now that they had been targeted.

"Where is it?" I asked, bounding up the steps to their front porch.

"Inside," he said. His face was hard, like he was as pissed off as I was. He held the door open for me and I stepped inside to see Daphne, still in her wedding dress, sitting in front of a pile of wedding gifts.

"Where is it?" I repeated.

"There," she said, pointing to an unassuming gift box sitting on the coffee table. "He sent us a wedding present."

I noted how pale and shaky she looked and instantly felt sick. I hoped she looked that way because this had brought back memories of the last time she was threatened, not because of whatever was in that box. But I knew that was unlikely.

Janet walked out of the kitchen, carrying two tea mugs. She looked startled to see me, for just the briefest moment, before straightening and putting on that damn mask of hers again.

"Sheriff Morrison," she said, nodding in greeting without even making eye contact as she crossed to Daphne and handed her a cup of tea.

Daphne took it gratefully and held on to it with both hands, like she needed the comfort. Janet turned and headed for the chair in the farthest corner, like she wanted to be as far away from the box—or from me—as possible. Either way, I didn't like it.

I pulled an ink pen out of my pocket and walked to the box, using the pen to pull away the top. My stomach turned as I got a glimpse of what was inside. On top were a couple of loose photographs. Tiny ones, but the images were clear. They were of the wedding: a shot of Daphne walking down the aisle and a shot of me and Emerson standing at the altar together. Worse, beneath them was a dead rabbit with a slit throat.

The threat was clear. He had been there tonight, had slipped past me even though I had been looking for him. He'd had us in his line of sight and could easily have taken us out.

And the dead rabbit? Well, that was clear enough.

"No note this time?" I asked.

Daphne shook her head. "No. Not even a card on the box. I–I shouldn't have opened it. As soon as I touched it, I knew something was wrong."

"It's alright," I said, not wanting her to blame herself for any of this. "Who else touched it? I'll need to check for prints." It was likely a waste of time. Most people who did something premeditated like this were smart enough to wear gloves, but I would check anyway.

Emerson had taken his seat by his bride, putting a protective arm around her. They looked at each other helplessly.

"Anyone there could have touched it," Daphne said finally. "If it was on the gift table, lots of people who brought gifts were over there, moving things around as they added their own. Alex and Cole loaded everything up for us before we left, and the three of us unloaded them here. But, really, anyone at the wedding could have touched it."

I nodded, frustrated. She was right. There could be a dozen unknown fingerprints on that box, and likely none of them would belong to who we were looking for.

"I'll be right back," I said, turning on my heels to walk out the door.

I went straight to my truck and grabbed a pair of gloves and fresh evidence bags. I wanted a closer look at those photographs.

I came back in and snapped a couple of pictures of the box exactly as it was before I moved anything, just in case. Then I slipped on the gloves and carefully removed the photographs, sliding them into a clear evidence bag where I could inspect them more closely.

I didn't like what I saw.

"It's hard to tell with these being so small," I said, scowling. "But it almost looks like they were taken by someone sitting with the guests." If true, that greatly reduced my list of suspects. The guest list had been small, reserved for only Daphne and Emerson's closest friends and family. But that would complicate things in a different way, as it didn't make sense for anyone there to be threatening us.

Daphne rose to take a look. "It does look that way," she confirmed. "But that doesn't mean anything."

"Why not?" I frowned.

"They may not have been taken by the guy himself," she explained. "Everyone there was taking pictures and immediately posting them on social media. He could have pulled the pictures from there."

A little relief flooded me. "You're right. So he may not have been there at all."

She shook her head. "I can look through everything we've been tagged in so far and see if I find a match."

"Do that," I agreed. "And I'll have Jackson do the same."

Jackson had his own social media accounts and would be up for the task. I personally stayed away from all of that, thinking it was pure insanity that anyone would post so much of their life on the internet for the world to see.

"Also," she added, "the photos are small because they were printed on an instant photo printer. I'll show you." She walked over to the desk in the corner of the room and pulled something out of a drawer.

"That's a printer?" It looked almost like a cell phone.

"Yeah," she replied. She put it down on the table and pulled out her own cell phone, tapping quickly on the screen. Within seconds, a small photograph, just like the one in my hands, came out of the little thing on the table. "It works on bluetooth," she explained. "So you can quickly print any photographs from your cell phone, including ones you saved from social media."

I scowled again. "So that means he didn't visit a photo lab tonight to get these printed."

"No," she said, biting her lip like she was holding back a grin. "Technology has come a long way. Lots of people have their own photo printers now."

"Is there any way to trace them?" I asked.

"Not that I know of," she said, shrugging.

"I'll add that to the list of things for Jackson to look into," I said, shaking my head again.

The guy was a ghost, and I found it infuriating.

"Greg, do you have any problem with us going on our honeymoon as planned?" Emerson asked, breaking into the conversation.

I weighed it momentarily. "I think going on your honeymoon is probably the best thing you can do," I said finally. "I like the idea of you guys getting out of town and away from all this while I hunt this guy down. But let's think it through. Who all have you told where you're going? Is there any way he could target you there?"

Emerson grinned, finally relaxing. "Not even Daphne knows where we're going. We're driving and it's a place my family owns. We'll be safe there."

Daphne smiled. "It's true. He told me what kind of clothes to pack, but that's it. Nobody will know where we are."

"Perfect," I said. "Are you guys planning to head out tonight?"

Emerson nodded confirmation. "Yeah. We're driving a couple of hours tonight, staying at a hotel for the evening, then heading to our final destination tomorrow."

"Good. I'm going to stay here until you get on the road, just in case. Janet," I said, turning my attention to her. "Are you safe to drive? I think it's best that you get on the road tonight too and head on back to Arkansas early. Maybe do the same and grab a hotel on the way if you can't handle the whole drive. But I don't want you staying here tonight."

"Agreed," Daphne said. "I have a bad feeling about this whole thing. Mom, I don't think you should stay here."

Janet paled and looked from my face to Daphne's and back again. "I—I can't drive home," she said, more flustered than I had ever seen her. "I'm not going back to Arkansas."

"Now don't be stubborn," I began. "I know you were planning on staying here and taking care of the dog while they're gone. Emerson told me. But don't worry about that." I glanced Emerson's way. "I'll take Thor out to my place and take care of him for you until you get back. You don't have to worry about a thing."

Emerson nodded agreement. "Really, Janet, that might be best," he said. "We'll be worried sick about you staying here with all of this, now that we got a threat too."

"Too many people know where I live," Daphne added. "And if they know you're here alone, they might try to get back at me by hurting you. I don't want to take that chance."

Janet shook her head again, looking even more flustered. "I can't," she repeated. "I can't go home."

"Why not, Mom?" Daphne asked gently.

Janet's face was bright red. I could tell she really didn't want to answer the question. "Because I don't have a home to go to," she finally spit out.

"Wait," I interrupted, confused. "What do you mean you don't have a home to go to?"

She let out a sigh and bit her lip, keeping her eyes on Daphne. "I was going to tell you all of this when you got back. I didn't want to take any focus off the wedding by making today about me. But I have news." Her face reddened again. "I was offered a new job, and I'm moving. I've already sold my house. In fact, the movers have already come and gone, and I gave the key to the new owners the day before I drove here. I quite literally don't have a home to go back to."

I looked back to Daphne, who was shocked but smiling.

"I knew it!" she said. "I dreamed about you packing your house up, and I just knew you were moving here! Didn't I tell you?" She poked Emerson in the arm, grinning.

Janet reddened even more. "Daphne, I'm afraid you're confused," she said.

My stomach dropped. I could tell by the look on her face that her plans did not include Rosemary Mountain and she was trying to figure out how to break the news to Daphne. I had already decided to write the woman off as a snob and move on from any thought of her, so why did knowing she wasn't going to move here after all feel like such a punch in the gut? Even after everything this weekend, I still wanted her to move here. Still wanted to get to know her.

Still wanted her, period.

Daphne's face dropped too, and I immediately felt bad for the girl. Emerson had told me how excited Daphne was about how she and Janet had been working on building a healthy relationship. Janet was the only family Daphne had left. She had loved the idea of Janet moving here. I could see the disappointment all over her face.

"Where?" Daphne asked. "Where are you moving?"

"Paris."

One word. One little word that felt like a bomb dropped in the middle of the room. The woman was moving to Paris. It made sense. She was perfect for a place like that. I could see her in my mind's eye even now, walking the streets of Paris in those heels she loved to wear, sipping coffee in some fancy café.

I loved Rosemary Mountain. It was a damn good place to live. But it was no Paris.

It felt like someone had thrown a bucket of cold water over the last remaining coals of hope—hope I hadn't even realized I was still carrying. I could never live up to the excitement and romance of Paris. I didn't have a chance in hell with Janet Sullivan, and I needed to just get over the whole thing.

The word had obviously affected Daphne too. "Paris?" she asked in a squeaky voice. "Wow. That's incredible. I'm really happy for you. But... Mom... Paris? I mean. That's just so far away."

Janet nodded slowly. "It is. But I'll fly here to visit at least once a year, and hopefully you'll come see me too. It really won't be that different from me living in Little Rock, right?"

I could see from both their faces they knew it would be different indeed. And it didn't seem like either of them was actually happy about it.

I cleared my throat. "Well, I know you two have a lot to talk about, but we still need to figure out a plan. Janet, you're saying you don't have a place to go back to in Arkansas? Can't you stay with a friend there?"

She looked at me blankly, then shook her head no. "I don't even have my own car," she said. "I already sold it. I flew into Asheville and rented a car. My flight to Paris is already booked. I leave from Asheville after Daphne and Emerson get back. It doesn't make any sense for me to go back to Arkansas when I have to come back this direction anyway."

"Okay, well, how about you drive to the airport and switch your flights?" I suggested. "Leave for Paris early."

I could immediately see she and Daphne were both against that.

"I don't have anywhere to stay in Paris if I get there early," Janet protested. "Plus, I planned the whole thing so I could have a couple of days here with Daphne before I go. It's going to take me some time to settle into the new job. I don't know when I'll be able to travel back."

I looked from her to Daphne again and saw the devastation on both faces. A thought hit me out of nowhere, and it came spilling out before I had the good sense to stop it.

"Alright, well, why don't you come stay with me until they get back?" I suggested. "I've got a guest room and a top-notch security system. I'm already taking care of the dog. It won't be a big deal for you to come too." *Real smooth, Greg. Real smooth. Comparing her to taking care of the dog? Seriously?*

Janet looked shocked and immediately began shaking her head no, but Daphne and Emerson jumped in to convince her.

"That's a great idea," Daphne said, relief flooding her face. "That way I'll know you're safe, and we can still have our time together before you leave."

"How do you know I'll be safe?" Janet sputtered. "After all, he's the one who received the first two threats."

"Because," Daphne said, giving her mom a pointed look, "I know, Mom. You'll be safe staying with him. I *know* it."

That discomfort immediately crept in as I realized she was referring to her "sight" again. I was also already regretting my offer and hoping Janet would turn the whole thing down once and for all.

But Janet seemed to take as much stock in Daphne's "knowing" as Emerson did. Daphne's words seemed to take all the fight right out of her. She opened her mouth to say something, then closed it and nodded tightly.

"Alright," she said. "Thank you for your offer, Sheriff Morrison. You don't have to worry. I'll stay out of your way. You won't even know I'm there. I do appreciate having a secure place to stay. I'll go get my things ready." Her tone was formal and distant, as if she were already putting lines in place between us. Clear boundaries, with a clear message.

She got up and walked toward the stairs, her head held high. Meanwhile, I stood there wondering what the hell I was thinking, signing up to watch over a woman who couldn't stand me and damn near drove me crazy.

CHAPTER ELEVEN

Janet

I WALKED TO THE GUEST ROOM AND STARTED EMPTYING the drawers I had just filled this morning, tucking things back into my suitcase. I was fuming. It was bad enough that this...this *person* unknown had threatened my daughter on her wedding day. But now? Being shuttled away to be babysat by Greg, the very man I had promised myself I wouldn't have to see again after today?

It was unacceptable.

I paused my packing and called down to Daphne, asking if I could see her for a moment. I would simply have to put an end to this. The threat had been toward Daphne and Emerson, not me. Surely the man knew they were leaving on their honeymoon. The house should be safe. This whole thing was ridiculous.

A little warning nudge inside told me I was being as stubborn as Daphne usually was. I knew I had no business staying here alone under the circumstances.

But staying here didn't feel nearly as terrifying as moving in with Greg.

"Mom?" Daphne asked, sticking her head through the cracked door. "Do you need help packing or something?"

I motioned for her to come in and closed the door behind her when she sat on the bed. "Daphne," I began, letting out a breath, "I think we made this plan in haste. I'm not this man's target, and anyone in their right mind knows you and Emerson won't be here this week. I will be careful, but really, I think it's fine for me to stay here."

Daphne immediately shook her head no, her mouth set in a thin line. "I think you're wrong," she said. "Mom, when I touched that box..." She shuddered, trailing off.

"Did you have a vision of something happening?" I asked, more curious than anything. I still didn't fully understand Daphne's gift of the sight, but I was learning to trust it.

She shook her head. "No. Not then. I just felt a lot of darkness surrounding that box. Whoever is behind this is dangerous, Mom. But when Greg offered you a place to stay? I just knew. That's where you're supposed to be right now. He'll protect you, Mom."

"Daphne, I can't stay with him," I whispered, feeling my face go red again. "You don't understand. Maybe I just need to go get a hotel in Asheville or something, then drive back here when you return. That way I'll be safe and out of the way."

She shook her head again. "No. We already know Mr. Boddy had connections in Asheville. Big connections. And unlike here, where that network has almost been destroyed, it's still going strong there. If whoever is doing this is part of that network, it will be even easier for them to get to you there."

"But I'm not his target," I repeated.

"It doesn't matter," she said, growing frustrated. "You don't understand how they work, how they'll hurt or kill loved ones just to make a point. Look, you're a grownup. I can't make you do anything. But right now? All I know is what I felt. You're supposed to stay with Greg. He's a good man. I trust him with my life. And I've been to his place. He's not kidding about his security. Please, Mom."

I sat down on the bed beside her, defeated and miserable. "I am dreading this more than you can possibly know," I said.

"Why? I thought you liked Greg. What happened?"

I shook my head. "It doesn't matter. We're just very different people, and it's going to be difficult to stay with him."

Daphne bit her lip, like she was fighting back a smile. "Maybe it won't be as bad as you think."

"Maybe you need to get that second sight of yours tuned up," I said, smirking. "Because I assure you, it will be awful."

I carried my suitcase downstairs with my head held high, trying to maintain some semblance of dignity. Greg's eyes widened when he saw the size of my bag, no doubt because he was unaccustomed to traveling with a woman. He probably just stuffed an extra pair of jeans into a backpack when he traveled. If that.

"I'll be happy to load that up into the truck for you," he offered, coughing like he was covering up a laugh.

"No need," I replied, my tone frosty. "I'm quite capable of managing my luggage on my own."

Greg reached over to grab the suitcase I had just sat down, accidentally grazing my hand as he did, sending unwelcome shivers up my spine. "I'm aware you're capable of handling it, but my mama raised me to be a gentleman. Good grief"—his tone changed drastically as he lifted the bag—"what the hell do you have in here?"

I gave him an icy smile. "Everything I need until my things arrive next month in Paris. There's another bag upstairs. I'll go get that one while you put this one in my car. Daphne, my keys are in my purse." I motioned for her to help him and turned on my heels to go back up the stairs. Let him carry my bags if he wanted. It didn't change anything.

Greg just shook his head. "Is the second one smaller than this one?"

"Larger," I replied, still giving him that frosty smile.

He squeezed his eyes shut hard for a minute, fighting for control before speaking. It almost made me want to giggle.

"Jackson, get this one," he finally said. "I'm going to carry her apparently even larger one down the stairs."

"I'm perfectly capable—" I began, but he cut me off.

"Just lead the way," he said, his jaw tight.

I rolled my eyes and walked back up the stairs, feeling him follow me with heavy footsteps. The man had offered to let me stay, but now he seemed as reticent as I was about the whole thing.

We didn't speak when we got to my room. I simply opened the door and pointed to the bag. He took a deep breath, as if praying for patience, before picking up the bag as if it weighed nothing. I let him lead the way back down the stairs, telling myself it was because I didn't want to be in the way if he dropped the admittedly oversized suitcase—not because I wanted to check out the way his muscles looked as he carried it.

Before he could carry the second one out, Jackson came back in with a somber look on his face. "Look at this," he said, handing an evidence bag to Greg.

Greg's face clouded with anger. "Where did you find this?"

"I found that one on Emerson's driver's-side window," Jackson said. "And this one"—he pulled a second bag from his pocket—"was on her windshield." He pointed at me.

"My car?" I asked, blanching. "Are you serious?"

He nodded, his face grim.

"What is it?"

"More photos," Greg said, staring at them. "Any chance these were on there when you guys drove home?"

"I–I don't know," I said. I really wasn't sure. The photo was small and I hadn't looked closely at my car.

"Definitely not on mine," Emerson said, his voice strained like he was fighting to keep control. The anger was written all over his face.

Greg scowled. "Then he's been here, sometime since you guys got home." He and Jackson instantly pulled their weapons and headed out without even speaking, apparently to see if the guy was still around.

Emerson followed, leaving me and Daphne speechless in the living room.

My daughter was apparently a magnet for criminal activity.

The men returned later, all three even more irritable than before.

"No sign of anyone," Emerson explained, that anger still on his face. He immediately went to Daphne's side and embraced her.

I watched her melt into his arms and felt a stab of loneliness. What was it like to have someone like that, someone you could just melt into and trust to catch you as you fell? I had never experienced that, not even as a child.

Greg let out a weary sigh. "He had to have been here, but there's no sign of him now. Seems like he had to come in on foot, or you guys would have heard his vehicle pull up. So he can't have gone far, but there's nothing we can track. It's like he disappeared into thin air."

Daphne paled. "What about Fiona? You don't think he would have hidden at her house, do you? Should you check on her? And Patricia? Her house is close, too."

Fiona lived just down the lane from Daphne, with a shortcut trail connecting the two properties so they could go back and forth easily. Patricia Kistler was Daphne's closest neighbor and now a widow living alone. Patricia considered Daphne an enemy because of Daphne's investigations. But for some reason, Daphne still had a soft spot for her.

Greg held up a hand. "Already did. Fiona's fine, other than a little pissed off that you got threatened. I kind of wish he would have gone there," Greg admitted. "She probably would have held him by shotgun til we arrived. Patricia's fine too. Didn't see or hear anything and just wanted to get back to her Saturday night movie. He must have disappeared into the woods somewhere. But with miles of wilderness around here, we don't have a chance in hell of finding him tonight."

Emerson's face was angry. "I can't believe he showed up on our property. He's playing with us now."

Daphne turned to me. "See? There was a photo on your car, too. You are a target, simply for being family. You have to promise me you're going to stay with Greg. No more ideas about going and getting a hotel or something."

Out of the corner of my eye, I saw Greg's face turn sharply, but he didn't say anything.

"Whoever this was probably thought the car was yours," I argued, not wanting to believe it.

Greg marched over and held the photo up where I could see it. It wasn't from the ceremony—it had been taken at the reception, while I was dancing with Greg.

"Still think you aren't a potential target?" he asked. "The man took a photo of us together and put it on your car. I don't think he got confused. I think he left you a message."

I could feel the blood run out of my face, but I refused to show my fear. I crossed my arms tight, putting on the bravest face I could. "Fine," I agreed, turning to Daphne. "I'll stay with him until you guys get back. In return, I'd like for you to think about coming with me to Paris. Just temporarily," I said, holding up a hand when I saw her face. "I know Rosemary Mountain is your home. But you and Emerson both could come stay with me for a bit while all of this settles down. That way I'll know you're safe, too."

Daphne and Emerson exchanged looks.

"We'll definitely talk about that," Emerson said, nodding. "Even if I can't get the time off of work, it's not a bad idea for Daphne to disappear for a while."

"But—" she started to protest.

"You can all talk about that later," Greg said, interrupting. "For now, let's do what we've got to do report-wise. Then I want you two to hit the road." He turned to Jackson, who had just come back in. "Does everything else look good with their vehicle?"

Jackson nodded. "Yep, looks secure. They should be good to go."

"Good." Greg's voice was firm and authoritative. "Take down an initial report. Keep it quick. I want them on the road ASAP. We'll finish up here. Then you can follow me home, Janet."

"Okay," I agreed. I was done arguing. It unnerved me more than I could even say that to know that someone had been watching me and had left a message like that. I never would have expected to be any kind of target. But I guess Daphne was right. Just being her family made me one.

It made me more sure than ever that Paris was the right place for me. And if I could manage it, maybe it would be the right place for Daphne and Emerson, too.

Chapter Twelve

Greg

Emerson and I loaded Thor—Emerson's elderly German Shepherd, a war veteran in his own right—and all the dog supplies up into my truck. I tried to pay attention to Emerson's instructions about food and what not, but in the end, I told him he better text them to me. With my mind consumed by threats, I knew I would never remember.

It had nothing to do with all the thoughts running through my head about Janet Sullivan staying with me for the next two weeks.

What the hell had I been thinking? This was a terrible idea. I was just asking for two weeks of misery, two weeks of her put-downs and snobby ways.

Two weeks of wanting something I couldn't have.

But once I'd said it, I couldn't take it back, especially when I had seen the relief on Daphne's face. Then when Jackson had discovered that Janet was a target after all, well, I really couldn't take it back.

It was my job to keep her safe, and that meant keeping an eye on her. Even if it was better for me, personally speaking, to never lay eyes on her again.

On the drive to my place, I ran through a mental checklist. As luck would have it, I had put fresh sheets on the guest bed just a couple of days ago. There had been talk of one of Emerson's Air Force buddies needing a place to stay for the wedding, so I had prepared. The guy ended up not getting leave after all, which meant the guest room was fresh and ready for Janet.

At least, I hoped it was. Had I known she was the one who would be staying in it, I probably would have taken a few extra minutes to make sure it was spotless.

The guest bathroom had been cleaned too, and it even had a fresh hand towel hanging up.

All it was stocked with was bar soap though. Guy soap. I sure hoped she had whatever lady things she needed. Surely she did, considering the size of her suitcases. But Daphne probably kept the bathroom stocked with lady things like fancy body wash and girl shampoo. Any fancy hotels Janet stayed in would have those things too.

I figured I might need to make a trip into town.

I let out a groan and scrubbed my hand over my face. This was going to be more complicated than I needed right now.

I drove slowly, knowing Janet wasn't used to these dark mountain roads. She kept up though. I had to give her that. She pulled into my driveway just seconds behind me, and despite my misgivings about the situation, I breathed a sigh of relief. She'd be safe here.

I climbed out of my truck and called out to her. "Let me just get the house unlocked and the dog in. Then I'll come back and get your bags."

"I can manage," she said, her tone clipped.

"I know you can. I'll get them just the same."

She seemed to soften a little, because she didn't insist on getting them herself. Just pulled her purse from her car and walked to the porch, where she waited for me to lead the dog up and get the front door unlocked.

I felt a wave of nerves before she walked through the door. I wanted her to like the place, but that was just stupid. It wasn't some chic apartment in Paris or some luxury condo with spa amenities. It was a good house, a solid house. Not the kind of house that would impress the likes of her.

But I wanted it to.

Whatever she was thinking, she didn't say a word as she entered. I caught her looking around with her lips closed in a tight line as I typed in the code to disarm the security system. She was probably judging the place, comparing it to the kinds of places she was accustomed to. But she didn't say a thing.

"Uh, let me just show you the guest room real quick," I said, unclipping Thor's leash. I locked the door behind us—I wasn't taking chances, for even the minute it would take me to show her where she was staying —then led the way down the hall.

"This is your room," I said, feeling more than a bit awkward as I held the door open for her. "It's got its own bathroom, just through there. Take a look and let me know if you'll be needing any, uh, supplies or anything. You know. Soap. Shampoo. Whatever you use. I can make a trip to town tomorrow, pick up whatever you need. There's towels and washcloths, too, but if you need more, just let me know. I don't know, you know, how many..." I cleared my throat awkwardly. "Anyway. Make yourself at home. I'll be right back with your bags."

I exited gratefully, feeling like a damn fool, barely able to form a proper sentence around her. This woman had gotten in my head and I didn't like it one bit.

Two tours in Iraq, yet I was pretty sure this was going to be the longest damn two weeks of my life.

Chapter Thirteen

Janet

I debated putting on my pajamas and going straight to bed just to avoid spending time around Greg, but that was silly. I would be living at his house for potentially two weeks; it wasn't as if I could avoid him the entire time. Better to get it over with and face him tonight.

Besides that, I knew I needed to thank him for letting me stay here. As uncomfortable as I was with the whole situation, I knew it had to be just as uncomfortable for him, if not more so. I regretted being so rude to him at Daphne's, when he had sacrificed his privacy and comfort to offer a solution that would allow me to stay here and see my daughter again before I left town. My anxiety had gotten the better of me once again.

I took my time changing out of my dress though. Facing him was inevitable, but I could at least delay it a bit. Walking out in my silk pajamas felt entirely too intimate, so I changed into chinos and a light sweater. I spent a few minutes getting settled into the room, then squared my shoulders and walked out with my head held high.

The living room was empty though, to my relief. Perhaps he was avoiding me as well.

I took the opportunity to take a better look at the living room and a quick peek into the kitchen. Truthfully, I was surprised by his home. It was neat and clean, with an elegant masculinity. The real wood floors shone, and the furniture had been thoughtfully chosen and properly placed. The color scheme was calming—steel-blue walls, dark wood trim, bronze fixtures, and sage-green accents. The back wall of the living room had floor-to-ceiling windows, promising a beautiful view when the sun rose the next morning. All in all, it reminded me of an upscale ski lodge. It was unexpected and elegant.

Just like him, when he had led me in a waltz at Daphne's wedding.

He came in as I was studying the wine rack in his kitchen, startling me.

"Sorry," he said, "I didn't mean to scare you."

"It's fine," I said, brushing it off, even though my heart was pounding—and not just from the scare. He had changed too, but apparently he had gone straight to his version of pajamas—gray sweatpants that rode low on his hips and a well-cut white t-shirt. Another shock, and one that had me flustered all over again. Both pieces fit him entirely too well.

He must have caught me staring at him, because he looked down at his outfit then looked back at me. "Um. Sorry," he said, running his hand over his head. "I thought you had gone to bed."

"It's fine," I repeated. "Listen, I'd like to apologize. I was rude and didn't properly thank you for your offer." I took a deep breath, hating how vulnerable I felt. "I really appreciate you making a way for me to stay in town and spend time with Daphne before I head to Paris."

He held my gaze for a moment before nodding. "It's fine," he said. "Glad I could help."

I turned my attention back to his wine rack, attempting to recover. "You seem to have decent taste in wine," I said.

He snorted. "Decent? Gee, thanks."

I looked up and realized my compliment had come off as an insult. "That's not what I meant," I started to say before he interrupted me.

"Doesn't matter," he said, raising his hands. "Listen, since you're up, let's go over a few things." His tone switched to all business.

"Sure." I nodded.

"Pantry is over there," he said, pointing to a small doorway off the kitchen. "Help yourself to whatever you want. I think it's best if you don't go into town by yourself, but like I said, I'll make a trip to the store tomorrow." He walked to a drawer and pulled out a pad and a pen. "Make a list of anything you need and I'll pick it up."

"Thank you," I said quietly. "I'll put some cash by the list to cover the cost of my items."

"Not necessary. I can cover it," he said with a flicker of annoyance in his eyes.

It seemed I had unintentionally offended him yet again.

He turned to the pad and scribbled something out before ripping the page off and handing it to me. "That's the security code," he explained. "I'll show you how to set and disarm it. I'll set it before I leave tomorrow. You'll need to remember to disarm it whenever you let Thor out to do his business, then reset it once he's back in. I want it on at all times. It will alert me directly if anyone breaks in."

I nodded as the gravity of the situation hit me.

He must have noticed the look on my face, because his own face softened. "I know this is a lot to take in," he said gently. "And I don't want you to feel like you're a prisoner here. But, Janet, the threats are escalating and we have to take that seriously. Good news is nobody outside our group knows you're staying with me. But we need to take precautions anyway."

"I understand," I said before swallowing hard.

"Speaking of precautions, I'd like to park your car in the barn out back. That way, if anyone comes snooping around, it will be out of sight. Mind if I borrow your keys?"

"Of course. Good idea," I agreed. "They're in my room. I'll go get them."

"Great. One more thing. I think, if you're agreeable, I'd like for me and Jackson to spread a rumor that you left town early. We'll say you got an early flight out after Daphne and Emerson received a threat."

The ramifications of that hit me immediately. "That means I have to stay hidden, doesn't it?"

He nodded slowly. "I'm afraid so. Look, you'll be off his radar. If we play our cards right, you'll stay that way. And that's good for both of us. Good for you because you'll be safe. Good for me because I'll be free to try to track this guy down instead of being stuck here playing bodyguard."

I stiffened at his words. "I apologize for being an inconvenience."

This time, he was the one who tried to apologize. "I didn't mean it that—"

"It's fine," I said, holding up a hand to stop him. "I get it. This really is inconvenient for you, and I'll do what I can to make it easier. Speaking of which, I'm going to get my car keys for you. Then I think I'll turn in. It's been an extraordinarily long day."

With that, I turned and walked toward my room. I heard him call my name, but I ignored it.

Better for both of us that I just stay out of his way.

I WOKE EARLY THE NEXT MORNING, RESTLESS AND EDGY, with a piercing headache. My sleep had been fraught with nightmares of a madman chasing me—and with dreams of being swept away to safety in the strong arms of a certain man with gorgeous gray eyes.

I wasn't sure which dreams annoyed me more.

I felt entirely too tired to dress properly, so I threw a robe over my pajamas and headed to the kitchen, in desperate need of a good cup of tea and a couple of aspirin. The champagne had flowed freely at the wedding, and I was paying the price for it.

Greg was in the kitchen, leaning up against the center island, sipping on a cup of coffee. The smell of freshly ground beans was intoxicating— and tempting considering my headache. But I knew if I indulged I would pay the price for that later, too.

"Good morning," he said, raising his cup to me in greeting. "I made a pot of coffee. Help yourself."

"Thank you," I said. "Would you happen to have any tea? I cut out coffee years ago."

He blinked a few times, like he was trying to process the idea that anyone would willingly give up coffee. "Tea," he finally said. "Um, yeah. I think I have some. Hold on a sec." He placed his cup down on the counter and disappeared into the pantry, rummaging around for a bit before emerging triumphantly with a box of family-sized iced tea bags. "Here you go," he said, handing them to me.

I looked at it and looked back at him. "This is for making iced tea," I said.

"Yeah."

"Do you have any hot tea?"

He stared at me for a beat before replying. "I don't know if you know this," he said, "but you've got to boil the water to make tea. You want it hot, by all means, drink it while it's still hot."

I could tell by the little twinkle in his eye that he was teasing me, but considering my pounding headache, I wasn't in the mood.

"You know what I mean," I said, irritation in my voice. "Do you have any teas meant for drinking hot?"

"I'm afraid this is all I've got," he answered, unaffected. "I've always been a coffee person. Tea is tea, the way I see it."

"Well, then, that's the first thing I'll be adding to the list," I said, heading straight to the pad on the counter to write down the Darjeeling tea I loved.

"Pots are in that cabinet," he said, pointing, "if you want to make a pot of tea. Mugs are in that one."

"No teakettle?"

He laughed. "Nope."

"Then I won't even bother asking about a proper teacup."

"Probably best you don't," he said, chuckling.

For some reason, his easy attitude was irritating me even more. *He* obviously hadn't been up half the night, tortured by dreams of me. And as much as I hated to admit it, I wished he had been.

Chapter Fourteen

Greg

I HAD BARELY SLEPT A WINK, KNOWING JANET WAS ACROSS the hall, sleeping in a bed that belonged to me. I told myself it was just nerves, that I was on edge because of the escalating threats. But that wasn't true.

The woman was a snob. She was downright annoying. She obviously thought she was better than me. She was uptight about damn near everything.

I couldn't stop thinking about her anyway.

So I had woken up bright and early, dressing before heading into the kitchen—no need to scandalize her again by wearing sweatpants *in my own home*. The woman probably didn't even own a pair of sweatpants. Good grief. Last night, she had changed from her wedding finery into the kind of outfit you might wear to a casual country club lunch. I couldn't imagine what she would come out in this morning.

My mind might have wandered a bit, imagining a few interesting possibilities on that front.

Still, I was unprepared when she walked out of her room wearing a silky blue robe—a short one that stopped a full inch above matching pajama shorts, showing off those killer legs again.

It was almost better than my fantasies.

We bantered back and forth a bit over coffee versus tea. Who in their right mind would ever give up coffee, anyway? Not anyone normal, that was for sure. Then she turned away from me and stretched onto her tiptoes to reach the only delicate-looking cup in my cabinet.

I almost dropped the mug in my hand.

Maybe my dry spell had gone on entirely too long, but the sight of that woman in her skimpy little robe, stretching for something in my kitchen... Well. I needed to get the hell out of there before I embarrassed myself.

"Just add anything else you need to that list," I said, forcing myself to look up at the ceiling as she bent over to get a pot from the bottom cabinet. "I'm going to head out in just a minute. I'm heading to the office today, keeping everything looking normal. But I'll stop at the store on the way home."

Her voice brought my eyes back to her. "Well, I shouldn't order anything too out of the ordinary, now should I? If it's a secret I'm staying here, I can't exactly send you to the store for anything particularly feminine. From what Daphne's told me, that will be sure to get the town gossips talking."

This time, her eyes were the ones twinkling, as she seemed to realize just how uncomfortable the mere thought of picking up female supplies might make me.

I cleared my throat. "Well, that's true. Anything like that we might need to enlist Fiona's help for."

She waved a hand, brushing me off. "Don't worry. I don't need anything that will alert the world you have a woman staying with you. Just some tea, please. And"—she walked to the fridge and peered in, frowning—"some fruit and vegetables. Unless that's too outside the norm for you."

"Everybody eats fruits and veggies. Even me, believe it or not," I said.

"Excellent." She walked to the list and made a few more notes. "I like apples. A few lemons would be lovely, and maybe a nice olive oil.

Salad greens. Organic, please. I saw some chicken breasts and mushrooms in the fridge. I'll put together dinner tonight, and a salad will go nicely with it. Get some oregano if the store has fresh. Dried fruit, but only if it doesn't have added sugar."

"I'll see what I can do," I said, refraining from reminding her that this was Rosemary Mountain, not some big city with upscale markets. That comment would only have been to rub at her anyway.

Truth was, we had people growing lots of organic produce here. It supplied our own markets, our growing "foodie" tourism, and some of it even got driven over to some of the neighboring cities. Rosemary Mountain might not have had all the amenities of a big city, but we did food right.

I poured the rest of my coffee into a travel mug, grabbed Janet's list, and showed her how to set the alarm on my way out the door.

I was in a hurry to get away from her. But once I left, all I could think about was getting back to her as fast as I could.

I KEPT MY DEMEANOR AS NORMAL AS POSSIBLE WHEN I headed into the office, knowing there was a chance the person who had sent those threats was someone who worked for the department. It could very well have been paranoia and trust issues, but I wasn't ready to let my guard down.

The plan was to debrief my people on the direct threats today, primarily so I could gauge their reactions. I would leave out the parts about thinking someone had tampered with my desk and my locker. I wanted everyone on the inside to think I was searching for someone on the outside. If that meant playing dumb about everything that wasn't an obvious threat, then so be it. Let the guy think he was getting away with something.

I'd get him in the end.

WHEN I WALKED INTO THE STATION, THERE WERE MORE than a few raised eyebrows and glances between the people on shift. I knew they hadn't been expecting me today, but I wasn't ready to give them an explanation. Not until the meeting, when I could see them all at one time to watch reactions.

I lingered in the main area, pouring myself a cup of coffee and saying hello to people, instead of heading straight to my office. Parker, one of my deputies, came around the corner and nearly dropped the box in her hand when she saw me.

"Sorry, sir," she stammered, "I wasn't expecting you today."

"Just needed to take care of a few things," I said, noting her odd reaction. I felt certain there had to be an innocent reason for it though. She didn't even rank on my suspect list.

She exchanged glances with Tracy, our other female deputy, and went to her desk.

"Conference room in ten minutes," I called out, taking a minute to make eye contact with everyone in the room. There were nods of acknowledgement and a few glances, but no one said a thing.

I headed to my office and unlocked it, taking a quick glance around. My senses immediately went into overdrive. Someone had been in here. The differences were small, almost imperceptible, but clear enough now that I was paying attention. My desk chair had been moved, slightly, and the papers on my desk were stacked neatly. I had left them in a stack, but not a neat one.

Someone had been through them.

Only two people had a key to this office: me and our cleaning lady. She only cleaned my offices on Tuesday nights, so she shouldn't have been in there over the weekend. Still, it was possible she had changed the schedule and I just didn't know about it. I made a note to find out.

With it being a Sunday morning, the number of deputies on shift was even lower than normal and our admin staff was out. That gave me fewer people to debrief than I would have preferred, but I would at least be able to play close attention to their reactions. When everyone gathered, I gave them a quick rundown of the notes and the gift. I also went ahead and started the rumor that Janet had already left town. Lying to people who worked for me and trusted me felt terrible, even though I had to do it. I despised the corruption that had touched this place, and I hoped with all my heart that I was wrong about someone here still being involved.

I told them Daphne and Emerson were safe, but we were going to keep an eye on their place while they were gone and try to figure out who was threatening them—the key word being *them.*

As I gave them the information, I saw two deputies, Miller and Tracy, exchange glances. No overtly guilty looks, but it was interesting, just the same.

"Any questions?" I asked after finishing my speech.

Miller raised his hand. He was a fairly experienced guy, having been here for nearly ten years. He was effective but also a bit cocky, and I didn't always care for the attitude he had when dealing with townspeople. Since he had worked under the former sheriff, he was one I had been concerned about from the beginning. TBI had cleared him, but I still didn't fully trust him.

"Yes?" I asked, turning my attention to him.

"Sir, can I ask... Where is Ford this morning? Wasn't he scheduled to work today?"

"He is working. He's at the reception venue interviewing potential witnesses. Anything else?"

Miller exchanged glances with the female deputy, Tracy, sitting next to him. She had a weird look on her face, too. Tracy had always been real quiet, and I had never quite figured her out, as she kept herself so closed off. She was a Rosemary Mountain native, and I got the feeling she was one of the ones who resented the fact that an outsider had gotten elected sheriff. There was a group of residents who hated that this had become a tourist town and had grown so much in recent years. They all looked down on outsiders and kept them at arm's length.

Tracy was exceptional at her job though, and unlike Miller, she seemed to connect easily with the townspeople. She had also been cleared by TBI, like everyone else who remained employed by the office. Still, I added her to my mental list of people to talk to. The looks they were exchanging were interesting, to say the least.

"Any other questions?" I repeated, turning my attention to the two other deputies in the room, Parker and Sanchez. They both wore poker faces.

Everyone was silent, so I dismissed them, and watched as they left the room. I wanted to see if there was any whispering or conversation about the matter, anything unusual at all. But other than the glances between Miller and Tracy, I didn't notice anything. During the entire meeting, there had been no signs of guilt, no signs of already knowing what I had been about to say.

Nothing suspicious at all.

But I wasn't about to let my guard down.

I WENT BACK TO MY OFFICE AND TEXTED EMERSON TO MAKE sure they had made it safely to their destination. Within minutes, he texted back, telling me they were safe and to leave them the hell alone. He was on his honeymoon and had much better things to do than talk to me.

I grinned, knowing that meant they were okay and I didn't have to worry—about them, at least.

Truth was, it had bothered me to leave Janet alone at the house today. I knew she would be fine. No one knew she was there. I had a state-of-the-art alarm system. And while Thor was on the elderly side, I had no doubt he could still do some serious damage if someone did try to break in. He belonged to Emerson, but he knew to protect the people Emerson loved. Janet was on that list, and I knew Thor would do his part to keep her safe.

I had every reason to believe she would be fine and every reason to keep to my normal routine.

But the thought of her being out there alone and probably scared, well, it gutted me. She was a snob, yes. She wasn't interested in me, no. But she didn't deserve to go through any of this. She was just a woman who loved her daughter and just happened to find herself caught up in a bad situation.

Snob or not, I would do my part to try to make it easier on her.

Even if spending time with her meant making it that much harder for me.

Chapter Fifteen

Janet

I HAD BEEN PREPARED FOR A MISERABLE DAY TRAPPED AT Greg's house like a prisoner. To my surprise, I found myself enjoying it. His home was lovely, and despite the lack of proper tea, I started feeling like I was on a retreat—a much-needed one, considering the stress of the last several months. I had been in go mode for months now, first helping Daphne deal with her father's death and the subsequent sale of his home (thank God *that* was over), then the chaos of her investigations, and then everything that went with a new job and an international move... I had barely let myself breathe.

Greg's home was beautiful—truly—but it was far surpassed by the view from his windows. I knew that Daphne loved her little spot in the woods, but it felt too closed in for my taste. Greg's house was situated in the valley, with a view of the mountains so perfect it looked like a painting. When I let Thor outside to do his business, I sat on the deck and just gazed at those mountains, feeling the warmth of the sun on my face and the breeze in my hair. I breathed deeply for the first time in months and felt some of the stress begin to ease.

Ironic, considering I was only here because someone was threatening me and everyone I loved.

But all of that barely felt real here, in the shadow of the mountains. Here, I only felt peace. All the worries I had carried for months began to fade.

And when Thor and I begrudgingly took ourselves back into the safety of the house with its security system, I had Greg's books to entertain me.

I had to admit his possessions were making me more and more curious about the man. I wouldn't have taken him to be a reader, but he had a bookshelf full of fascinating books. All non-fiction, sadly—romance novels were my secret guilty pleasure, and I had only packed one, which I was trying hard to save for the flight to Paris. But his non-fiction collection spoke of a man who was fascinated with the world around him and wanted to learn everything he could about it.

There were true crime stories and psychological profile books, both of which I would have expected for someone in law enforcement. But there was also a wealth of history books and various encyclopedias about the natural world. I pulled one about the caves in Appalachia, curious considering Daphne's recent experience in one, and spent an hour enthralled by the photographs and information.

I WAS SITTING ON THE DECK AGAIN, SOAKING UP THE afternoon sun in a wooden rocking chair, when I heard the door open behind me. My body immediately tensed as I remembered why I was here in the first place. I jumped and looked behind me, relaxing when I saw Greg had returned.

"It's just me," Greg called out as he strode toward me.

I put my hand on my heart and laughed. "You scared me."

He took the rocker next to me, making my heart twist with a sudden shot of longing. My grandparents, one of the only truly happily married couples I had ever known, had always sat together in their front porch rockers every afternoon while they sipped their sweet tea and reconnected after the day apart. I hadn't thought of that in years, but that image flashed through my mind as I watched Greg beside me.

"Sorry for scaring you," he said with an easy smile. "Next time I'll text you, let you know I'm on my way home, so you know to expect me."

My heart twisted again. "Ah, yes, you are home early, aren't you?" I stammered, trying to force my mind away from the unwelcome—and unrealistic—images of him coming home to me every day, of us sitting right here, sipping our tea, and talking.

I couldn't even imagine where those images had come from. It was ridiculous, really. I closed my eyes and pictured Paris, forcing my daydreams to change to my future life there. Paris was my future. Paris would be my love. Paris...

Paris was so far away.

"Nah, not for a Sunday," Greg explained. "I just needed to put in a few hours. Probably would have been back sooner, but Old Man Murphy got in a tiff about someone trespassing on his property. Most of the deputies are terrified of him, so I handle those calls myself. Had to make a trip up the mountain and cool things down."

"Why are they scared of him?" I asked, curious.

He grinned. "Old Man Murphy's half crazy, I think. Lives alone on the mountain, totally off-grid. Has long hair and a long beard. Likes scaring hikers away by pretending to be Bigfoot. He's harmless, I think, but he's got everyone convinced otherwise."

I just smiled and shook my head. "This is an interesting place to live."

"Yep. But I sure love it. By the way, I stopped by the store on my way home. The things you wanted are on the counter in the kitchen."

"Wonderful. Thank you," I said. "I can go get started on dinner right away." I stood up to leave, but he reached up and grabbed my arm, stopping me, sending a thrill up my spine.

"Sit," he said. His voice was firm but kind. "It's only four. No need to rush off and get to work."

I looked down to where his hand was still on my arm as his thumb rubbed my wrist absentmindedly, like he had forgotten who we were or why we were stuck here together. Like he genuinely wanted me to stay.

His eyes followed mine and he immediately let go. But I could still feel where his hand had been. It felt as if my entire body came alive every time he touched me.

"Sit down," he repeated. "Tell me about your day here. Were you too bored, or did you find a way to entertain yourself?"

I obeyed, sitting back down beside him in the rocking chair. *Paris, Paris, Paris.* It was like being in one of those silly meditation classes, trying so hard to focus on a mantra and let everything else go when all my mind wanted to do was wander elsewhere.

"It was fine," I said, keeping my eyes focused on Thor, who was slowly making his way back up the deck stairs.

The dog came over and dropped down at Greg's feet, practically smiling at the man. When Greg reached down and scratched between his ears, Thor flopped over, exposing his belly. Greg just grinned and gave the dog all the love he was looking for.

Meanwhile, I was watching, and my heart was continuing to betray me. Thor was an intuitive dog. He obviously trusted Greg completely, adored him even. I wasn't surprised by that—I knew Greg was a good man. But something about being here with him, now, and watching Thor's adoration for him...

It just felt like too much.

"I–I really need to start dinner," I stammered.

He looked over at me, his easy grin having changed to a frown. "You hungry? Did you not find anything to eat here today? I should have checked on you to make sure you had lunch."

My heart squeezed again. When was the last time someone had checked on me to make sure I was taken care of? I was usually the one doing the checking.

"No, I did. Find lunch, that is. Thank you." I felt abnormally shy and awkward. It was a strange feeling for me. I was used to walking into any room and feeling like I belonged. I was normally able to be charming and carry on conversation in any arena. It was practically a requirement for my job. But this man was constantly knocking me off-balance, sending my mind—and my heart—in a million unfamiliar directions, leaving me feeling like a boat adrift on the ocean.

"You seem tense," he said, still looking at me with that frown on his face. "Did something happen here today? Did someone see you or threaten you? What's going on?"

I took a deep breath and let it out slowly, scrambling for a response.

It's not as if I could just be honest. *No, Greg, there was no threat. Tense? Yes, I'm tense. But not because of a madman. I just find myself flustered beyond belief every time I'm near you.*

No, that wouldn't do.

"It's just a stressful situation," I said, finally settling on an answer. He didn't have to know that the stress was primarily from my internal war of feelings for him.

He nodded, letting out a breath of his own. "I know. I've been thinking about that. Look, I needed to go in today to keep things normal looking. But I felt bad leaving you here all alone. I worried about you..." His voice trailed off, and he frowned.

"I was fine. Really." I suddenly wanted to reassure him, wanted to bring back his relaxed smile. "I–I enjoyed your home. I took the liberty of exploring your bookshelf and read a book on the caves around here. And this deck, with this view..." I trailed off myself, turning my eyes away from him and back to the vista before me. "It's really beautiful," I said finally.

"It is, isn't it? This place was a lucky find," he agreed. "As soon as I saw it, I knew it was the place for me. I was ready to make an offer before even looking at the inside of the house." His smile returned, and I relaxed back into my chair.

"I don't blame you," I said. "Most views like this seem to have been snatched up by vacation rentals or other businesses. It's dreamy to imagine actually living in a place like this all the time." I bit my lip, realizing I had just nearly given away the fact that I really *had* imagined it earlier, before forcing my thoughts back to Paris. "So, ah, you've heard about my day," I said, quickly changing the subject. "How was yours? Find out anything new at work?"

His face changed, hardened, as he shook his head. "Not really," he said, glancing over at me. "The rumor has been set that you left town already, so that makes me feel better."

"That's good," I agreed.

He quickly explained about the meeting he called and the purpose behind it.

"But you didn't notice any weird reactions?" I asked.

"A couple of deputies exchanged looks, and one of them asked where Jackson was." He paused, silent for a moment, as if thinking it over again. "I don't know. I need to talk to each of them privately. But I want to give it more time."

"Why?" I asked, curious.

"Watch and wait. That motto has always served me well. A lot of times, you find out more by just watching than you do by questioning. I kept my eyes and ears open today. Wanted to watch how everyone went about their shifts before I did any talking. Besides that, I don't want any of them to know I'm looking internally. As far as they're concerned, I'm looking for someone on the outside."

"That makes sense."

Time seemed to stop for just a moment as he looked at me and our eyes met. Thoughts of Paris faded away, replaced by this, here, now—the warm breeze, the valley grasses swaying in the wind, the soft blue mountains surrounding us, and this man. This man who sat beside me in a rocking chair, telling me about his day as if it were the most natural thing in the world. I found myself leaning toward him, pulled in like a magnet.

Thankfully, I quickly came back to reality when Thor scratched loudly on the back door.

"Oh," I said, moving back, hoping I hadn't completely embarrassed myself. "I guess he's ready to go inside."

"He's probably ready for some water," Greg agreed.

"Yes. Water. I could use some too. I really will get started on dinner now." I stood up and stepped away from the rockers, flustered yet again.

"I'll come help," he said, standing.

"Oh, no," I protested. "I've got it. You just relax." I wanted to put a little distance between us, wanted to be alone again, to get my head on straight.

He looked at me like he could see right through me, then nodded and sat back down. "Okay," he said. "But the offer stands. Change your mind and want some help, I'm here. And I've got dish duty. That's non-negotiable."

I nodded, then slipped away to the refuge of the house.

Paris, Paris, Paris.

CHAPTER SIXTEEN

Greg

I SHOOK MY HEAD AND SIGHED AS JANET WALKED BACK INTO the house, practically running away from me. Again. For a moment there, I had let myself forget that the woman wanted nothing to do with me. When she had leaned in, staring at my lips like that, I'd actually thought she was going to kiss me.

Before Thor had interrupted things, I had nearly beaten her to it.

I had gotten caught up in the moment, that was all, and it wasn't just the possibility of that kiss. Sitting out here with her, talking about my day, well... It had felt *right*.

It had been a long time since I had someone to sit and talk with like that, and I missed it. Sure, I talked things over with Emerson and even Jackson. They were solid buddies, and I appreciated the friendship.

But it was a different thing altogether to come home to a woman and talk about my day with her.

I just needed to remember that Janet Sullivan had no intention of ever being that woman.

I forced my thoughts away from her and back to the case. I hadn't told her yet about the conversation I'd had with Jackson when he had gotten back to the office. He hadn't had any luck getting video surveillance of the places where threats had been left, but he had found a waitress at the restaurant who said she'd seen a tall man wandering around the parking lot the night of the rehearsal dinner. She had only noticed him briefly when she took out the garbage and wondered if he was struggling to find his car. She had called out to him, asking if he needed help, but he waved her off without turning around.

It wasn't much, but it was something, and the tall factor matched the guy I had seen pass by the doorway that night. I still had a nagging feeling that he reminded me of someone I knew, but I hadn't yet placed it. It was driving me nuts.

I needed to find out who was behind this before Daphne and Emerson got back from their honeymoon and I had even more people to worry about keeping safe.

I WAITED AWHILE BEFORE HEADING INSIDE. IT FELT WRONG. I didn't want Janet to think she had to "earn her keep" by cooking for me while she was here. I wanted to be in there, helping her.

But I also wanted to respect the fact that she didn't want to be anywhere near me. She also probably didn't want me anywhere near the dinner she was making. Probably assumed I would screw it up, since she seemed surprised anytime I did anything right.

This had to be a tough situation for her, stuck living with someone she didn't even like, in a town she didn't care for, either. She liked my valley though. And if that made me feel a swell of pride I hadn't earned, well, it was just because I loved this place.

It wasn't because I secretly wanted her to love it too.

THE KITCHEN SMELLED AMAZING WHEN I WENT IN. I WASN'T a bad cook, but I had to admit my simple dinners didn't smell like *this*. It was almost a shock, coming in from the fresh mountain air to the savory aromas of whatever she was cooking up in here.

"Smells great," I commented, watching her busy at work. Although busy wasn't quite the right word. She seemed downright relaxed about the whole thing, like it was a dance she had rehearsed a thousand times. One hand held a skillet, casually flipping the food like it was no big deal. The other hand held a glass of white wine, which she was sipping ever so daintily.

"Thanks," she said, blushing. "I hope you don't mind. About the wine, I mean. I chilled a bottle that would go nicely with the chicken."

"Don't mind at all," I answered. "Dinner's always better with something to perk up the taste buds."

"Exactly," she said, smiling. "Can I pour you a glass?"

"A small one. Thanks." I couldn't resist enjoying her full meal, but I needed to keep my wits about me tonight.

And not just because of the threat we were facing.

She rested the skillet on the stove and moved to pour me a glass of wine. When she handed it to me, our fingers brushed for the briefest second. She blushed again, and it took everything within me to not pull her to me. I wanted to run my hands through her hair, wanted to press my lips to hers and taste that pretty mouth.

And I needed to stop all these thoughts in their tracks. *The woman doesn't want you.*

She backed away and went back to the skillet, awkward yet again.

"What's cooking?" I asked, taking a larger sip of the wine than I intended, hoping it would cool me down a bit.

"It's just chicken," she replied.

"It smells great. You look like a real chef, handling that skillet the way you do."

She was still avoiding looking at me, but I saw the way the corners of her mouth turned up in a pleased smile. "I've been taking cooking lessons," she said like she was confessing a secret.

"Oh yeah? What for?"

She shrugged. "It probably sounds silly. I felt like I needed to have a bit more skill in that area before moving to Paris. I grew up on ramen noodles and pasta kits. Switched to takeout when I could afford it. I never really learned to cook more than a few basic meals, and food is such an important part of French culture. Before hosting people in my apartment, I wanted to make sure I could produce something that wouldn't have them rolling their eyes about the American woman who didn't know her way around the kitchen."

"That's not silly at all. I think it shows a lot of character actually."

"Really?" she asked, finally looking at me with curiosity on her face.

I nodded and took another sip of the wine. "Really. It's not unlike what I do in my job in a lot of ways. People are more apt to connect with you, trust you, if you care about what they care about. I came here as an outsider. But I love this town and I prove it to the people here. I show up for all the festivals. I hike trails with them. Hell, I even went to the school play last year despite not having a kid in it. Showing respect and appreciation for the people you're serving goes a long way. Shows you aren't just in it for yourself."

"I love that," she said quietly. "Thanks for understanding."

I just nodded and tipped my wine glass toward her.

"So," she asked a moment later, "is that why you wear jeans all the time? To fit in with the people here?"

I grinned. "Janet, I wear jeans because they're damn comfortable."

Chapter Seventeen

Janet

I KNEW I SHOULD KEEP MY DISTANCE FROM GREG. I DIDN'T know what I was thinking, cooking dinner for us like this. I guess I hadn't thought it would feel this, well, *intimate.* When I was married, Lonnie and I had dinner together almost every night.

That had never felt intimate at all.

Family dinners with Lonnie and Daphne had always felt tense, strained, and distant. Lonnie and I would take turns asking Daphne about her day, but we never talked to each other. Daphne had always been a sort of buffer between us, helping us pretend we were a normal family.

But this, with Greg, felt different. I cooked in front of people all the time at my evening cooking classes, but cooking for him, here in his kitchen? Yes, it felt completely different indeed.

It felt...right.

He was talking to me and smiling like he wanted to be here. Like he genuinely wanted to spend time with me, like he thought I was interesting.

It was confusing in a thousand ways.

He offered to set the table while I put together the salad. Then he surprised me once again by pulling out real cloth napkins. I hadn't expected as much from a single man living in the mountains.

But, then again, Greg Morrison seemed to be a constant surprise, a study in contradictions that kept me on my toes.

I plated our meals and carried them to the table, feeling surprisingly happy about the whole situation. I knew I was playing with fire, letting myself enjoy playing house with a man with whom I had no future. But I couldn't help myself. I *was* enjoying it. And for once, I decided to just relax and let myself.

"Oh, wow," Greg said with a little moan as he bit into the chicken. "Okay. Those cooking classes were well worth whatever you paid for them. I normally think chicken's a little, well, bland. But this is anything but."

"Thank you," I said, blushing despite myself. I couldn't seem to stop blushing around him. "I'm glad you like it."

"Listen," he said, suddenly serious. "I've been meaning to tell you something."

"Yes?" My heart sped up, wondering what on earth he was about to say and hoping, somehow, it was about *us* and not about the case that had thrown us together.

"That night, at the rehearsal dinner. I know I pissed you off. I'm sorry. I'd like to explain."

I raised an eyebrow, surprised by the turn. "Okay."

"I had a bad feeling that night about those threats. Couldn't relax. Something in my gut told me he was close. While you were talking, a man I didn't recognize passed by the door to our room three times."

"Oh," I said, suddenly understanding his perspective. "I–I thought you were just bored."

He shook his head and chuckled. "No, Janet. I've felt a lot of things around you, but never once have I felt bored."

The look in his eyes made me believe him. It was a look I had seen in them more than once—a look of wanting. But it was a want that went deeper than the physical. It made me feel like he wanted *me.* All of me.

And if he kept giving me looks like that, I was going to end up in big trouble.

"It's fine," I said, shaking it off and starting up the internal *Paris* mantra yet again. "Don't worry about it."

"I'm not sure how badly I came off that night, but I just want to apologize for it," he said, his eyes sincere. "And now that I know how I made you feel, I'd like to doubly apologize. I'm sorry, Janet. I can get laser focused on work and miss what's right in front of me."

I shook my head, smiling slightly. "I can relate to that. Really. Don't worry about it. What you were focused on was more important anyway. Do you really think this man you saw is the one who threatened us?"

He shrugged, his face turning hard. "I don't know. But he might be." He relayed the conversation he'd had with Jackson about the man in the parking lot. "Can't say for sure she saw the same man I did. Can't say for sure, even if she did, that he's the man leaving the threats."

"But your gut thinks they're connected," I said, prodding.

He nodded slowly. "Yeah. But I need more than that. I need evidence. And I need a name."

"Hmm…" I mulled it over, nibbling the chicken dish I had put together.

He was right; it *was* tasty. It amazed me how some of the most delicious dishes could be created with just a few simple ingredients. And while I had zero intentions of ever again becoming someone's wife—which in my experience was just a prettier-sounding word for live-in maid and cook—part of me was rejoicing over the fact that I had made him such a nice dinner.

Paris. Paris. Paris.

"What are you thinking over there?" he asked.

"Just thinking about the case," I replied, a little white lie to protect myself. "I don't know how much you can talk to me about it. But if you can, I'm happy to be your sounding board."

He grinned. "Got an investigative streak in you like your daughter does, do you?"

I returned the grin and shook my head. "Not at all. I prefer to stay well out of danger, thank you. But I do have some experience helping her talk through her investigations, and I would like to know more about this situation that has turned my own plans upside down."

His face turned serious again. "Yeah. I'm sorry about that, too. I don't know if making you come here was the right choice or not. I feel terrible thinking about you stuck somewhere you don't want to be. But selfishly, I'm glad to know you're safe."

Our eyes met and an unexpected wave of butterflies coursed through me. It mattered to him that I was safe. I could see that all over his face. And I knew, somehow, it wasn't just because of his job title.

It felt like *I* mattered to him.

I found myself leaning toward him again before catching myself and coming back to reality. "So what can you tell me?" I asked, bringing the subject back to the case and my wine glass up to my mouth. I needed something to do with my hands, and I needed a barrier between us before I embarrassed myself.

He leaned back in his chair and put his hands behind his head, a contemplative look on his face. "I feel like I'll mostly be repeating things you already know," he said.

"That's okay. You never know when talking things through will spur a new thought," I said, encouraging him. I really did want to hear about it. Partially because I was interested, and partially because I needed to get the conversation on to a safe topic.

"Okay," he agreed. "Well. Let's start at the beginning. Daphne came here and stirred a hell of a lot of things up." He winked, letting me know he wasn't angry at my daughter for everything that had happened.

"Yes, I'd say she did," I said.

"You know the basics there. While investigating her mother's death, we uncovered corruption, going back decades, and all leading to the same man."

"Ahhh, yes. The infamous 'Mr. Boddy,'" I said, filling in the blank.

"Exactly," he agreed. "He set up a drug trafficking and money laundering organization here. Small beans compared to the big players in the city, but he was incredibly successful at what he did, in part because he was so damn good at getting people in his pocket. Everyone who knew him either didn't know what he was and adored him, thinking he was just some benevolent older man with some quirks, or they did know and were afraid of him. Either way, he was good at getting people to do what he wanted."

"And you really think this all goes back to him?" I asked. It was something I was curious about—and, frankly, scared about as well. What little I had heard put me solidly in the terrified camp.

He leaned forward, putting his elbows on the table and running his hands through his hair, making it stand on end. I smiled, realizing I was seeing him in his thinking mode, with that edge of professionalism disappearing. This was Greg off duty yet still thinking about the work to which he had dedicated his life. It was endearing and, frankly, sort of adorable.

"I don't know," he confessed. "The language in the notes makes me think it is. The guy said he owns this town. That's how 'Mr. Boddy' thought of it. In his mind, Rosemary Mountain existed to serve him and his family, to give them a legitimate business front and a steady stream of customers. He owned it and everyone in it. And now this new guy is saying the same."

"Hmm..." I mused again. "So maybe someone who was under him, wanting to take over?"

"That's my thought," he agreed. "Problem is finding out who. We've pretty much rounded up everyone already."

"There's no one left?"

"No one that I have any proof of having been involved."

My heart picked up when I realized there was something here. Someone he suspected but hadn't named. Maybe I had a little of Daphne in me after all, because this was fun.

"What are you not telling me?" I asked, smiling to let him know I was interrogating him all in good fun.

He grinned back. "Oh, I see how it is."

"That's right," I teased. "Tell me what you know."

He turned serious again. "Daphne told me that when Luke was ordered to kill her, there was mention of someone named Billy."

"Billy?"

Greg nodded slowly. "We haven't yet found a Billy involved. There's one man named Billy that I know in town, but..."

"You're talking about Bill Brinksley's son, aren't you?" I was well aware of who Bill Brinksley was, thanks to my daughter's investigations.

Greg nodded confirmation. "There's no proof at all that Billy Brinksley was involved, but it fits in some ways. He's an angry man, and he has money. When I questioned him, he denied any involvement. FBI looked into him when they took over. They said he was clean. But I still wonder."

"Did the man you saw look like this Billy guy?"

Greg shook his head. "Not really. Billy is in his fifties and nearly bald. The man I saw was forty, tops, with a head full of greasy hair. He's also thinner. More rough looking. Billy has a real polished, professional look. This guy didn't."

"What is it?" I asked, seeing there was something else he was thinking over.

He just shook his head again. "The guy I saw. It's driving me crazy. He seemed so familiar. I didn't recognize him. I don't think he lives here. But something about him feels familiar."

"I sure hope you figure it out quickly," I said, shaking my head.

A look flashed across his face. Then he slipped back into professional mode. "Yeah. I know you're ready to get out of here and back to your life," he said, his tone different. It wasn't cold, exactly. Just professional. Distant. "We'll get things wrapped up as quickly as possible. In good news, it won't be long until Daphne gets back, and then you can get out of here no matter what."

"Yeah," I agreed, feeling an odd ache. I hadn't meant to insinuate that I wanted the case solved so I could leave. The truth was, I wasn't in a hurry to leave at all. And as he reinstated the distance between us, I found myself missing the Greg I had just seen, the one who talked to me like we were friends.

Because despite how different we were, I really wanted his friendship.

If I was being entirely honest with myself, I wanted more.

Chapter Eighteen

Greg

Janet and I finished up dinner, chatting the whole time. Conversation turned away from the case and back to her job, with her finally telling me all the things she had tried to tell me at the rehearsal dinner, when I was distracted by the man walking by.

I had never been so disappointed to see a meal end.

The food was delicious. But more than that, I was just enjoying her company. I had thought she was a snob, but I was starting to see a different side of her. I began to wonder if that other side—the perfect, uptight version of herself—was just a sort of armor, a hardness she had conjured up to protect herself from something. Because the Janet I was seeing tonight was soft. Gentle.

Fascinating.

But she had also reminded me that she was eager for us to solve the case so she could get out of here. It was something I needed to keep at the forefront of my mind, because when we were talking, I quickly found myself forgetting she was only here because she had to be. Our conversation was so easy and enjoyable that it would be too easy to forget that she would split the first minute she had a chance.

. . .

I HAD PROMISED TO DO DISH DUTY, BUT SHE INSISTED ON helping. We found ourselves side by side, with me washing and her rinsing, quickly falling into a rhythm as we worked. I felt happy, and lighter than I had in years. All the stress of work, all the responsibility I normally felt for this town and these people, somehow faded when I was with her. Not that I would ever let go of the responsibility. But somehow, it didn't feel so heavy a burden to carry with her around.

I had her giggling while she rinsed, telling her some of the stories of crazy calls I had gotten as sheriff in a rural mountain town. She seemed to be particularly fond of stories about Old Man Murphy, so I told her all about the ways he tormented hikers. Hell, he had even gotten his picture in one of the newspapers once, with the words "LOCAL BIGFOOT SIGHTING" in bold letters across the front page.

With every story, she giggled harder. I don't know what got a hold of me, but I was downright intoxicated by her sweet laughter, and I wanted to keep it going. I pulled up a scoop of bubbles in my hand and turned to her, putting them right on her nose.

She blinked hard and looked at me, shocked, before her face broke into a wide smile. "Oh, you're getting it now," she said.

"Oh, am I?"

"Absolutely. You forgot something very important."

"What's that?"

She grinned. "That I'm the one with the sprayer."

With that, she squeezed the trigger on the water and sprayed me right in the face. I couldn't believe she had it in her. I laughed and dove for her, grabbing the nozzle out of her hand, fully intending to get her back. But when I realized I had my arm around her waist and she was staring up at me with those big hazel eyes, I dropped the sprayer. Before I knew what I was doing, I put my other arm around her and pulled her to me, running my hands up her back.

"Greg," she said nervously, putting two hands on my chest like she meant to push me away.

I dropped her waist instantly. "I'm sorry, Janet. I didn't... I just—"

"I'm leaving soon," she whispered, still staring at me. Her hands stayed on my chest, and she didn't pull away after all.

"I know," I said.

"I should go to bed," she said, finally taking her hands off my chest.

"It's only eight."

"I've got some work to do on my computer." She took a step backward.

"Okay."

She turned around and walked out, practically running from me again.

The alarm went off way too early the next morning. I groaned, not wanting to face another day at the office. Truth was, I wanted to stay right here.

With Janet.

I let my mind briefly play out that scenario. Would she welcome it if I took a day off to stay here with her? Not likely.

Not that any of it mattered anyway. With a new threat in town, I couldn't hide out here, playing house with her, no matter how much I wanted to.

I sighed and dragged my tired body out of bed. Sleep hadn't come easy the night before. I wanted to get back to the days when this town felt a whole lot closer to Mayberry than it did right now, when keeping the peace was a lot more about maintaining good relationships with my townspeople and a lot less about tracking down people intent on hurting them.

I went to the kitchen and started my coffee, then pulled out the teakettle I had bought the day before. It was a silly thing to do. It wasn't as if Janet would be here longer than two weeks at most. But I wanted to make her smile, and I wanted her to have things the way she liked them while she was here. So I had picked up the teakettle and hidden it in a cabinet before going out on the deck the night before. Now, I washed it carefully, filled it with water, and put it on the stove to heat. It would be ready for her to brew up whatever kind of Darjeeling she wanted when she woke. After all, I had bought every brand the store carried.

Next, I washed the dainty little teacup I had bought for her and tucked it into the cabinet with my coffee mugs.

I couldn't wait for her to see it.

I didn't have to wait long, thankfully. Just as I was pouring my own cup of coffee, hoping the strong brew would keep me from getting arrested myself today, she floated gracefully into the kitchen, wearing that silky robe again.

And once again, I almost dropped my coffee.

It wasn't fair how damn gorgeous that woman was first thing in the morning. Clean face, sleep still in her eyes, hair piled on top of her head in a messy clip—not at all put together the way she normally was—and yet I almost liked her this way better.

Couldn't help but wonder what it would be like to wake up next to her, with that messy hair spread over my pillow.

"Good morning," I said, forcing my thoughts back to the present. "I started the teakettle for you."

She stopped suddenly and looked at it. For a moment, she didn't say a word, just stared. I was starting to wonder if I had made a mistake. Maybe what I thought was a teakettle was completely different than what she had meant? Maybe she wanted some fancier thing, like those cast-iron ones the fancy tea shops in the city sold.

"You bought me a teakettle?" she finally asked, her voice small.

"Just wanted you to be comfortable while you're here," I said. *And wanted to see you smile, not standing there looking devastated like you are.*

"I–I saw the different kinds of tea you bought in the grocery bag," she said, finally tearing her eyes away from the stove and looking at me. "That was incredibly thoughtful. As is this. Thank you."

She finally smiled, but it was a different kind of smile than I had expected. It was almost sad. Wistful.

And damn if I didn't want to move straight to her, pull her into my arms, and get her to tell me what the matter was.

"Are you sure you like it?" I asked. "You don't seem happy."

"Oh, no, I am," she said. "I'm sorry. It's just that nobody has done anything like that for me in a very long time." Her voice was quiet.

"Well, you deserve more than that," I said gruffly. The words came out unexpectedly, but I didn't regret them.

"Thank you," she said, looking at me for a long time. Then she walked over to me tentatively and planted a light kiss on my cheek.

It was the last thing I'd expected, and it nearly knocked me off my feet.

More than a few women in Rosemary Mountain had kissed me on the cheek since I had been here. Most were older women, grateful for my help with something simple but meaningful to them. A few had been women my age—or even a bit younger—who were obviously flirting with me, hoping to make something happen.

Not once had it left any sort of impression on me.

But Janet's kiss? It felt like a gift, a prize, a trophy.

And I wasn't sure I would ever recover from it.

"You bought me a teacup, too." Her voice brought me back to earth as I turned my eyes to where she was standing, staring into the cabinet.

"Um. Yeah," I said, my voice thick. "Wanted you to have the full tea experience."

She withdrew the cup and held it in her hands, tracing the flowers with her finger. "Did I tell you why I don't drink coffee?"

"Um. No? Health reasons?" I was still a bit off my game, struggling to focus on what she was saying. All I could think about was that little kiss.

She smirked and set the cup on the counter, choosing a box of tea. While she spoke, she put together her drink, putting the teabag in and pouring the steaming water on top. I watched every bit of it, entranced by her every movement.

"You can find as many health reasons for drinking it as you can for cutting it out," she said, one side of her mouth twisting up into a painful smile. "I use health as an excuse now. And it's been so long since I've had that amount of caffeine, it really would keep me up all night. But that's not why I stopped drinking it."

"Why did you then?"

She let out a little sigh, then told her story. "I've always preferred tea, but I used to drink coffee too. I would switch back and forth in college, depending on how much sleep I had the night before." Her eyes were unfocused, like she was gazing into the past. "Then I met Lonnie."

"Daphne's dad?" I asked even though I was well aware of the family history.

"Right." She sighed again, a deep one this time. "I was in college. Young. Stupid. So very stupid." She shook her head, a look of deep regret on her face. "I met him at a coffee shop. I was there studying. He came in with his adorable little daughter, and I was instantly attracted. He was older than me and seemed so, well, fascinating. The coffee shop was full, but I was at a table alone, with my books spread out. He asked if he could sit there since there wasn't an empty table. I said yes."

She went silent for a moment, remembering. "I thought it was my lucky day. I was over the college boys who ran around in basketball shorts and sweatshirts, using the worst sort of language and the crudest jokes in an attempt to look cool. Here was this *man,* in an actual button-down shirt and sweater vest, talking to *me.* He obviously adored his daughter. Absolutely doted on her, which of course made my little heart swoon."

"Go on," I said, wanting to encourage her to talk but not knowing at all what to say.

"I was studying for a history test," she went on. "And he was a history buff. He told me stories about what I was trying to memorize that brought it to life for me." She cracked a little smile finally. "I aced that test."

"So what happened?" I asked. This was one part of the family history I didn't know. I knew that Lonnie had left Rosemary Mountain when Daphne was a toddler, shortly after his first wife, Eileen, had been murdered. I knew he and Janet had married not long after and divorced basically as soon as Daphne was old enough to stay home alone. But the years in between were blank for me.

"I fell hard," she said, her face flat now. "Everyone tried to tell me it was moving too fast, that I should date boys my own age. But I didn't listen. I thought I knew better than them. Besides that, I was very attracted to the life he promised me." She sighed in a way that spoke of a lifetime of regrets. "I had grown up rather poor, in a home with parents who were always fighting about money. I always wanted a different life than what I seemed destined for. I wanted to be elegant, sophisticated. Different from my parents, who were so unhappy. I worked so hard to get a college scholarship, hoping to create a better life for myself. But then this man entered the picture, promising me the world. Promising me the life I had always dreamed of. Promising me the happy family I had never had. I felt like I had won the jackpot."

"Did he... Was he..." Even though I asked these questions all the time in my line of work, it somehow felt wrong to ask her what I was thinking. Frankly, she presented like a woman who had been abused somehow, but I didn't know how to ask her about it.

She looked up at me. "You mean, did he hurt me?"

I nodded.

"Only my heart," she said. "Within three months, we had eloped. I thought I had found myself a happily ever after. I loved him. Truly. Loved everything about him. The problem was, he didn't love me." At that, her voice became strained, like it was painful for her to say. Painful to admit.

"I don't understand how that's possible," I said. I really couldn't. What wasn't to love?

She snorted, raising her eyes to me again. "Thanks. But it turns out, all he was looking for was a cheap nanny and housekeeper. He was suddenly a single father and didn't know what to do."

She went quiet again, and I just stood there, giving her space to continue.

"I don't blame him," she said, finally sighing. "Not really. I mean, part of me does. What he did to me was wrong. But I do understand his position. He was just trying to do what was best for Daphne, and in his mind, she needed a full-time mother figure. He couldn't stand the thought of putting her in a crowded daycare where she might be neglected or even harmed. I don't think he sat down at my table intending to trick me into marrying him. I think I fawned over him and Daphne both and he suddenly realized he might have a solution to his problems."

"Did you go into the marriage realizing that's what you were? A solution to his problems?"

She shook her head. "No. I thought it was a whirlwind romance, that he was the love of my life and I was his. I was too stupid to realize Eileen was his love and always would be until after we had signed on the dotted line." She shook her head again, this time looking angry. "Anyway. After we married, he let me know what my role was in our partnership. Part of that included making him coffee every morning."

"He told you that?" I was flabbergasted.

"Not in so many words, but he made it clear," she said, rolling her eyes. "And for years, I did it. I got up and made him coffee, just the way he liked it, every single morning. I thought if I was good enough, if I took care of him and Daphne well enough, that eventually he *would* fall in love with me. That he would look at me and see I was what he wanted all along. That the fairytale I wanted would really happen, that he would look at me with love in his eyes and actually want to be with me. But that never happened. I went from the unhappy home of my youth right into another one."

"Lonnie was an ass," I said before I could stop myself. Anger rose up within me at the thought of Janet as an innocent young girl being trapped with someone who didn't see how damn lucky he was to have her just because he needed cheap childcare. I had never met the man, and since he was dead, I wouldn't get the pleasure. Which was probably a good thing, since all I wanted right now was to punch him in the face over the look he had put on hers.

Janet laughed suddenly. "He was, wasn't he? I hate to say that. Daphne adored him. He was truly a wonderful father to her. Much better than I was at being a mother. But, as far as I was concerned, yes. He was an ass."

"I can see why you don't like coffee," I said, raising my eyebrows.

She laughed again and nodded. "I drank it our whole marriage. If I was already making it for him, it seemed pointless to make something else for me. It was a symbol in a lot of ways of how I gave up everything I wanted for him and his preferences." She went quiet again, fiddling with the string on her teabag. "I even had to drop out of school to take care of Daphne for him so he could go back and get his degree."

"I'm sorry," I said. It didn't feel like enough. I was beginning to understand the armor she wore—not because she thought she was better than everyone else, but because a sorry excuse of a man had convinced her she was worthless.

"Ah, well," she sighed and dipped her teabag into the cup, shrugging. "It's in the past. But the day we divorced, I went out and bought myself a teapot, and I haven't had a single cup of coffee since." Now, her eyes twinkled a little bit, and I relaxed.

"Reclaimed that part of yourself, huh?"

"Exactly. I was never again going to settle for something I didn't really want just to make someone else happy." She took a sip of the tea in her hands, and I felt even more glad I had bought it all for her.

Because standing there in the kitchen with her, I realized something. I wasn't just attracted to her.

I was falling in love with her.

But I couldn't ask her to stay here, somewhere she didn't really want to be. She had already given up everything she wanted once before.

I could never ask her to do it again for me.

CHAPTER NINETEEN

Janet

I DIDN'T KNOW WHETHER TO FEEL RELIEVED OR SAD WHEN Greg left for work. I had enjoyed spending time with him—too much, in fact.

He wasn't anything like I'd expected. I had felt drawn to him from the very first time we met, even though I couldn't understand why. But now?

I was drawn to him because of who he was.

It felt wrong somehow to constantly compare him to Lonnie, but I couldn't seem to help doing it. Lonnie had never once helped me wash dishes.

My marriage had always felt like a business arrangement. An arrangement I hadn't understood at all when I'd signed the contract. But nevertheless, that's what it was. My responsibility was to take care of Daphne and our home. That meant cooking *and* cleaning. I'm not sure it would have even crossed Lonnie's mind to take dish duty.

In return, I got a nice car, free room and board in a beautiful home, and eventually, when school was behind us and Lonnie had a decent income, a generous personal budget for buying whatever I wanted.

I had the elegant life I had always wanted but found it to be a poor substitute for the love I craved.

Thanks to the wisdom that comes from age, I knew I should have seen the warning signs before marrying him. They were certainly there. Had I been older, with more life experience—had I ever had a real relationship with a man—I would have seen it. I would have seen the grief he was still carrying, grief that nearly tore him apart. Had I been wiser, I also would have seen the selfishness, the lack of investment in our personal relationship, and the many ways in which our courtship was essentially a trial run as a supervised nanny.

But I hadn't seen it.

Now, though? Now, all I could see was Greg and how thoughtful he was. How he'd insisted on helping with the dishes.

How he had gone out of his way to make sure I had the tea I loved.

And now, with him at the office, I found myself missing him. I wanted him back here, wanted to get back to joking around and telling stories, connecting in a way I never really had with anyone.

Sure, there had been men since Lonnie—a string of short-term, emotionally distant, mutually beneficial "relationships." I was the kind of woman who looked good on a man's arm at a social function, a woman who had connections with the major players in town and attracted men who wanted to leverage that and become known.

What I had never seemed to attract was real, honest-to-goodness love. Experience had proven I simply wasn't the kind of woman men fell in love with.

But last night, Greg had looked at me the way I had always wanted someone to. There was so much emotion in his eyes—emotion he seemed to hold back and never voice. But it was there. It was there, and crazily enough, it seemed to be for me. When he had put his arms around me and pulled me to him, it was different. Different from someone just trying to seduce me.

It felt like what Greg wanted was to hold me—to love me.

And this morning, he had given me a teacup and a kettle.

He would probably never know what that had meant to me. It was such a simple thing, but to me, it felt like the world.

If I wasn't careful, I was going to lose my heart to him.

. . .

I HAD BARELY FINISHED MY TEA BEFORE PHILIP—MY NEW boss—showed up on my caller ID. It felt like stepping into a cold shower. Until now, seeing his name on the screen had always filled me with excitement and made this unbelievable opportunity actually feel real. But while I was curled up in Greg's easy chair, my heart sank when I saw his name.

Philip was calling to update me on the Paris transition and to get the details of my flight so he could meet me at the airport personally, something he clearly expected me to view as a high honor. I was professional, of course, but my heart wasn't in the call at all. I tried to summon up my previous excitement about the move by closing my eyes and imagining myself walking on cobblestone streets, eating in Parisian cafés, and shopping at the best boutiques.

But when I closed my eyes, all I could see was me standing on Greg's deck, the valley breezes blowing through my hair, and him coming up behind me to wrap his arms around my waist, making me feel safe. Loved. Happy.

Those images did nothing to help excite me for my new job.

Not long after the phone call with Philip, I heard a sharp knock on Greg's door. Thor's ears pricked up and he barked once, then looked at me as if waiting for instructions. I froze, not knowing what to do. Nobody could know I was here. I moved behind a corner, out of sight from the front window, in case whoever was there decided to peer in. Unexpected fear coursed through my body, making my hands shake uncontrollably, as my mind flashed back to the poor rabbit in the gift box. I hadn't realized how afraid of this threat I really was.

The knock rang out again. Then came a voice I'd have known anywhere. I let out a breath and relaxed.

"It's just me!" Fiona called. "I brought sustenance."

I went to the window and checked just in case, grateful to see Fiona standing alone on the front porch with a basket in hand.

I quickly deactivated the security system and moved to the door. Thor's body went on alert when I put my hand on the doorknob. I bit my lip, wondering if he would be an issue.

"It's okay, Thor," I said awkwardly, feeling rather stupid to be talking to a dog like he was a human who could understand me. "It's just Fiona. You know her. She's a friend."

At that, he relaxed and laid his head back down on his bed, making me wonder if he was more intelligent than I had realized.

I opened the door and let Fiona in, still shocked she knew where I was. "It's so good to see you," I said, meaning it with all my heart. "How did you know I was here?"

She gave me a tight hug. "Daphne popped by my house real quick as they were leaving for their honeymoon. Told me what was going on and asked me to check on you."

"I'm glad she did," I said. I had never been so happy to see a friendly face. "But Greg might not like it. No one is supposed to know I'm here."

Fiona brushed it off. "Who am I going to tell? Your secret's safe with me. Besides, he can't expect you to just sit here all day every day by yourself, like a prisoner. A woman could go crazy doing that!"

"But what if someone sees your truck here and wonders why you're at the sheriff's house in the middle of the day while he's at work?"

"I came to let the dog out, silly," she said as if it were obvious. "Poor thing can't stay cooped up all day, now can he? Stop worrying. What you need is to take your mind off all this mess." She pulled the cloth off the top of her basket, revealing the treats inside. "I brought blueberry muffins and fresh-squeezed lemonade. Thought we could sit outside and have ourselves a nice treat. Also brought over some tea and good honey to go in it—harvested it myself. There's some dried fruit, dark chocolate, and greens from my garden. Those things are for you to keep here. Daphne told me a few of your favorites and wanted to make sure you had what you like while you're here."

Tears pricked my eyes. "She did?"

Fiona nodded, then cocked her head. "Why do you look so surprised?"

How could I begin to explain it? "I don't know. I shouldn't be surprised. She's a thoughtful girl."

Fiona looked at me with narrowed eyes. I squirmed beneath her gaze, feeling like she could see too much.

"Boy, Lonnie did a number on you, didn't he?" she said after a moment, shaking her head. "You know, Janet, at first glance, you seem like a real confident woman. Someone who knows who she is and has it all together. But that's not quite true, now is it?" Her voice softened, and compassion—or pity—came into her eyes. "Does it always surprise you when someone does something nice for you?"

I swallowed hard, unable to answer. She was right. Dead right, as always. But I didn't trust myself to go there without breaking down, so I changed the subject.

"Let's take this outside," I suggested, avoiding her eyes. "Thor hasn't been out in a while, and it's a lovely day. I'll grab some glasses and plates and meet you on the deck."

I hurried away from her, grateful to have a minute to compose myself. Fiona was a dear, and I was truly grateful she had visited. But she wasn't the type to just let things be, and right now, everything felt so raw and painful.

And confusing.

CHAPTER TWENTY

Greg

I STOPPED AT THE FRONT DESK, CHECKING IN WITH OUR administrative assistant, Aubrey Hall. She was a strange lady who had apparently inherited the position from her great-aunt a few years prior. From what I had heard, the elder Ms. Hall had worked for the office since the beginning of time and never would have retired if not forced. Aubrey seemed to have inherited more than just the job. She couldn't have been older than forty, but she was one of those women who was probably born with a purse filled with hard candy in hand. Showed up before anyone else every morning, dressed in one of her "vintage" dresses and big glasses. Reminded me of a librarian in the fifties or something. She loved to gossip and was entirely too hungry for attention. But she also took a great deal of pride in her job, and she was damn good at it. Truth was, I didn't know what we would do without her. She ran a tight ship, taking on more than was strictly necessary for her job title, and I was grateful for it.

Even if I found her to be one of the most annoying people on the planet.

"How are you today, Sheriff?" she asked, beaming up at me from her desk when I stopped by.

"Doing great, Ms. Hall. And you?"

"Oh, just fine and dandy," she replied, reaching for her purse.

I stifled a groan, knowing exactly where this was going.

"I adopted a new cat this week," she said, beaming as she pulled out a picture to show me. The woman was obsessed with her cats.

"Very nice," I said automatically as she handed me a picture of a cat that, to me, looked exactly like all her other cats. Technically speaking, the city only allowed her to have five. I knew this one made at least number nine. But nobody would have the heart to turn her in. Not even me.

"I named him Darcy," she said, practically cooing. "He's a good boy, yes he is."

"Oh, like Mr. Darcy from *Pride and Prejudice*?"

She gave me a confused look. "No, after Mark Darcy from *Bridget Jones' Diary*."

"Ah. Gotcha. Great name." I cleared my throat. "Anyway, I have a favor to ask of you." I handed the photograph back to her.

She took it almost reverently and put it back into her wallet. "What can I do for you, Sheriff?"

"I need to call a meeting this morning. Ten sharp in the conference room. Let everyone know, will you?"

"Will do. Did something big happen?" Her eyes sparkled. She was always looking for tidbits of gossip she could pass on to her friends without breaking any confidentiality rules.

"Nah," I said, flashing her a grin. "Just need to have a quick chat with everyone. Hey, I do have a question though."

"What's that?" she replied, beaming at me.

"Do you know if our cleaning lady changed her schedule?"

She looked confused for a moment, then nodded. "Oh, yes, I forgot about that. She needed to come in this past weekend. Some family thing threw her off schedule."

"Great. Thanks." One mystery solved. I rapped my knuckles on her desk and headed out before she thought of another cat story to tell me.

• • •

I KEPT MY EYES OPEN WHEN I WALKED THROUGH TO MY office, looking for threats—and for evidence. As I walked through, I noted Miller and Tracy were whispering in a corner.

Interesting.

Parker was sitting at her desk. She looked up when she saw me, giving me a strange look before quickly turning her eyes back to her paperwork.

One of my other deputies, Sanderson, was busy at work on his computer, but a quick glance told me something was off about him. His face was redder than normal, and his pupils were a bit too dilated for the light in the room. I studied him as I walked by and made a mental note to watch him.

Jackson was waiting for me by my office door. We greeted each other with a head nod. Then he followed me into my office and closed the door.

"Have a seat," I said. "Any updates?"

Jackson sat down. "Unfortunately, no. Not since we talked yesterday."

I let out a frustrated sigh. "Alright. Well, at least nothing else has happened."

"Yet."

"Yet," I agreed.

"Have you identified any other potential suspects at this point?"

I sighed and leaned back in my chair, putting my hands behind my neck. "No," I finally admitted. "Not really. Something's up with Miller and Tracy. And Sanderson looks off today. I'm keeping my eye on all three, and I'm calling a meeting at ten to discuss the threats again. With more deputies on staff, maybe I'll get more. But I can't let go of this guy I kept seeing at the rehearsal dinner. My gut says he's involved. It's going to bother me until I find him."

"Could it have been Miller or Sanderson, maybe in disguise?" Jackson suggested. "You said the guy seemed familiar."

My initial reaction was no way. I would have recognized him if it had been either of them. But I took the suggestion seriously and thought it over just the same. "I don't think so," I said when I had made up my mind. "The guy was skinnier than Miller. Moved differently, too.

Miller moves like a cop. This guy didn't. He kind of skulked around if you know what I mean. Reminded me of an overgrown teenager. Sanderson is the right build, so theoretically, it's possible. Sanderson also has a less confident walk in general. But he doesn't normally skulk like that. I don't think it was him, but it's something to keep an eye on either way."

"Did he remind you of Sanderson in any other way?" Jackson asked, continuing to pry. I didn't mind it at all. This was how the two of us worked, bouncing ideas off of each other.

I leaned back again, contemplating. "Maybe? But I don't think that's why it's nagging at me so much."

"I'm just thinking if Sanderson is behind this, maybe he has help," Jackson suggested. "One of his brothers, or a cousin maybe. He's got a pretty big family living here in the area."

"That's a good point," I admitted. "See if you can talk to him today. You know, like a buddy. I don't want to go accusing anyone who works for me unless I have a damn good reason. See if he opens up to you about what's going on that has him looking so off. And let me know what you find out."

"Will do," Jackson said, nodding. "And, sir?"

"Yeah?"

"You do realize Miller and Tracy are dating, right?"

I blinked a few times. "Dating?"

Jackson nodded. "At least, I'm pretty sure. They haven't said anything to anyone. But you aren't the first to notice them whispering and talking. They normally keep a lid on that when you're around, but they talk a lot when you're gone. I also saw him coming out of her house late one night while I was on a jog."

"Hmm." I frowned. "I hope that's all it is, but I'm not sure a secret relationship makes me feel any better about them."

"I'll keep an eye out," Jackson said. "There's something else I think you should know."

"What's that?"

Jackson fidgeted a few times, obviously struggling with whatever he was going to say.

"Spit it out," I said, not having the patience to wait around.

"I know we're looking for a man," he said, "but what are your thoughts on Parker?"

My eyes narrowed. "Why are you asking?" Parker was a good deputy. She was smart and strong as a whip, and she handled herself like a pro. A lot of people underestimated her because she was tiny—five-foot-two and barely a hundred pounds soaking wet. But she was a third-degree black belt and could lay out a man twice her size without breaking a sweat.

"I'm not saying this means anything," he said, still fidgeting. "But I went to a bar in Asheville my last weekend off, and she was there too, with a man. Sheriff, he called her Billie."

All the color must have drained from my face. "Billie?"

Jackson nodded. "I'm guessing a nickname for Belinda."

I stared at my desk, my mind racing. "Belinda Parker. I never even thought about her name being shortened to Billie. TBI cleared her."

"They did," he agreed.

"I never had a single reason to think she was involved. Did you?"

"No," he said, shaking his head.

"Why didn't you tell me this sooner?"

His face turned crimson. "I'm sorry. But like you said, TBI cleared her. And she and I are friends. She...she and I have similar histories. We talk a lot. I really don't think she's the Billy involved with the organization. But with everything that's just happened, I felt like I had to mention it."

I ground my teeth, stopping myself from scolding him for withholding this. As he said, TBI had cleared her, and I had never had reason to think she wasn't completely above board. But I would have to take a second look now.

"Anything else you need me to do?" he asked, breaking the awkward silence.

"Not yet. I'll keep you posted."

"Yes, sir." He rose, knowing he was being dismissed.

I waited for him to close my door again and gave myself ten minutes to mull over what he had just told me before forcing myself to tackle one of my least favorite parts of the job—paperwork.

Chapter Twenty-One

Janet

I took my time gathering things from the kitchen while Fiona went outside with the dog. When I felt in control of myself, I joined them, smiling the minute the sun hit my face. This deck was quickly becoming one of my favorite places on earth. There was a sense of peace here in the valley that I couldn't begin to explain. All I knew was that when I was out here in the breeze and the sunshine, I felt like I could breathe more deeply than I had in years.

I had never been particularly into nature, had never liked camping or hiking or any of those outdoor things so many people seemed to thrive on. But here, in Greg's valley, I could almost begin to understand people like that. I found myself inexplicably wanting to walk through the valley grasses, toward the mountains ahead, trailing my fingertips along the tall weeds and wildflowers. It was beautiful and, somehow, so very *alive.*

"I didn't take you to be an outdoorsy kind of person," came Fiona's voice, pulling me out of my thoughts.

"I'm not," I said with a laugh, feeling lighter already. "But I think this is one of the most beautiful spots on the face of the earth."

"It sure is pretty," she agreed. "Me, I prefer living on the mountain. But Greg's got a view—I'll give him that."

"Daphne likes living on the mountain too," I said, taking the seat beside Fiona and passing her a saucer.

She pulled muffins from the basket and placed them on our plates, then poured us tall glasses of what appeared to be ice-cold, delicious lemonade. "It's in her blood," Fiona remarked.

The comment stung, though I knew that wasn't Fiona's intention. It was simply a reminder that Daphne wasn't mine—not really. She was very much the daughter of the woman who had given birth to her on that mountain. I had only been a stepmother and barely that.

It was a reminder that, when it came down to it, I didn't really have a place in her life.

"Now, Janet," came Fiona's voice again. "I see how your face just changed. Come on. Tell me what's going on in that heart of yours?"

I sighed and shook my head. "Nothing you don't already know. I just need to get through these two weeks and get to Paris."

"Is that what you need?" she asked, her voice indicating she thought otherwise.

"Of course it is," I said. But I knew I wasn't convincing. Because the truth was I had started wanting something very different. It was pointless though, and I needed to remember that.

"Janet, why are you still letting Lonnie control you all these years later?"

"What?" Her question caught me off guard. "I don't let him control me."

"Seems to me you do. He's still in your head, isn't he? Telling you you aren't Daphne's real mom. That you'll never live up to Eileen. That nobody cares about you. That you aren't wanted. That you aren't worthy of the love you're obviously desperate for."

She said the words calmly, quietly. But every one of them felt like a dagger to the heart.

I opened my mouth, then closed it again. I turned my eyes to the mountain and stared at it, silent.

Fiona waited.

"Three years of expensive therapy and not once did my therapist ever hit the nail on the head like that," I finally said with a painful laugh. "You're right. I never saw it as that or even realized he took up so much space in my brain. But you're totally, completely, painfully right."

"Of course I am. I'm always right," she retorted, making me laugh again.

This time, it was a little less painful, and I was grateful for it.

"Honey," she said, "you're never going to be free unless you stop believing all that. I understand you made some mistakes parenting Daphne. She understands that too. You were critical and controlling—sorry, but it's true," she said in response to my wince.

"Yes, it is true," I said softly.

"And there's a lot of hurt there over you leaving," Fiona continued. "Wounds in her heart, so much worse because she had already lost one mother. And hurt from the years you and Lonnie lied to her. Mistakes were made. You can't change that now. But Daphne loves you. She does. Beyond that, she understands you were practically a kid yourself, in a painful and confusing situation, and you didn't know what to do. I think she realizes that more than you do. And whether you see it or not, she wants you to be her mom now, no matter what happened in the past."

"I don't know how," I confessed.

"Sure you do," she said, patting me on the leg. "Just be there for her. Like you were when all the trouble happened. You showed up like a mom then, didn't you? And wasn't she grateful for it?"

"Sometimes I just feel so terrible at love, in all its forms," I said, shaking my head again.

The pain of it all was easing, and for the first time, it felt good to say these things. Like opening up an infected wound to clean it out. It hurt, but in a cleansing way. A healing way.

"I'm terrible at all relationships that aren't strictly professional," I continued with a little laugh. "I'm so much better with work. I think that's why I'm such a mess right now. It feels awful to be in this in-between phase, without a job anchoring me. I know who I am in my professional life. I have confidence there. I know how to manage people, how to make things happen, and how to navigate professional relationships. But right now, without that? I feel lost at sea."

"You're out of your comfort zone, for sure," Fiona agreed. "But I think some of that is Lonnie's voice still. I think he made you feel like a failure in your marriage and even as a mom. It benefited him for you and Daphne to have some distance in your relationship, you know? I don't think he wanted you to replace Eileen there, either. But, honey, I don't think you're the one that failed. He did. Oh, I know it's never that simple. But from what I've heard, both from you and Daphne, maybe it is this time. He was a broken man who didn't know how to deal with his grief, and he broke you in the process. But you don't have to stay broken, you know."

I took a long drink of Fiona's lemonade and leaned my head back on the rocking chair, closing my eyes and resting in the warmth of the sun. "So, oh wise one," I finally said, smiling at the grin on her face. "How do I get rid of his voice in my head? How do I become good at relationships? How do I learn to be who Daphne needs me to be?"

"Well, to start with, I think you've gotta stop running away from it all," she said. "That's what Paris really is, isn't it? Running away?"

She was right, but it didn't matter.

"I've already committed to the job in Paris," I said. "I signed a contract. There's nothing here for me—job wise, anyway."

She patted my hand. "Maybe you need to stop worrying about the details. Maybe you need to stop controlling everything and be open to possibilities."

"Easier said than done," I said, attempting to laugh. "The one time I was open to possibility, look what it got me. I only have what I have now because I started controlling my own life again."

"I know, dear."

We sat quietly for a bit, until Fiona spoke again.

"That's the hard thing about the world, isn't it? There's good and bad, pain and joy in just about everything. That was the first lesson I learned as a midwife. Childbirth is a pain no one would willingly sign up for, and yet women do all the time because after that pain comes a joy unlike any other." Fiona smiled tenderly.

"That's true," I said. "Although I've never experienced that myself."

"Not literally. But we all experience it metaphorically. You might be birthing a new version of yourself right now. And that's painful. But it's worth it."

"I know why my daughter adores you," I said, smiling at her.

"Everybody does," she laughed.

FIONA STAYED FOR A WHILE, CHATTING ABOUT EVERYTHING and nothing while we enjoyed the treats she'd brought over. It was the most pleasant morning I had enjoyed in quite some time, and I found myself surprised at how easy Fiona was to talk to. She had a million stories, most of which made me laugh out loud, like she was deliberately soothing my soul the way she knew I needed most.

I knew from Daphne that Fiona was an herbalist and midwife known all over Rosemary Mountain for her healing abilities. But I had never realized how much of her medicine came from just spending time with her. She was gentle and fierce, wise and silly, serious and funny, all at the same time.

By the time we had polished off the lemonade, I was feeling truly happy again. More than happy—content. It was an interesting feeling, especially considering the situation in which I found myself. I was here only because someone had threatened my family, yet I felt a sense of peace and contentment I hadn't felt in ages.

Fiona was part of that, but I knew that Greg was too. I didn't want to look too deeply at those thoughts yet though.

As Fiona began packing up her picnic basket to go, she asked if there had been any progress on the case.

"Not really," I said, unsure whether to feel frustrated or relieved. As much as I wanted the threat to be over, part of me was glad I was still "stuck" here with Greg.

But I couldn't look too deeply at those thoughts yet, either.

She nodded, her face serious. "You know, I've been thinking a lot about the wedding. I haven't talked to the sheriff about this yet, but there's been a little something bothering me about it."

"What is it?" I asked, my pulse quickening. Fiona was as sharp as a tack, more observant than most people. If something was bothering her, there was a good chance it was important.

"There was a lady there dressed like the rest of the servers. I noticed her though because she was wearing a wig."

"A wig?" I thought back to the wedding, trying to remember if I had noticed any staff members obviously wearing a wig. But my whole focus had been on Daphne that evening.

Well, and Greg, if I was being honest.

"Yeah. A wig and a whole lot of makeup. Have you seen those videos on social media where the girls use makeup to look like a different person and trick people into dating them?"

I bit back a smile. "Yeah, I know what you're talking about. The ones where they brag about catfishing people?"

"Right! Catfishing. What a silly word for such a thing. But anyway, I was paying attention to her because that's what it reminded me of. She reminded me of one of those internet women."

"I'll tell Greg, but it may be nothing," I said. "Honestly, a lot of young girls wear entirely too much makeup these days."

"Isn't that the truth?" she agreed. "But here's the part that sticks out to me. I distinctly remember her organizing some of the wedding gifts."

My pulse picked up again. "Are you sure?"

She nodded firmly. "Absolutely I am. I kept an eye on her because I thought, if she was one of those catfishing women, she might be tempted to steal something."

"That's definitely something I'll tell Greg," I said. "And I'm sure he'll want to talk to you about it as well."

"Anytime," she said, nodding. "Now, I've really got to go. I've got to go check on Laura Kistler. She's about ready to pop!"

"Laura Kistler," I repeated. "That name sounds familiar."

"She and Daphne are friends," Fiona said. "She's married to Matthew, the new minister at the church."

"Oh, goodness," I said, suddenly making the connection. "Of course. Matthew as in Luke's brother." I shook my head, reeling from that bit of information. "I didn't realize she and Daphne had become friends. I guess I'm surprised, considering everything that happened."

"Oh, they don't blame Daphne for a bit of that, and Daphne doesn't blame them, either," Fiona said, waving it off. "Matthew and Luke may be brothers, but they are about as different as different gets.

Laura's real timid and quiet, but she and Daphne hit it off somehow. I guess opposites do attract!"

"Why weren't they at the wedding?" I asked, curious.

"Well, *they* don't blame Daphne, but Patricia—that's Matthew's mother—still does. And they're still trying to salvage a relationship with her, though I can't imagine why." Fiona sniffed, appearing disgusted. "She's an awful woman. But for whatever reason, Matthew's trying to build some kind of bridge there. So I think they declined out of respect for her, but that's just speculation on my part."

"I see. Well. Good luck with Laura," I said, smiling. It was hard to believe Fiona was seventy-two years old and still working actively as a midwife, but the woman was probably in as good of shape as I was, and continuing to work was likely part of that.

"And good luck with Greg," she said, winking as she leaned in to squeeze me in a tight hug. "You keep your chin up, Janet. You're a lovely person, and you deserve happiness too."

My eyes filled with tears. I hadn't realized how much I'd needed to hear that. I hoped I would someday really believe it.

"Thank you," I whispered.

I said goodbye and locked the door behind her, barely able to wait for Greg to come home so I could tell him about the mystery woman who was messing with the presents.

Chapter Twenty-Two

Greg

When 10:00 finally rolled around, I pushed away from my desk, happy to have a reason to walk away from it.

I was the last person to walk into our small conference room, which was just as I'd planned it. I wanted them to have time to whisper without me there, knowing Jackson would report back if anything interesting was said.

Sanderson was still as red as a beet when I walked to the front, with beads of sweat trickling down his face.

"You okay, Sanderson?" I asked, staring at him.

"Yes, sir," he choked out.

"Need a minute? A glass of water or something?" The man looked like he was about to be interrogated.

"No, sir." He shook his head and averted his eyes, clearly wanting me to stop talking.

Sanderson had never been particularly confident. Sometimes you worked with people and wondered why they had gone into law enforcement in the first place. Sanderson was definitely one of those guys, shy to a fault and anxious in general. But he had also never caused problems, unlike Miller.

This kind of reaction was new though.

"Alright. Well, most of you already know why we're here, I'm sure," I said, looking around the room, taking a moment to make eye contact with everyone there.

Jackson was about the only one who looked completely normal. Miller looked angry—though, frankly, that *was* halfway normal for him. Tracy looked defiant. Parker looked bored, like she resented having to hear it all again. Kennedy, one of Miller's buddies, was mirroring his anger.

It was all interesting to watch.

I quickly recapped what I had already told everyone. There was no surprise on anyone's face. That didn't mean anything though. I had known that the news would spread after the meeting yesterday.

Miller raised his hand.

"Yes?"

He cleared his throat. "I'm assuming Ford will be investigating these threats?"

I nodded. "He will indeed be assisting me on this investigation. However, I'm taking the lead on this one."

There was a flash of something on his face. I knew he was annoyed I had put Jackson over our newly instituted investigative "unit." The word unit felt like a joke with how small our department was. We all had to do a little bit of everything. But putting Jackson in charge of something had riled Miller up, understandably so. Miller had more time served under his belt. But he wasn't half as smart as Jackson, and he never got far investigating anything since he didn't know how to talk to people without immediately putting them on edge.

"Anything else?" I asked.

From their faces, it seemed that they were all full of questions. But the room was silent.

AFTER THE WORLD'S STRANGEST MEETING, I LEFT THE OFFICE and drove straight to the venue where the rehearsal dinner had been held. I knew it wouldn't be open this early, but with any luck, maybe someone would be there—someone who could give me something, anything to work with. Jackson had already talked to them, and I trusted his work. But it wouldn't hurt to check again.

For once, I got lucky. There was a surprising number of cars in the parking lot for this time of day. I walked up to the glass doors and spotted what appeared to be a meeting happening. The manager, Louise Hamilton, recognized me and ran—well, her version of running anyway, hips swaying and high heels clacking—to the door to let me in.

"Sheriff! What an honor. Come on in. How can I help you?"

"Hi, Louise. You have a meeting of some sort going on?" I asked, gesturing at the people behind her who were all looking at me with open curiosity.

"Yes, we have a luncheon scheduled today at eleven," she said, the words spilling out with bubbly excitement. "The Asheville Garden Club. Such a fun group of society women! They're driving into Rosemary Mountain to tour Alva Jean's gardens. She grew some rare flower —don't ask me what it's called, I don't know a *thing* about gardening— but it's very special, and they're coming here to see it, and they rented the whole place for their luncheon! And there will be photographs, and we'll be featured in Asheville's local magazine!" She finally paused to breathe, beaming up at me, her false lashes fluttering.

"Oh. Wow. That sounds like an exciting day," I said, smiling politely. "Is there any chance MaryAnne is working today? I'd like to chat with her about something."

"Oh," she said, seemingly caught off guard. "Why yes, she's here. MaryAnne, come on over here for a minute." She beckoned to the girl who gracefully rose from her chair and walked over to where we were standing. "Sheriff Morrison needs to speak with you. Sheriff, if you need privacy"—she raised her eyebrows—"you can use my office. Right through there." She pointed at a doorway off the side of the restaurant.

"Let's just step outside and get some sunshine," I suggested instead, getting the distinct feeling that, if I went into the office, she had every intention of listening at the door. And while she probably already knew the reason I was here, if there was any chance she was unaware, I wanted to keep it that way.

Louise Hamilton was one of the biggest gossips in Rosemary Mountain.

I held the door open for MaryAnne and followed her outside. "It's a nice day," I said.

"It is," she agreed. "I'm guessing you want to hear about the man I saw the night of the wedding reception."

Straight to the point. I liked it. "I am," I agreed. "I know you already gave a statement, but I'd like you to tell me about it, if you don't mind."

She shook her head. "I don't mind. It was my night to take out the trash." She shivered involuntarily. "So creepy at night. I wish they would make the guys do it, but we all have to take turns. Anyway, I tend to keep my eyes open, you know?"

"Smart girl," I commented.

She gave me a half smile. "Anyway, I had just dumped it in the big dumpsters over there"— she pointed at some black dumpsters at the edge of the parking lot—"and was on my way back when I saw this guy kind of wandering through the lot like he wasn't sure where he was going. He was walking slowly, and I wondered if he was a wedding guest who had too much to drink. He turned and looked at me, so I called out to him and asked if he needed help." She blushed a little. "This self-defense class I took said that we should make eye contact and let people know we see them. That way, they're less likely to try to take us by surprise."

"That's right," I said, agreeing. "Did something about him make you nervous?"

She shook her head. "Nothing in particular. Not then, anyway. But still."

"Got it. So he turned and looked at you—did you get a good look at him?"

"No," she said, shaking her head again. "He was over there in the middle of the lot, away from any of the lights. I can tell you he was tall, with dark hair. Thin. Bad posture. But I couldn't see his face clearly."

"Okay." That matched with the guy I had seen as well. "So what happened after you called out to him?"

She shrugged. "He immediately turned away and put a hand up, waving me off. Didn't say anything. I guess I got a weird feeling then, because I walked as quickly as I could back to the door. I kept my eye on him the whole time, but he just stood there, pretending to unlock his car."

"Pretending? How do you know?"

She shot me a look. "He was standing beside a fairly new SUV. You don't need to pull out a key and put it in the door to unlock it. Just stand beside it and push a button."

"You're observant and smart," I said, grinning. "Want a job?"

She grinned back. "I don't know. Maybe. I mean, I've always been interested in law enforcement, but my dad said girls weren't cut out for that kind of thing. You think I could..." Her voice trailed off, like she was insecure even asking, but I could see the little glint of excitement in her eyes.

"Some of the finest officers I've known have been women," I said. I pulled one of my cards out of my wallet. "If you're really interested, give me a call. I'll hook you up with one of my female deputies. You can spend a day with her, see what the job is like, and decide if it's something you're interested in pursuing. If you are, we'll get you on the right track."

"Are you serious?"

"Dead serious. Now, think back to that night. Is there anything else you remember, anything at all? Anything that stood out to you as unusual in the slightest."

She paused and thought hard, wrinkling her brow in concentration. "Actually, something weird did happen. Not that night though. It was the night of the wedding. And honestly, I doubt it has anything to do with what you're investigating."

My ears perked up. "That's okay," I said. "Tell me about it anyway."

"There was a man and a woman fighting. I didn't see them, just heard them. They were in one of the storage closets. I walked past it, going to put some trays away, and heard them arguing."

"What were they arguing about?"

"It sounded like they were arguing about a gift. She was saying it wasn't big enough, that they should have done more. He said they would do a bigger display later. Honestly, couples fight all the time at weddings." She rolled her eyes. "Something about watching other people in love makes unhappy couples even more miserable. But it was really odd to me that they snuck off to a storage closet to argue. I mean, there's a million other places they could have had a private conversation."

"That's really interesting," I said. "And you're also proving to have good insight into how people work. Now, let's go back inside before your manager has a fit." I grinned conspiratorially. "I'm going to have a word with her about handling the trash situation differently so no women are walking out here alone at night. Because you're right—that's not a good situation. I wish that weren't the case, but that's the reality of the world we live in."

She gave me a grateful smile. "Thanks, Sheriff Morrison. For everything."

It felt good to be able to solve one person's problems.

I only wished I could solve this damn case.

CHAPTER TWENTY-THREE

Janet

I WAS CURLED UP WITH A BOOK WHEN MY PHONE BUZZED with an incoming text. I smiled, seeing Greg's name on the display.

Greg: Hey Janet. Just checking in. Everything okay there?

I held the phone for a minute, thinking about how to reply.

Janet: Everything's good here. Fiona visited today–Daphne apparently told her I was staying here. She brought treats and entertained me with stories.

Greg: Of course Daphne told the biggest gossip in town where you're staying.

I giggled. Greg was right, but he was also wrong. Fiona Flanagan definitely loved to gossip, but she was as trustworthy as they came. My secret would be safe with her. She had saved my daughter's life. I trusted her completely.

Janet: Don't worry. We can trust her.

Greg: I know. I'm just teasing. I'm heading home in a few minutes. Need anything from the store before I do?

My whole face lit up. He had remembered to text me that he was on the way home. It was such a simple thing, but it meant so much.

Janet: I don't think so. I can put together dinner with what we have here.

Greg: Don't lift a finger. I'm bringing dinner home.
Janet: Oh?

Greg: It's pizza night. What kind is your favorite?

Janet: Thin crust with all the veggies.

Greg: The healthy kind. I should have known. Alright, one veggie special and one meat lovers pizza, coming up. Probably a bad idea though. If I order a veggie special, they'll know for sure I've got a woman at my house. Maybe I'll have Jackson put in the order. Be home soon.

I grinned as his final text came through. He was teasing, but it didn't feel like he was making fun of me. Everything happening between us felt...fun.

More fun than Paris.

Everything Fiona had said earlier had made a bigger impression on me than she probably realized. Part of me was starting to wonder if maybe Paris wasn't what I wanted after all.

I put my phone down and walked outside onto the deck, seeking the peace of the valley again. What did I want? If I wasn't worried about what I *should* do or what I *should* want, what would I really, truly want?

I leaned on the railing and closed my eyes, basking in the sunlight on my face.

Peace.

I wanted this kind of peace.

I shut down all the other voices in my head and let myself just imagine for a moment. I had said there was nothing for me in Rosemary Mountain, but was that true?

Daphne was here. Daphne and Emerson and, someday, hopefully, their children.

Fiona was here, and I was beginning to feel like she and I could be true friends. Not the kind of friends I had in Little Rock, where interactions were carefully planned in order to impress each other and prove who had the best life. No, with Fiona I felt like I could have a real friendship, a friendship where we talked about things that were true and deep and meaningful.

I hadn't had a friend like that in over twenty years.

And of course, there was Greg.

My feelings for him had gone way past the initial attraction I had felt when we first met. He made me smile. He made me feel seen. But it was even more than that. Living here with him, even for this short time, had shown me what kind of person he was. Not that there was really any question about that. Like Fiona, he too had put his life on the line for my daughter. He had chosen a life of service, and I had felt him to be a good man from the start.

But here in his home, I saw so much more than that. I saw how smart he was and how varied his interests were. I saw how Thor adored him almost as much as he adored Emerson.

I saw how thoughtful he was and how hard he tried to make me feel comfortable.

It was ridiculous and it was happening way too fast, but I was falling for him. And that made me seriously question whether Paris would truly make me happy.

I closed my eyes and tried to picture myself there again. But those images felt false. They didn't feel like the real me. I let them go and tried to picture a future here in Rosemary Mountain, wondering what that would look like.

It looked like home.

I was still on the deck when Greg arrived.

"Looks like this is your favorite place," he said, opening the door to join me. "Pizza is hot and fresh. Ready to eat?"

"Yes," I said, blushing as he came to stand beside me, so close our bodies touched as we both leaned against the railing. I stepped away first, but his hand went to my back, his fingers trailing my spine as he walked beside me, reaching the door first so he could open it for me. I wasn't even sure he realized what he was doing. It was just automatic for him to be a gentleman. But I loved every second of it.

Two boxes of pizza were sitting on the counter. One veggie, one meat lovers, just like he'd said.

I laughed when I saw them. "Did you really have Jackson order them?"

"No," he said. "But I should have. The lady questioned me like it was a police interrogation. I had to lie and say I was trying to go on a diet but was only ready to give up half my meaty goodness."

I giggled and shook my head. "Wow. Just wow."

"Better than her starting a rumor that the sheriff has a date at his house tonight. That would break the hearts of half the women living here." He gave me a wink.

"Uh huh." I laughed it off but felt an unexpected flicker of jealousy.

Greg probably did have half the town fawning over him. Emerson had certainly had his fair share of women fawning over him when he moved to town. Daphne was the first—and only—woman here he had taken on a date, and she'd had waitresses practically refuse to serve her because of it. It was probably the same with Greg.

"So, how was your day?" he asked, handing me a plate and motioning for me to help myself first.

"It was nice," I said. "Oh, and I have some information for you! Fiona came to visit me today. She remembered something from the wedding she thought was important."

"Oh yeah?"

"Yes." I quickly relayed what she had told me about the woman who was wearing so much makeup.

"That's interesting," he said slowly when I finished the story.

"Think it's important?" I asked.

"It might be," he said. "On one hand, I see your point that lots of women wear too much makeup these days. But the waitress who spotted the guy in the parking lot also told me about a fight between a couple." He told me the story she had told him.

"Wow. So they could have been talking about the present they left." I took his plate and carried both of them to the table while he pulled a fresh bottle of wine from his rack.

"I'm wondering," he said. "Maybe we aren't looking for a single guy. Maybe we're looking for a couple. I found out one of my female deputies has the nickname 'Billie,' at least in some circles. She was completely cleared by TBI when they investigated, but that's something I can't ignore."

I shivered. "If one of your deputies worked for Mr. Boddy, that's terrifying."

He shook his head. "I would have a hard time believing that of her." He blew out a long breath. "Sanderson has a wife," he mused. "I've met her a few times. She's a real piece of work. I could see them hiding in a closet, arguing. And something is definitely going on with him. He was sweating bullets at the meeting today."

"Well, there's a lead to look into," I said.

"Yep. And another one of the deputies I'm watching, Miller, is apparently dating within the department. He and Tracy have been whispering together the last couple of days. Maybe they're working together, and she made herself up so I wouldn't recognize her."

I moved back to the counter, where he was pouring two glasses of Chianti, a perfect choice for our pizza. "If it was one of your deputies, don't you think you would have recognized her even if she had worn an extraordinary amount of makeup?"

He turned his eyes toward me, letting me see the heat in them. "Janet, my deputy could have walked into that wedding in full uniform and I still might not have noticed. You see, I was terribly distracted that night." He came closer, brushing my cheek with his hand and tilting my face up to look at him. "The only thing I could see was you."

I felt like time had somehow frozen as I stared up into his eyes. Yes, this whole thing was ridiculous. Yes, it was probably too good to be true. Yes, it was happening too fast.

But it was happening. There was no denying that. And I was tired of fighting it, tired of denying everything I truly wanted.

I put my hands on his chest and stepped forward, knowing he would kiss me. Knowing I wanted him to.

But at that very moment, like fate was slapping my hand, reminding me to not ask for things it had never allowed me to have, Greg's cell phone rang and interrupted us.

He cringed. "I'm sorry. I've got to get that. Job hazard."

I immediately dropped my hands and pulled away, nodding.

He frowned when he saw the screen. "It's Jackson. He doesn't call me at night unless something's going on."

Daphne. I could feel my face go white. Had this man found her somehow?

"What is it?" Greg asked as he answered the phone, his voice strained. He leaned back against the counter and closed his eyes, listening to the report. Then he hung up, then turned back to me with a dark look on his face.

"Please tell me it's not Daphne or Emerson," I said, my voice quivering. I was terrified something else had happened to her. There had already been too many close calls.

"No," he said, reaching out again, this time putting his hands on my arms to steady me. "Everything's fine. Nobody is hurt. This isn't about Daphne or Emerson."

"But it's about this, isn't it? I can see it on your face."

He nodded slowly. "I'm afraid so. Looks like things are continuing to escalate."

"What happened?"

"John, the owner of O'Malley's, left work tonight and had a note on his car. It said something similar to the one on mine. Said someone new was in charge, and he had a choice to make. Pay one hundred dollars a week for protection or face the consequences. He has twenty-four hours to decide. His window was busted out and there was another dead rabbit inside his vehicle."

"Extortion?" I frowned. "Did Mr. Boddy do that?"

Greg shook his head. "Not to local businesses, no. That's one of the reasons he got away with everything for so long. He was an asset to the local community, a true friend to other business owners. He blackmailed a few people when he needed specific things from them. But nothing like this."

"What are you going to do?"

He let out a deep sigh. "I don't know yet." He scrubbed a hand over his face, suddenly looking very tired. "I need to think it over."

Chapter Twenty-Four

Greg

"Morning, Sheriff!" Ms. Hall's cheerful voice rang out as I walked through the doors of our building. I stifled an inward groan. I wasn't in the mood to talk cats today.

"Good morning," I said, forcing a smile and hoping it didn't come across as insincere.

"It's going to be a good day today," she said. "Can't you just feel it in the air?"

"I hope you're right." My gut was saying the opposite.

I went straight to my office and closed the door, needing a minute to get my head on straight. Last night had been amazing. When that call came in, Janet had stepped in and had done something I never would have expected—she had taken care of me. It was a weird feeling, honestly. I was used to being the one to take care of everyone else. But last night, she had seen the weariness in me, and she had set about easing it.

Truth was, had she not been there, I would have gotten in my truck and headed straight for O'Malley's to take care of things, even though Jackson was already on scene and had already handled it before he called me. He'd assured me he didn't need me, but I would have gone anyway. Janet had told me that was silly, that I was obviously exhausted and needed to "put on my own oxygen mask first." She made sure I ate, entertained me with funny stories of her own, then suggested we play a board game. We played until late in the night, with her giggling like a schoolgirl every time she beat me. As we played, we swapped life stories and got to know each other. And somehow, she eased the tightness in my soul in a way I wouldn't have thought possible.

The woman was incredible.

We had grown up in completely different worlds. My family vacationed in the Hamptons, while Janet grew up in a trailer park in Arkansas. Night-and-day backgrounds, but I was beginning to see how similar we really were. I had rebelled against my parents' world by going my own way, working myself up from the lowest ranks to where I was now, wanting to earn my respect instead of being given it because of my dad's accomplishments.

In a way, Janet had done the same thing. She wanted more for herself than the world in which she was raised, a world that told her life was hopeless and she should resign herself to a bleak future of hard work and poverty.

The hard work didn't scare her. That was obvious from how hard she had worked to climb the ladder in her industry. As a nineteen-year-old girl, she had "taken the easy way out," as she described it, by marrying Lonnie. But when that imploded, she built a new life for herself from the ground up. I admired her for it, and I was starting to understand why she felt the need to dress the way she did and surround herself with nice things. This life still felt fragile to her in a way. She was still looking for evidence that she had really done it, that she had created something for herself.

I understood that all too well. Hell, I had done the same thing in my life, just in a different way, and it was the reason I could look at myself in the mirror every day. Knowing she had done the same made me like her even more.

The only problem was how hard it had been to tear myself away from her this morning. We had taken our morning drinks—coffee for me, of course, and tea for her—out on the deck and watched the sunrise together. Then we had talked non-stop until I had to force myself to leave so I could drive into work.

I couldn't wait to go back home to her.

The one thing we hadn't talked about was my marriage or my late wife. It rubbed at me a little bit, knowing I had evaded conversation about a major part of my life that had shaped me into the person I was. Janet had been refreshingly open with me, and it felt wrong to not reciprocate. But some things were just too hard to talk about.

A knock on the door interrupted me before I really felt ready to put thoughts of Janet aside and step into my role. But I sighed and called for whoever it was to come in. Jackson entered and closed the door.

"Sit," I said, "and tell me what the hell happened last night. Why did John call you instead of me? He's got my cell." It annoyed me more than it should have that he hadn't reached out to me directly. Jackson was exceptional at his job. He was my right-hand man, but I still liked to handle town business personally whenever possible. And in this situation, I needed to be involved.

Jackson sat down. "He didn't. I was eating at the pub when it happened."

"Gotcha. Did you see the guy?"

"Nope. Not a thing. Nothing suspicious at all in the parking lot when I arrived. I was having my last drink when John decided to leave early and let Marie close up. He came right back in and brought the note to my table." With that, Jackson slipped the evidence bag out of his jacket pocket and put it on my desk so I could see.

"Same handwriting," I commented. "Same kind of verbiage. So it looks like our guy is getting around, huh?"

"Looks like it," Jackson agreed.

I stared at the note for a minute. "See if you can find a discreet way to get a sample of Billy Brinksley's handwriting. Just in case. Better compare this to Miller's, Parker's, and Sanderson's handwriting, too. I have reason to believe we may be looking for a couple, so keep that in mind as we go forward."

"Will do. Anything else?"

I shook my head. "No. But I'm going to go see John today. You're welcome to come with."

He nodded. "I'll plan on it."

MINUTES AFTER JACKSON LEFT, ANOTHER KNOCK ON MY office door interrupted me.

"Come in," I called out, stifling a groan. At this rate, I would never catch up on paperwork.

Miller stuck his head in. "Can I have a word, sir?"

"Sure. Have a seat."

I watched him walk over and sit down. The guy was nervous, that was certain, which was a change for him. He was also angry, which wasn't a change at all. His biggest problem in the job had always been his attitude. It got him in trouble sometimes, thinking he was better than everyone else, including the citizens he served. But the nerves were new and interesting. I was glad he had approached me, knowing it would give me a good opportunity to feel him out.

"What's up?" I asked, keeping this casual and letting him take the lead.

"Well, sir, this isn't easy for me," he said before clearing his throat awkwardly. "But I've been thinking about things and, well, I have some concerns."

"Concerns?"

He nodded. "The, uh, threats you told us about yesterday in our meeting. I have some concerns they may be somehow connected to the drug trafficking ring you took down a few months ago."

I kept my face blank. "What makes you think that?"

He shrugged. "Who else would be making those threats? Daphne Sullivan is an ordinary citizen except for the fact that she might end up being a witness in a federal trial against a major player in the drug world. Of course it's his people threatening her." He looked at me like I was stupid. "They need to shut her up before the trial."

I shook my head, just slightly. "I understand what you're saying. However, Daphne won't be testifying against him. He's *not* a major player in the drug world. He's a bad dude, but his operation was relatively small. Feds gave him immunity in exchange for a chance at the big guys, and he's already in protective custody. Daphne *will* have to testify against Luke Kistler for trying to murder her. But he was basically nothing in the organization. A new guy, a hired hand, with almost no information. I'm not sure anyone even cares if he goes to prison other than his mother. *She's* mad as hell, but as far as we can tell, she didn't have any connections to the organization at all."

Something niggled the back of my brain a bit, but I had to keep my focus on Miller.

Miller looked a little like the wind was let out of his sails, but he quickly recovered. "I still think it's connected," he insisted.

"And you may be right," I said, trying to soothe without being condescending. Truth was, I thought this was connected somehow, too. Even now, it felt like puzzle pieces were swimming in my brain, just waiting to connect. But I didn't want to give any of my cards away to Miller until I knew for sure he was clean.

"Sir, if you will allow me to speak frankly..."

"Feel free," I said.

"I'm concerned you've allowed corruption to go unchecked." His face turned red and he said the words quickly, spitting them out like he had practiced them.

My eyebrows rose. "What makes you think that?"

"Frankly, sir," he said, gaining steam, "I think you're too close to see what's right in front of your face."

I kept my calm, even though he was clearly losing his. "So fill me in," I said. "What am I missing?"

"Ford," he spit out with a flash of anger in his eyes.

I was taken aback. "Jackson? What does he have to do with this?"

Miller glared at me. "Well, sir, you tell me. Look at it from my point of view. Here comes this guy, relatively new to the job with only a few years of experience. Sidles in and buddies up to the new sheriff. Quickly rises to the top and all of a sudden he's your right-hand man instead of those of us who have actually worked here and put in the time. It's not fair to the rest of us. Not fair to me. I'm ranked higher than him. Hell, I'm the highest ranking officer here, next to you. And it got me thinking. Maybe he had the organization's power behind him, helping him rise so quickly. Or hell, maybe you're both dirty and you've kept your distance from the rest of us so we don't figure it out."

Shock flashed across his face after his last sentence, like he hadn't meant to actually say it.

"You better watch what you say," I said, my tone firm but calm. I wanted to hear everything that was going to come spilling out of him now that he was worked up like this, but I couldn't allow him to accuse me of corruption.

"Sorry," he said with a look that said he wasn't sorry at all. "But you've got to admit. It looks bad. Jackson was at both the reception and the wedding when the threats were left, wasn't he?"

"He was," I said calmly.

Triumph flashed on his face.

"Anything else?" I asked, unable to keep the warning tone out of my voice.

"No. Sir." he said, adding it on like it was an afterthought.

"Good. Listen, I'm going to do you a favor. I'll try to forget the fact that you just accused me of bad judgment, at best. At worst, you've accused me of corruption and conspiring with the very man I was responsible for taking down." I raised my eyebrows pointedly. "Not the smartest statement you've ever made, huh? But I understand we're all nervous considering everything that happened. We're all looking at everyone around us, wondering if anyone slipped by the investigations. I've done it too, which is why I can extend you a small amount of grace on that one."

A look of relief flashed on his face before being replaced again by anger.

"But to be clear, that's as much grace as I've got for the moment. So you need to watch yourself. As far as Deputy Ford goes, maybe another time, when you're cooled off, I'll explain exactly why he's earned a level of trust and respect from me that you haven't yet. It has nothing to do with any imaginary connections you've come up with and everything to do with how he handles himself on the job—and frankly, how badly you handle yourself comparatively. But I don't think either of us needs to have that conversation right now."

His eyes grew angrier with every word I said, but he simply nodded and got up, walking out and shutting the door behind him with more force than necessary.

I let it go, mainly because I needed to think things over while it was all fresh in my mind.

Was Miller the one I was looking for and this was his way of throwing Jackson under the bus in an attempt to keep the focus off of him? Was this whole scene one big show, faking indignation and righteousness to make me think he was above corruption?

Or did my own people really suspect I might be dirty, too? The thought gutted me. My integrity was everything, and I had worked hard to win the respect of the people in Rosemary Mountain.

Worse, the things he'd said about Jackson hit a little too close to home. Jackson had been there at the wedding, at the rehearsal dinner, and even in Daphne and Emerson's driveway when they'd gotten the new threats.

He had also been at the pub, which Miller apparently didn't even know about yet.

Jackson was the one person here I had trusted completely. But Miller's words were like poison, sliding in and coloring over the memory of everything that had happened so far.

While I didn't want to believe it, I had to at least consider that I had made the biggest mistake of all.

CHAPTER TWENTY-FIVE

Janet

Greg: Good morning. Just checking in. How's your day going?

Janet: Everything's fine here. I got in my workout and a shower, and now I have a whole lot of nothing to look forward to. How about yours?

Greg: I know it's got to be boring being cooped up there. I'm sorry. Weird morning here. Had a confrontation with the deputy I told you about, Miller. I'll tell you all about it later.

Janet: I'm not bored. It's actually nice to have nothing on the to do list for once. Sorry about your weird morning. Anything I can do?

Greg: I started to say no, but honestly? You're already doing it. I like talking to you, Janet.

Janet: I like talking to you, too, Greg.

I SMILED AS I PUT MY PHONE DOWN. TEXTING BACK AND forth with Greg was becoming one of the highlights of my day. I loved how he checked in throughout the day and kept in touch like... Well, like we were a couple, honestly.

Yesterday, I had started wondering what my life would look like if I stayed here. The truth was, I wasn't even sure it was possible. I had signed a contract, after all. Breaking a contract was something I had never even considered before this.

I wondered if I could at least have some more time. A month instead of two weeks. Two months at most. That was a lot to ask of a company. But this was an international move, and they had expressed understanding that it wouldn't be a quick transition. Maybe they could give me a little more time here.

Something was happening between me and Greg and it felt important enough that I wanted to see where it was going. Throwing away a job opportunity at this early stage of an undefined relationship would be a terrible idea. But maybe I could push back the start date in order to have just a little more time to see where this was going.

I checked my watch. It was just four in Paris. It was at least worth calling Philip to see if we could push my start date back a bit. I wouldn't know unless I tried.

He didn't answer, so I shot him an email, explaining that there was a family emergency concerning my daughter and asking if we could push my start date back. I felt a little guilty about the email, but it wasn't exactly a lie. There *was* a legitimate emergency.

He didn't need to know that it wasn't at all the reason why I wanted to stay.

Chapter Twenty-Six

Greg

The confrontation with Miller had soured my morning to the point where I couldn't focus on the paperwork in front of me even if I tried. I pushed my chair away from my desk, grabbed my keys, and walked out.

After everything, I felt self-conscious stopping at Jackson's desk. I could feel the glare from Miller across the room and had to wonder—was everyone pissed off about how closely I worked with Jackson? And if so, was one of them angry enough to be behind these threats? I looked around and realized none of the faces here truly looked friendly, other than Jackson's.

Even worse, had Jackson fooled me all along? He had lied to me once already, by omission anyway, keeping his biological family a secret. But I understood that. I understood the reasons why he hadn't disclosed his past when I'd hired him, and I knew how terrible he'd felt about it when he'd told me the truth. And during the time he had worked for me, he had been nothing less than exceptional in his job.

I couldn't let Miller's words taint that now.

"I'm heading out now," I said as Jackson stood.

He looked down at the papers scattered across his desk. "Okay," he said. "Do you mind if I meet you there in a few? I need to finish up this report before I lose my train of thought on it."

"That's fine. Take all the time you need," I said. I felt a wave of relief about it, actually. I didn't want to let Miller's words get to me, but I wouldn't mind having a word alone with John before Jackson arrived.

Just in case.

"Alright. I'll meet you at the pub in half an hour," he said, not bothering to be discreet.

I cringed, not wanting the whole department to hear. Sanderson had definitely overheard though. I could tell by the slight raise of his eyebrows, even though he kept his eyes focused on his computer.

Hopefully that was only because he disapproved of my going to get a drink first thing in the morning.

"YOU'RE LEAVING ALREADY?" MS. HALL CRIED OUT AS I walked toward the doors. "I haven't gotten to show you the new pictures of Darcy I took last night!"

"Uh, yeah," I said. "Sorry. Duty calls. Rain check on those cat pictures though." I pointed my finger like I meant it and gave her a friendly grin, hoping this wouldn't put me on her bad side for too long.

Her bottom lip stuck out in a pout.

I figured I might have to get her flowers or something to smooth things over. Although God knows I didn't need her getting the wrong idea. I'd have to talk to Janet about how to manage it. She'd know.

Janet.

Just the thought of her seemed to wash over me like peace itself, smoothing over the raw edges of the morning. Knowing she would be there at the end of the day felt good.

Too good.

I needed to get a grip and remember that this was just temporary. She had other plans and they didn't include me.

But man, how I wished they did.

* * *

I PARKED MY TRUCK AT THE BACK OF THE PUB'S PARKING LOT. Doing so only gave me an extra ten seconds or so on the walk in, but I was grateful for every one of those extra seconds in the fresh air just the same. When all this was over, I was due for a vacation. A real one.

I loved this town and its people. I was damn grateful to wake up in such an amazing place every morning, knowing how lucky I was to live in a place so beautiful it drew tourists by the thousands every year.

But a trip away would do me some good. I tried to imagine it, thinking I would picture myself on the coast of Maine—one of my favorite getaway spots—bourbon in hand as the wild waves crashed against the rocky shoreline.

But instead, the image that flashed through my head was of a sandy beach, all sun and gentle waves, with Janet lying next to me in some impossibly tiny bikini, holding one of those fruity little umbrella drinks in her hand.

Get. A. Grip.

I blew out a breath and forced the image out of my head as I pushed the pub door open and stepped back into my real life.

"Be with you in a moment!" John called from the back.

"It's just me," I called out. "Take your time." I slid onto a barstool and waited for him to emerge from his office, using the time to think through the case thus far.

"Sheriff," John said with a nod of acknowledgment as he walked to the bar and immediately grabbed a towel, wiping it down even though it was already pristine. "Thanks for coming."

"Of course. I would have come last night had you called me. You know that."

He nodded. "And I would have, had young Jackson not been here already."

I winced as Miller's words came back, washing a shade over everything yet again.

"Tell me what happened," I said. "Everything you can think of. Even if you don't think it's related, you never know what detail might help."

He shrugged. "It was a fairly normal Monday night. You know the citizens of Rosemary Mountain don't drink on Sundays, so they have to make up for it on Monday." He grinned.

"Yeah, sure they don't," I said with an eye roll. I had seen too many domestics and DUIs during my time here to believe that for a second. "Did you see anyone out of the ordinary?"

He mulled it over. "No, not really. All locals, except the few tourists who found our little hole. Jackson was here, having a late dinner. Old Man Murphy stopped in for a pint. A couple other regulars—no one I would be worried about at all."

"Okay. Do you have security cameras in the parking lot?"

"I do, actually," he said. "And I pulled up the footage already. You're welcome to see it, but I don't think it will do any good."

"Why's that?"

He winced. "I wasn't parked in the parking lot. My SUV was pulled up around back."

"In the alley?" I groaned. That made things considerably harder. That back alley was full of dark hiding spots, and I knew there wasn't a camera back there. I had installed one myself—twice—out of the sheriff's office budget, as the alley was the number one crime spot in Rosemary Mountain. But the good citizens who frequented that alley had removed it—twice—and I had given up after, resorting to frequent patrols instead.

"Yep. I know, I know." He waved his towel at me. "A bad idea even in normal circumstances."

"You're right it's a bad idea. That's just asking for your SUV to be stolen or broken into."

"I know. But I had bought some new glassware in Asheville and needed to carry it in last night. I parked there to make it easy." He shrugged. "Besides, I don't usually get any trouble here. You know that."

"I know."

John was a favorite among the locals. On top of that, he was built like a linebacker and had made it clear from the beginning he was able to handle any "nonsense," as he referred to it. Not once had I ever gotten a call about a brawl or anything else at the pub, even on its rowdiest nights. He didn't tolerate bad behavior, and everyone knew and understood that. The few tourists who found the place and came in looking for trouble in the name of a good time quickly learned. He always handled it, then made them wash dishes as a penance.

That was one reason it surprised me he had gotten a threat at all. Not many people would be bold—or stupid—enough to threaten him. It made me think the threats were from someone who didn't actually know Rosemary Mountain all that well. That, or someone who was just crazy.

"I'll take a look at the footage anyway," I said. "You never know. How long had Jackson been here when it happened?"

He shot me a funny look. "I can't say for sure. I'm not sure what time it happened, to tell you the truth. It was about seven when I left and found the note. But I hadn't been out to the truck since five. It could have been put there anytime during those two hours."

"Got it. Knowing the time frame we're working with is at least something," I said, making note of the hours on my phone. "Have you noticed anyone new coming around?"

He shrugged. "It's tourist season. The main restaurant has new people every night. We get one or two here every now and then, but no repeats here."

"Got it."

John had two restaurants in town—the bigger, ridiculously tacky Irish pub on the main strip that catered to tourists looking for an Irish-themed experience with Americanized food and this one, the place he had built specifically for the locals to make their own. This one was subtle and discreet, and it didn't get advertised in any brochures.

Which was in direct contradiction to my earlier thought about it being an outsider who had targeted him.

"Do you have any thoughts about who might be behind this?" I asked, genuinely curious. He was a Rosemary Mountain local through and through, born and raised here after his parents had emigrated from Ireland. And as a pub owner, he knew the pulse of the town. He probably heard more secrets than the local priest.

He leaned over the bar, sighing, with a contemplative look on his face. It was a look that said he knew something but was holding back from saying it for whatever reason.

"Come on. Let's have it," I said.

He shook his head. "Sheriff, I know most people were shocked to find out what was happening in this town. But I wasn't. There were always rumors. Quiet ones, told so you didn't know for sure if the person was serious or just joking around."

"Go on," I said, wanting to hear where this was going despite my irritation that not one Rosemary Mountain citizen had come to me with those rumors.

"Let's just say there's rumors happening again," he said, his face flat.

"What kind of rumors?"

He looked me straight in the eye. "Rumors that you're about to be out. Gone. Sheriff no more."

"What?" I shook my head, trying to process what John had just told me. Of everything he could have said, I had not been expecting that. "What are you talking about? Who's saying that?"

He just shook his head and went back to wiping the bar. "I'd tell you if I knew the source, but I don't. I'm hearing things third- and fourth-hand at this point. Little snippets of conversation when I deliver drinks. But I've heard it more than once. That things are happening and you're about to be out of here, just like our other sheriffs who resigned before the end of their term."

"I want to know where you're hearing this from," I repeated. "Because I don't plan on going anywhere."

"From your own deputies," he said, giving me a pointed stare. "But I don't get the impression it originated from them. I got the impression it's coming from somewhere else and they were just sharing the gossip."

"What people?" I demanded. "I want to know specifics."

But Jackson chose that exact moment to walk in, and John immediately went silent. I shot him a look, letting him know the conversation wasn't over, but I dropped it.

For the moment.

"Hey, Sheriff. Big John." Jackson gave us an easy grin as he strode over to where I was sitting at the bar. "Any leads yet?" he said, sliding onto the stool beside me.

"Not really," I answered, still keeping my eye on John. "We're thinking the guy left the threat sometime between five and seven."

"Yeah, that's what we talked about last night," Jackson said, agreeing. "And no footage of the incident, unfortunately."

"Unfortunate, indeed," I agreed, my bad mood getting worse.

I decided to leave Jackson to finish up the official report, realizing John wasn't going to talk to me any more with Jackson there. As much as I hated it, I needed to at least consider that Jackson might somehow be involved in this. Questions had been raised, and even though my gut said they were baseless, I needed to act like a cop first, friend second.

Although truth be told, I had always found that line to be a bit murky. When you worked so closely with people that you literally trusted them with your life, it was hard to think of them as anything other than a friend. I knew it would be near impossible for me to think of Jackson as possibly corrupt.

Which was why I needed to proceed as if it were a possibility, no matter what my heart and gut said.

I stopped in my tracks as I neared my truck, cursing silently. The passenger's-side window was shattered. All my senses went on high alert as I drew my pistol and scanned the area for signs of anyone. Seeing no one, I quickly squatted and checked underneath the truck, then took a wide circle around it, checking the bed in case anyone was there, waiting to ambush me. I went through the motions of clearing the truck before getting too close even though it was unnecessary. If someone really wanted to hurt me, he wouldn't have smashed the damn window and alerted me to his presence. He would have ambushed me when I was caught off guard.

Finally, I approached the truck, confirming what I had already suspected. This was another threat, another attempted show of power, from someone who wasn't ready to show himself.

But all it did was piss me off.

I pulled my evidence kit from the back of the truck and slid on gloves, rolling my eyes as I did. There would be no prints—again. But I had to try anyway.

I opened the door and found the note that had been left inside, grateful for no dead rabbits this time. This had likely been a crime of opportunity, without time to set the stage. The note was clear:

Stay out of my business, or next time, this will be your face. This is your last warning, Sheriff. You're not in charge anymore.

I ROLLED MY EYES AGAIN, UNABLE TO STOP MYSELF. "IS THAT a promise?" I muttered under my breath. Because the truth was, I was ready for him to come after me directly. Ready for him to finally show himself and give me a fair shot at him.

Then I could end this and send a message of my own that threats weren't tolerated around here.

I clenched my jaw and turned back toward the pub, hoping this time we might get a glimpse of the guy on the security camera footage.

Jackson and John both looked up in surprise when I walked back in.

"Forget something?" John asked.

I shook my head. "I need you to pull up your security footage from the last half hour."

"What's wrong?" Jackson asked, immediately standing, his eyebrows knitted in concern.

"Someone busted my window while I was in here," I said. "Another threat."

Jackson's eyebrows shot up. John's face was placid. I made note of both reactions. As far as I knew, only three people knew I was here—John, Jackson, and Sanderson. So unless the perp had just randomly driven by and seen my truck in the parking lot—possible but unlikely—he was connected to one of them.

Or *was* one of them.

"Did you see anything when you got here?" I demanded, looking at Jackson and searching his face, hoping beyond hope he was the Jackson I knew and believed in. It would kill me to learn he had fooled me these past couple of years.

He shook his head, looking shocked. "Not a thing. I pulled in at the front though. I noticed your truck was at the back of the lot, but I didn't look closely at it and I didn't register anything out of place. Didn't notice any damage. What window was it?"

"Passenger side."

"I didn't notice anything," he repeated, still with that shocked look on his face.

I stared at him, looking for any signs of dishonesty but not seeing any.

Would I though? Maybe Jackson was just an exceptional liar, one of those people so disconnected from reality that they could do something terrible in one moment, then fake innocence in the next and practically believe it themselves.

I just couldn't believe that about him though. I had worked too closely with him to believe he was behind this. There had to be another explanation.

"Footage is pulled up," John called from where he had stepped away from the bar into his makeshift office/supply room on the side.

I strode over and took the seat he offered me, peering at the screen as he played through the time I had been there. My truck was almost completely out of frame. At the back of the lot, we only had a partial view of my driver's-side bed. But I watched the whole lot carefully to see if any vehicles pulled in or any pedestrians walked by.

Nothing.

Just my truck sitting there in an otherwise empty lot until Jackson pulled in. The video showed him pulling in, getting out, and walking straight into the pub. Minutes later, I walked out, going straight toward my truck, then pulled my gun and went into alert mode.

But there was absolutely nothing on the video that showed the act itself or who was behind it.

I leaned back in my chair and put my hands behind my head, thinking it through.

Unfortunately, the video didn't clear Jackson. He had looked at security footage the night before. He would have been familiar with the coverage area and would have known it was unlikely to be spotted on my passenger side. He could easily have parked somewhere down the street and approached my truck from the back of the lot, then gone back to his truck and arrived shortly after.

John could have taken a look at the cameras before he came out of his office. Could have messaged someone working for him that I had parked out of the way and to leave me a message. His own threat had conveniently taken place where he was well aware there were no cameras. If he had decided to open up a less-than-legitimate side business, he could have faked his own threat just to add a sense of power to it. Or to throw me off course.

Sanderson knew where I was going. He could have waited for Jackson to leave, then made a move.

"Did Sanderson stay at his desk while you were there?" I asked Jackson, frowning.

Jackson pursed his lips like he was thinking. "No," he said, finally. "He got up shortly after you left. Headed toward the bathrooms. Was still there when I left."

"Was his vehicle still in the parking lot?"

Jackson's face flushed. "I didn't notice, sir."

"Rewind the footage," I said, wanting to look through it one more time for anything I might have missed—a flash, a shadow, anything at all.

But I couldn't see a damn thing.

THE VANDALISM TO MY TRUCK CHANGED THINGS IN A BAD way. The notes left for me before had been vague threats toward the town, not toward me specifically. I had toyed with the idea of calling in another agency, but thus far, I had been able to walk a fine line on that point and keep myself in charge of this investigation. It was a gray area, admittedly, especially when the threats shifted to my friends.

But now, the threat was directed toward me. It wasn't a gray area anymore. Officially speaking, I shouldn't work this case.

I knew it, and Jackson knew it too. He was more than a little awkward when he took my official statement. When I was finished, he cleared his throat and stumbled over his words.

"Just say it, Jackson," I said.

"Well, sir, you know what this means. Now that you're officially being targeted, you really shouldn't work the case anymore."

I nodded. "Right. Officially, it's in your hands now. Contact the TBI and ask for their assistance. We need another agency taking point."

He nodded, still looking distinctly uncomfortable.

"I'm taking off the rest of the day," I said. "Consider me off duty." With a pointed look, I climbed into my truck and started the engine.

"Sir," he began, "I don't think—"

"You don't think what?" I asked.

He opened his mouth to speak, then closed it again. "Nothing, sir."

I nodded. "Tell Ms. Hall to reschedule any meetings she's booked for me over the next couple of days. I plan on taking a few days off, now that I think about it."

Jackson swallowed hard. "Got it."

I nodded again and pulled out of the parking lot, leaving him behind. My rearview mirror showed him standing there, unmoving, just staring at me as I pulled away.

Maybe I was being a jerk about the whole thing, but I was beyond pissed at the situation.

There was no way I was going to let all this continue without doing something about it.

Chapter Twenty-Seven

Janet

I QUICKLY RECEIVED AN EMAIL BACK FROM PHILIP, although it wasn't what I'd expected. He didn't appear to have read my email at all. He sent a quick message saying they were excited to have me joining the team soon and that he had attached the latest sales numbers for the stores I would be managing so I could go ahead and start analyzing the data.

Did that mean he was ignoring my request or that he was fine with me working from Rosemary Mountain for a bit? I wasn't sure, nor was I sure how I should respond.

I stared at the screen for a bit, willing the email to give me more information than it actually did. Finally, I sighed, and decided I might as well take a look at the reports. It wasn't as if I had anything more important to do. Not until Greg came home anyway.

I found myself counting down the hours until Greg came home, and I didn't like it one bit. In the early days, married to Lonnie, I counted down the hours waiting for him, too. But it was always a letdown when he came home, clearly uninterested in anything except Daphne. As a young bride, I would wait for him by the door, only for him to blow right past me to scoop her up and dote on her, ignoring me completely.

Part of me had died a little every day.

So it made me uncomfortable that here I was, doing basically the same thing again. I decided it had to stop. Maybe the email from Philip was exactly what I'd needed. Work would get my mind right again, and it really would benefit me to spend some time getting familiar with what my new customers were buying. Little Rock shoppers were one thing. Paris shoppers were another.

I was deep in analytic mode when the door opened, making me jump.

"Just me," Greg called out, walking into the living room, where I was curled up on his couch with my laptop and notebook, furiously making notes.

"Hi," I said, quickly removing my reading glasses and putting them on the table beside me.

"Hey." He leaned against the doorway and looked at me—one of those looks that made me feel like he was truly seeing *me*—and let out a deep breath. "I didn't mean to scare you. I sent you a text that I was coming home early."

"It's fine," I said, laughing. "Just a mild heart attack." I picked up my phone and saw the missed text on it. "Sorry, I didn't see it. My new boss sent over some files and I got caught up in them."

He kept standing there, just looking at me, with a gaze that set me on fire. "Man, it's good to see you," he said.

I flushed, from both his gaze and his words. I wasn't used to being spoken to that way or seeing a man visibly relax in my presence, like he had just been waiting to come home to me.

"Hard day?" I asked, tucking my hair behind my ears and putting my computer away. When I did, he walked over and sat on the couch with me instead of taking one of the chairs. My heart pounded against my chest from being so near him.

"You could say that," he said before letting out a sigh and leaning his head back on the couch. He looked exhausted.

"Want to talk about it?"

He scrubbed his hand over his face and raised his head. "Where do I even start? First, Miller confronted me. Basically accused me of corruption. Then someone broke the passenger window on my truck while I was interviewing the pub owner. Left me a message to mind my own business."

My heart sank. "Oh, no. I'm so sorry."

"Me too." He pulled my feet into his lap and started massaging them. "Not because of the truck. That's easily fixed. But because it means I'm officially off the case. I'd been able to walk a line up until now, keeping myself in charge of the investigation. But there's no denying I'm a target now. We'll have to call TBI back in, and Jackson will be the one working with them." A shadow moved across his face as he spoke, trouble he wasn't telling me about.

I forced myself to concentrate on the conversation even though I was entirely distracted by his gentle massage. It felt like such an intimate thing to do, yet it didn't feel wrong for him to do it. I didn't want him to stop, especially when he started tracing circles on my ankle with his thumb.

"So what does that mean?" I asked.

"Officially, it means I'm taking a couple of days off. Unofficially..."

"You're still investigating," I said, finishing his sentence for him. I knew him well enough already to know he wasn't going to drop this until it was over.

"Damn right I am," he said. "Unfortunately, I can't use the weight of the badge or do anything that would interfere with the official investigation." He shook his head and groaned, then looked at me. "I hope you don't mind having me around more the next few days."

"I don't mind." I swallowed hard. "I like having you around."

Our eyes met in a look that seemed to last forever—until suddenly I was moving toward him, pulled in like a magnet. His hand came up to stroke my cheek, then slid behind my head into my hair, pulling me even closer. Then his lips were on mine, soft at first, then seeking more— taking more. I had imagined him kissing me a thousand times since we had met, but this—this was better than anything I could have imagined. It seemed to last forever, until he broke the kiss and pulled me into his lap, whispering into my hair.

"Janet, what are you doing to me? I can't stop thinking about you.

Can't stop wanting you. Can barely focus at work because all I think about is coming home to you."

"I–I know how you feel," I said weakly.

He looked into my eyes, searching. "Janet, are you saying you feel the same way about me?"

My breath caught. Then I nodded, once. "Yes. But—"

He closed his eyes. "I hate buts."

"I know. But I'm leaving soon," I whispered.

"I know," he said when I finally pulled away. He clamped his lips, seeming to battle himself before allowing himself to speak again. "I know you're supposed to leave in a few days," he repeated, "and I promised myself I wouldn't ask you to change your plans for me. But do you really have to go? I mean, is it really what you want?"

No, it isn't. But everything within me was at war.

"I don't know what I want anymore," I said, giving the most honest answer I could. "I'll admit I've wondered about that. But I signed a contract, and this job is the kind of opportunity that doesn't come around often."

He let out a sigh. "Yeah. Look, I know I can't compete with Paris. But, Janet, feelings like this don't come around often, either. Not for me at least. What I feel for you..." He trailed off, shaking his head. "I wish we had time to give this a shot. A real one. I'd love to take you on a proper date. Spend more time together. See where this goes. Maybe you could wait on Paris for just a little while? See if it's really what you want, or if, maybe..."

His fingers trailed up and down my spine, making me know *exactly* what I wanted—in that moment at least.

"I don't know," I said, shaking my head breathlessly, trying to somehow keep a grasp on reality despite the feelings he was stirring up in me. "I did email my boss earlier telling him I had a family emergency and that I needed more time here." I saw the instant flash of hope in Greg's eyes and felt I needed to tamper it somehow. "But he didn't give me an answer. Plus, you know my past. I already gave up my plans for a man once, and I've regretted it every day since."

"I get that," he said, sighing, dropping his hand. "I do. I'm sorry. I don't want to be someone who makes you give up anything." He leaned his head forward, resting his forehead against my chin.

I wrapped my arms around him and allowed myself to sink, temporarily, into the comfort of being held.

And I wondered, not for the first time—would any part of me really regret giving up Paris if I stayed?

Or would walking away from Greg be my biggest regret of all?

Chapter Twenty-Eight

Greg

Janet said she couldn't stay for me, couldn't give up her dreams for a man again. I understood that. Respected it. It disappointed me, deeper than I could possibly explain. But then again, I couldn't begin to explain the feelings I had developed for her. I had fallen fast, faster than I would have thought possible. Here I was, unable to even picture a future without her in it, while she still saw her future in Paris.

Disappointment wasn't even the right word.

Yet, despite her words, she hadn't pulled away from my arms, hadn't moved off my lap. She had snuggled in, letting me hold her, almost like she needed it as much as I did.

So I held her. I leaned my head back, closed my eyes, and kept my arms wrapped around her like I never wanted to let go.

'Cause I didn't.

We stayed that way, silent, for what felt like a long time, yet somehow it felt like not long enough. But eventually, she pulled away, reluctance on her face.

"I'm sorry," she said.

"For what?"

She looked at me blankly for a minute, then let out a small laugh. "You know, I'm not even sure. I just feel sorry."

I reached up and tucked her hair back behind her ears, allowing my thumb to graze her cheek, touching her gently like she was a precious thing—because she was. "You don't have to be sorry," I said. "I really do understand. It was selfish and stupid for me to even ask you to stay. I promised myself earlier that I wouldn't, then broke that promise the minute I saw you again. I meant what I said. I would never want you to give up your dreams for me. Not only would that be unfair, but it leads to resentment, and I don't want you to resent me. I want you to—" But I stopped short, knowing I shouldn't finish that sentence.

Her eyes were big, like she knew what I was going to say. She seemed to struggle within herself, wanting to speak but feeling unsure herself. She pulled away, back into the corner of the couch where she had been before I came in. I moved, turning to face her. I didn't want her pulling away, but I knew I didn't have a right to ask her to stay.

"I–I've been..."

"What, Janet? What is it?"

She hesitated, then shook her head. Whatever it was, I could see she wasn't going to say it after all. Instead, she changed tack. "I've been wanting to go for a walk through the meadow behind your house. Would you like to walk with me?"

I nodded. "Absolutely. Did you bring boots?" I eyed the fancy shoes she had discarded on the floor in front of the couch. Those would never do for walking out here.

She bit her bottom lip and smiled. "I think I have a pair somewhere in those giant suitcases."

"Alright. Put them on. I'll leash up Thor and we'll take him too. He'll enjoy it."

She swung her feet off the sofa and stood, bending down to pick up the heels from the floor. I stifled a groan and looked to the ceiling, reminding myself—again—that the woman had other plans. We might as well be friendly while she was with me, but I needed to keep things on a strict friendship level or else it was going to hurt even worse when she left.

Unless there was a chance I could convince her to stay.

I shut down the thought immediately. I wouldn't be that guy. I wouldn't woo her and convince her to change her plans just because it was what I wanted. That's what Lonnie had done to her, and I would never hurt her like that.

I would just have to figure out how to live with her and keep my hands to myself.

Easier said than done.

I distracted myself by getting the dog ready for a walk. Thor perked up as soon as he saw the leash, wagging his whole butt. I had him leashed up and ready to go when Janet returned wearing the most casual thing I had ever seen her wear—dark jeans so tight I could see every curve of her body, tucked into tall leather boots. It was the kind of outfit I had seen on girls half her age, but somehow, on her, it worked even better.

I embarrassed myself thoroughly by dropping Thor's leash the minute I laid eyes on her.

She blushed, pinking up those cheeks so prettily. "Ready?" she asked.

I cleared my throat. "Sure. Let's head out."

I motioned for her to head out the back door first, then set the security system and locked the door behind us. I wasn't sure how far Janet wanted to walk—she didn't exactly seem like the outdoorsy type, so I figured this was going to be a pretty short outing—but I wanted things to be secure just in case.

A visible change took place the moment she stepped outside. She turned her face to the sun and took in a deep breath, her shoulders dropping like she had just left the weight of the world behind her.

"That's how I feel out here too," I commented, giving her a grin.

"What?" she asked, turning back to me with a smile.

"The way you just instantly relaxed. It's how I feel here, too. It's the main reason I bought the place. I love this valley. No matter how much stress or chaos there is at work, when I get home, I can just come out here and feel instant peace. It's better than bourbon."

"You're right," she agreed. "Peace. That's what I feel out here. You're a lucky man."

"I am," I said, agreeing with her even though all I could think was that even my valley paled in comparison to the woman standing in front of me. Coming home to the valley was wonderful. Coming home to her was heaven.

She turned and walked down the steps of the deck and into the yard below. Thor and I followed her, letting her lead the way. This was her walk. She wanted to explore, and I wanted to let her go wherever her heart desired.

But she stopped suddenly at the edge of the mowed grass, peering into the taller grasses beyond.

"Is it safe?" she asked timidly, turning to look at me.

"What do you mean?"

"I mean, are there snakes out there?"

I nodded slowly. "Could be, yeah."

"Poisonous ones?"

"Venomous," I corrected. "Yeah, we've got a few bad ones here. But if it makes you feel better, they don't want anything to do with you, either. Just watch your step."

"Maybe you should go first," she said.

I grinned. "Okay. Look," I said, pointing off to the side. "You can see where I normally walk right over here. There's a path through the grass. Follow me."

Thor and I moved toward my makeshift trail. Janet followed—and surprised me by slipping her hand into mine.

I looked down at it and then looked at her, but her eyes were focused on the mountain in front of us. I turned my head forward too, fighting back a silly grin. I wasn't a teenager anymore, and this wasn't my first date. But the feelings felt similar all the same.

We walked quietly for a long while, up and down soft hills, her hand still in mine, until we got to the place I had in mind—a little dip in the valley with a small pond and the shade of an old tree. I took off Thor's leash and told him to go play, knowing he would come to me if I called.

"It's beautiful down here," Janet breathed. "I didn't even know this pond was here. I couldn't see it from the house."

"The hill hides it," I said. "The valley looks flat compared to the mountains around here, but you'd be surprised what all these hills can hide."

"It's so lovely. Is this all your land?"

I nodded. "Yes. Sixty acres. My dad left me some money when he passed. I decided the best thing I could do with it was to invest it in land in the place where I wanted to spend the rest of my life."

"Wise investment," she said, surprising me again by sitting down at the bottom of the tree.

I had figured she was too proper to sit out on the dirt like that, but she seemed like a different woman out here somehow—relaxed in a way she wasn't anywhere else. It looked good on her.

I sat beside her, just itching to put my arm around her. I didn't think it would be unwelcome—not after she had reached for me and held my hand the whole way here. But I was still struggling internally with what the right thing to do was, considering she had made her wishes known.

This woman was damn confusing, and all my normal confidence was gone.

"I've been thinking," she said, her voice breaking through the quiet.

I turned to look at her. She kept her eyes fixed on the pond, like she was afraid to look at me.

"What have you been thinking about?" I asked.

It was an interesting thing. Sometimes, the woman made a fun verbal sparring partner. I enjoyed poking at her, teasing her, ruffling up those pretty feathers a bit. But other times, like this, I found myself speaking to her the way I would talk to a wounded animal or a scared child. Quiet. Calm. Non-threatening.

It seemed to me like Lonnie had broken something inside her, and it made me furious.

"About what you said." She kept staring at the water, fidgeting with the hem of her shirt with her fingers.

"What did I say?"

"You said feelings like this don't come around that often," she said, speaking like she had practiced the words in her mind a thousand times. Finally, she turned to look at me, searching my face with those big eyes of hers. "Did you mean that?"

I nodded. "I did."

She looked back at the pond. "I'm not sure I've ever felt this way before," she admitted. "Not really. I know I told you how in love I was with Lonnie. And that was true. I was madly in love with him. But it was...different." She frowned. "I think, if I'm being honest with myself, I was more in love with the *idea* of being in love than anything else. Caught up in the romance of it all."

"Puppy love," I said, giving her an easy grin, trying to encourage her to keep going. I could tell whatever she was trying to say wasn't easy for her.

She smiled a little at that. "Exactly. Puppy love. It was real, but...but it wasn't deep." She shook her head, stopping herself again from saying whatever was on her mind. "I've dated other men since. Short-term, always casual. Always very socially oriented, you know. But I never let myself really *feel* anything for any of them. And I don't think they felt much for me."

"I doubt that's true," I said. "I imagine you broke a lot of hearts, keeping yours so locked up." I nudged her with my shoulder, wanting to see a smile on that serious face. I got it—a small one.

"I don't think so," she said. "But." She shook herself and took a deep breath, obviously gathering strength for whatever it was she really wanted to say.

I felt myself still, waiting, hoping beyond hope it was good news.

She looked into my eyes. "I feel different with you than I have with anyone, including Lonnie. You're different. I feel like you really see me."

"Hard not to when I can't stop looking at you."

She flushed a little, that touch of pink I loved putting on her face. "But it's more than that, isn't it? More than just the physical, I mean. I feel like you see me as a person."

I reached out and took her hand in mine, bringing it to my lips for a soft kiss. "I see you, Janet. I see an incredibly strong, sexy, smart, sophisticated woman—a woman who has worked her ass off to create a career for herself. I see a mother who is fighting damn hard for a relationship with her kid, and who dropped everything—twice—to come to her rescue when she was in trouble. I see a woman who's interesting and complicated, and who wears a suit of armor around her heart to keep from getting hurt again. I see a woman who was nearly broken by a sorry excuse for a man who didn't know what he had right in front of him—but who grew past that and built something for herself. I see a woman who's strong and soft and—"

But she cut me off, putting her mouth over mine. Before I knew it, she was in my lap again, straddling me this time in those skintight jeans of hers. Her lips crushed mine, hungrily seeking more. I put my hands on her waist, then slid them down, cupping her against me. It felt like being a teenager again, sneaking off into the woods to make out. All I could think was *more*. I wanted more, wanted everything she would give me. As she moved against me, driving me crazy, still kissing me, the world almost faded away—until it came back again with the sound of a twig snapping.

I stilled instantly and pulled back.

"What? I'm so sorry. Was that too much?" Janet looked flustered and embarrassed.

I put my finger against her lips and gave her a sign to be quiet. There it was again. Another snap. Something was in the brush. I looked over to where Thor was lying by the pond. He had heard it too. His head was alert, listening, as he looked to me for instruction.

I picked Janet up off my lap and put her to the side, standing and pulling out my service weapon. She backed against the tree, nervous too, as we both listened. Another snap, this time sounding like it was moving away from us, toward the mountain.

"Stay with her," I said to Thor in a low voice, hoping he would understand me. He seemed to, as he moved toward Janet and sat beside her. "I'm going to check it out," I whispered to Janet, who nodded silently and put a hand on Thor's head.

I moved toward the direction of the noise, slowly and methodically. The noises picked up, quicker now, as whatever—or whoever—it was moved away from me more quickly. I knew it was likely a deer or even a bear, which would make pursuing it one of the dumber things I had done.

But my gut said these noises were made by a human.

A human that had been hunting us.

Chapter Twenty-Nine

Janet

My heart pounded as Greg moved out of sight, through the tall grasses beyond the clearing. Thor seemed to sense I needed comfort. He moved to my side and I clung to him, fearing for Greg's safety. I couldn't believe he was just going after whoever had made that sound. It was his job, yes. But I had never witnessed this part of it. I had never seen him pull his weapon and walk fearlessly into an unknown situation.

He was so brave. He put his life on the line, day in and day out, to keep everyone else safe. He had gone to bat for Daphne and tried to get her help when none of us knew what was wrong.

He was a good, good man.

And he saw me. He saw more in me than I saw in myself, frankly. And despite seeing me, the good and the bad, he wanted me. Not to be a live-in nanny or glorified housekeeper, but *me*.

It was glorious and unexpected, and all I could think was that if he made it back safely, I needed to tell him the truth about what I wanted.

I needed to tell him I was falling in love with him and that Paris could wait until we figured out where this was going. Where *we* were going.

The thought made me almost giddy, despite the seriousness of the situation we were in.

Minutes passed by, slowly, until he finally emerged from the grass. I heard him barking orders on his cell phone before I saw him. He sounded angry, which I felt certain meant he hadn't found what he was looking for.

I stood when he reached me, brushing the dirt and leaves off my jeans, blushing as I remembered his hands on me earlier. We had practically behaved like teenagers, kissing madly in a field until we were interrupted. It was completely unlike me.

It was also the most fun I had ever had.

He finally ended his call and stuck his phone in his pocket, sighing.

"What is it?" I asked. "What did you find?"

"Nothing," he said flatly. "I can't even be sure it was a human out there. Odds are it was an animal. But my gut says it was him, stalking us."

"You should listen to your gut," I said. "I trust it."

He looked at me, then pulled me to him in a tight hug. "Are you okay? I'm sorry I left you like that."

"I'm fine," I soothed. "You did what you needed to do. Who were you talking to on the phone?"

"Jackson. I called the station and asked for him. I needed to know where he was."

"Jackson?" I frowned as I realized the implications. "Wait. You were concerned he's the one behind all of this?"

He took my hand and started leading me back to the house. "Earlier today, Miller suggested Jackson might be the problem. I've always trusted Jackson completely, but I had to admit he had opportunity. He was everywhere the threats occurred. He even could have been the one to break my truck window. So when my gut said whoever was behind this was in that field, I had to make sure it wasn't him."

"But it wasn't," I said, wanting to verify as much as anything.

He shook his head. "No. I called Ms. Hall at the office and asked for him instead of calling his cell phone, just to make sure. He was at the station, finishing up some reports. He's on his way here now. I asked if Miller was there. That was a negative. Asked about Tracy, Parker, and Sanderson too. All negatives. So right now, I'm thinking Jackson's in the clear and I need to focus on my original suspicions. But that means I'm nowhere closer than I was. And there are still other deputies I haven't even had a chance to interact with since all this went down."

"You'll find him," I said, knowing full well it was true. I had complete and utter confidence Greg would win this. "And it has to be a relief knowing it wasn't Jackson. I know he's practically a son to you."

Greg stopped suddenly and turned to me, tucking my hair behind my ears before pulling me close to him. It felt like he couldn't help himself, that he reached for me without thinking, simply because he wanted me close.

I loved it.

"And just how do you know that?" he asked.

"Because I see you, too," I said simply. "It's obvious you've mentored him, and he clearly thinks the world of you. Daphne told me how horrible his childhood was and how he went into law enforcement to be different from his father. He found something different in you. He would never betray you. You're like a dad to him. I see it every time you're together."

He let out a long breath and rested his forehead on mine. "You're exactly right. I've never thought of it that way, but yeah, that's how it's been. I shouldn't have doubted him."

"You were just doing your job."

He pulled his head back so he could kiss me right there in the field, with the prairie grasses waving around us. I wrapped my arms around him and sank into it, those giddy feelings returning as I relished every single moment of whatever was happening between us.

"I'm going to have a hard time letting you go, Janet," he whispered into my ear as he pulled me even closer.

"I don't know that I want to leave," I whispered back.

"Really?" He pulled away and studied my face like he wanted to be sure I meant what I was saying.

"Really," I said, my heart railing against my chest as I confessed the truth. "I don't know exactly what's happening between us or where this is going, but I want to find out. It feels bigger and more important than Paris. I keep hoping you'll ask me to stay."

He ran his thumb along my cheek. "If you mean that, I'm going to do everything I can to convince you not to go."

"I hope you do."

Threat or no threat, I was disappointed Jackson was on his way. I wanted to be alone with Greg, wanted to finish what we had started in the field. It was exhilarating and incredible.

It was like falling in love.

Was I really, truly falling in love with Greg?

The answer rang through me so clearly I couldn't possibly deny it. Yes. I was in love with Greg Morrison. But it was more than that. Deeper than that somehow. I had known Greg for nearly a full year now. More importantly, Daphne knew him even better than I did, and she had complete and utter respect for him. Emerson, whom I had grown to trust completely, also thought the world of Greg, and he had known him even longer. Greg wasn't a stranger, and this wasn't just a fling. It wasn't just the exhilarating feelings of puppy love or infatuation.

I knew who Greg was as a person. He was solid. Faithful. Good.

I didn't just love these incredible feelings or the fact that he looked at me the way I had always wanted someone to. I loved *him*. I loved his character and integrity. I loved what he stood for and how he was willing to fight for it.

I loved Greg Morrison. And that was worth way more than Paris.

Greg and I stole another kiss or two before Jackson arrived much too soon, in my opinion. Now that I knew my own heart, I didn't want to waste another minute. Forget waiting a week or two—I knew what I wanted. I was ready to call Philip and give him the bad news. It was crazy and foolish. After all, my things were already on their way overseas. I wasn't like Daphne. I didn't do impulsive things like this, didn't make rash decisions based on my feelings. Not anymore. But it felt *right.*

Those conversations would have to wait though because of this whole threat situation. I couldn't wait until all of this nonsense was wrapped up.

JACKSON'S FACE WAS GRAVE WHEN HE CAME INSIDE. "I've got something you need to see," he said to Greg before they even greeted each other. He gestured toward the dining table, where we all sat.

The dynamic felt off to me, with Jackson now essentially taking charge. I stole a glance at Greg, whose face revealed nothing.

Jackson flipped a laptop open and turned it so we could see. A video was pulled up—surveillance footage.

"That's your truck," I said, leaning into Greg.

"Sure is. Where did this footage come from?" Greg asked, looking at Jackson.

"One of the houses across the street from the pub. They have one of those video doorbells, and it happens to catch the other side of O'Malley's parking lot. We got a look at the man who broke your window."

"That's a good catch," Greg said.

I couldn't help but notice the hint of pride in his voice. I didn't know how he had never realized the way he saw Jackson. But I did—it was how I felt about Daphne. Neither of us were biological parents to our children, but the feelings were the same.

"Here he comes," Jackson said, pointing to a tiny image on the screen.

"It's not very clear. Can we zoom in?"

"That is zoomed in," Jackson explained. "We're pushing the limits of this camera right now. It's not great, but it's something."

Greg rewound it and watched again as the man slunk over to his truck, looked around, then went to work busting the window. It seemed to take him more effort than I would have expected. I wasn't sure if that said more about the strength of the window or the weakness of the man.

"I'm convinced it's the same guy I saw at the rehearsal dinner," Greg said. "The posture's the same. Height is right. Dark hair. I just wish I could see his face."

"Me too," said Jackson. "But in good news, I agree with you this guy isn't built like Miller. So it wasn't him. His build is the same as Sanderson, but his hair is too dark."

"Agreed," Greg said. "Sanderson has some brothers, right? What do we have on them? Any pictures on file?"

Jackson pulled the laptop over and did a quick search. "Younger brother has a photo here from some misdemeanor charges. Prank-type stuff. Nothing major." He spun the laptop around for Greg to see. "Darker hair. But he's shorter than the guy in the video. Nothing in here on the others. There's four brothers total, if I remember correctly."

Greg leaned back in his chair, in that pose I was becoming so familiar with. I could see the wheels spinning as he thought.

"We need to talk to his other brothers," he said finally. "See if any of them are the right height and hair color. See if any of them have an attitude. Do a little more digging into their connections. It's a long shot, I think, but—"

"I've contacted the TBI," Jackson said, interrupting him. "We'll handle it. I just wanted to give you an update."

I felt Greg tense beside me.

"Look, there's something else we need to talk about. When I was talking to John today, he said there were rumors—"

The sound of shattering glass filled the room, interrupting Greg and setting the alarms off. Greg and Jackson were both up in an instant, weapons in hand, as they moved toward the living room, where the sound had come from.

I stayed, paralyzed it seemed, feeling like my heart had stopped in my chest. My fingers gripped the wooden table as if it would somehow protect me.

THE ALARMS STOPPED, AND BOTH MEN RETURNED TO THE table quickly, weapons still in hand. Greg was carrying a brick with another note held in place with a rubber band. He quickly slipped the band off, not even bothering to put on gloves like he normally did, and read what the message said. His face paled and he looked at me, betraying a fear I had never seen in him.

"What is it?" I asked before swallowing hard.

He slid it toward me, letting me see for myself.

Attached to the note were pictures—more small pictures, like the ones from Daphne's wedding. But these were of me and Greg, in the field, kissing. Greg was right. He had been there. He had watched us, photographed us.

Hunted us.

It made all of this feel real in a way it hadn't before.

The note was clear:

I'm taking this town. I've already shown you I can get to you and everyone you care about. Get out of my way, or I'll take what's yours—starting with her.

MY HANDS SHOOK AS I PUSHED THE NOTE AWAY, NOT wanting to see it anymore. It was sickening.

"Stay with her," Greg told Jackson, his voice rough. "Protect her with your life. I'm going after him. He can't have gotten far."

"You can't—" Jackson started, but he stopped when he saw the look on Greg's face. "I'll protect her," he said quietly.

Greg nodded and turned, disappearing yet again, leaving me alone to pray as the man I loved walked straight into danger.

Chapter Thirty

Greg

ANGER BOILED INSIDE ME, THREATENING TO OVERFLOW THE minute I caught this guy. I wanted him. Wanted to slam my fist into his face and feel bones break. This kind of anger wasn't like me, and I knew I had to get it under control.

But he had threatened the woman I loved, had made her face turn white with fear when she saw those photos. And now I wanted more than just to stop the threats.

I wanted to see him pay.

He had run straight for the treeline on the left edge of my property. I could see his trail, the careless marks he had made as he had run from my house like a coward after throwing the brick through the window. His words didn't match his actions. For someone who was constantly threatening harm, he still hadn't done anything more than break a couple of windows and kill some rabbits. It was the one thing that calmed the rage I had felt at his threat against Janet.

He was all talk so far. I just had to make sure it stayed that way.

I cursed when I got to the treeline and the trail all but disappeared. I slowed my pace and looked closely, wishing I had Emerson's tracking skills.

"What would Emerson look for?" I muttered to myself, looking around.

Then I saw it—the broken twigs and a small disturbance in the path signaling that someone had been through here recently. I followed it, pistol drawn, more slowly than I had the obvious path in the grass. But I was on his trail. I was sure of it.

We were heading straight through a small section of woods that separated my plot of land from a newly built subdivision, pretty little cookie-cutter houses meant to attract new residents to town. I quickened my pace, knowing that a million things could go wrong if he beat me to that neighborhood. He could hide in any of the houses currently under construction—or, worse, break into some unsuspecting innocent's home to hide out. There were several young families with children living in the neighborhood, recent transplants who had been recruited to work at our growing hospital. I shuddered to think what might happen if he was desperate and there were any kids outside playing.

All I could do was hope he stayed in character, the coward he seemed to be, and that he did nothing more than hide from me. I didn't mind a long game of hide-and-seek. I just didn't want anyone to get hurt.

I broke the treeline and scanned the neighborhood, looking for any sign of movement. Tires squealed loudly as a car peeled out of the driveway of one of the houses currently under construction. It flew past, almost knocking me down as it did. I cursed again and started running.

Chapter Thirty-One

Janet

I insisted on sweeping up the broken glass even though Jackson said I shouldn't be by the window. There were windows everywhere, I argued, and I didn't want Greg coming home to a mess.

I also desperately needed something to do with my hands as I counted the seconds, worrying about Greg's safety. I couldn't rest until I knew he was alright.

Jackson seemed restless, too, and irritated to be stuck babysitting me. He paced the living room, scowling, with a hand resting on the weapon in his belt. He was as worried as I was.

"He'll be okay," I said with more confidence than I felt. It was the little bit of mother I had in me, wanting to soothe the kid who looked at Greg like a father.

It was a funny thing, really. Had Jackson not been here, I felt certain I would have fallen apart. But the need to be strong for him—even though he was a grown man wearing a deputy's uniform—was somehow more powerful than my own fear.

I wondered if that's how Greg felt about everyone he took care of.

Jackson stopped pacing and looked at me, relaxing just a little. "I know. But I don't like him out there on his own. And he's not exactly following protocol. He shouldn't be on this case. He should have stayed here with you while I went after the guy. I shouldn't have agreed to let him go. I screwed up."

"I don't think Greg's the type to stay behind while someone else does the hard work," I said with a little smile.

Jackson shook his head. "You got that right. He doesn't hide behind a desk, even when it comes to the kind of duties other sheriffs would push off on the lowest on the totem pole. Do you know, when it's storming outside, he'll take over traffic duty at the school? Stand there in the pouring rain, directing cars and school buses, just so nobody else has to."

I smiled. "I didn't know that, but it doesn't surprise me."

Jackson looked at me. "You really care about him, don't you?" He blushed suddenly. "I don't mean to pry or be rude. But the pictures..."

I blushed too, thinking of the pictures of me straddling Greg, making out with him like we were half our age. It was mortifying that Jackson had seen those. "I do."

"That's good," he said, nodding. "He's a good man. And it's been obvious to the rest of us that he's had a thing for you since the day you two met." He grinned, making me blush again.

"The attraction was mutual," I admitted. "But I don't know if anything would have come of it had we not been stuck here together. I guess, in a way, when all this is over, I need to thank the man who threatened us."

This time, Jackson laughed out loud. "Maybe Greg will too. He never said anything, but I could tell he was lonely."

I knew I shouldn't ask questions about Greg's private life, but I was curious and couldn't stop myself. "Has he dated much since you've known him?"

"No," Jackson said, shaking his head. "Not at all really. A casual date here or there, but nobody he seemed interested in. Honestly, I thought he'd stay single. Seemed like one of those types who would never get over his wife's death and would be faithful to her until the grave. Well, until you came along, that is."

The world seemed to stop spinning on its axis. I felt the color drain out of my face. "What did you say?"

He looked at me oddly. "Until you came along."

"I meant about his wife." I clung to the broom, feeling like I was going to be sick. "I assumed he was divorced. Or maybe had just always been single."

The idea of him being a widow had never even crossed my mind, although I couldn't imagine why it hadn't. He was attractive and completely wonderful. Of course he had been married, and of course it hadn't ended in divorce. Who would divorce someone as incredible as he was?

"Oh. No. He and his wife married young. He never talks about it. I only know the story because his brother confided in me when he visited. Said the grief about destroyed Greg when she died. He was never really the same after. She was killed by a drunk driver a few years into their marriage. It's one of the reasons he stayed in law enforcement," Jackson explained. "Wants to do what he can to make sure that doesn't happen to anyone else."

Jackson kept talking, oblivious to the fact that my whole world was caving in on me. A widow. A widow who'd married young and adored his wife and changed his entire life after she died.

It was like Lonnie all over again, and I had never seen it coming. No, Greg didn't want me for a nanny or housekeeper. But it didn't matter. Not really. I would never be able to compete with a late wife. I knew that game all too well. Death had a way of making people romanticize and idolize the spouse who died first. I had heard the same, time and time again, in the support group for second wives I had joined in one last desperate attempt to make sense of everything and save my marriage.

I had spent nearly a decade competing with a glorified late wife. I could never, ever do that again.

"What is it? What's wrong?" Jackson asked, finally pausing in his monologue about all of Greg's virtues.

"Nothing," I said, shaking my head. I knew I must have been as white as a ghost. "I'm just concerned. It's been a while since we've heard from Greg. I hope everything is alright. Will you excuse me? I think I need a minute."

With that, I got up and walked straight to my bedroom. I closed the door and collapsed on the bed, knowing I couldn't stay here after all.

Jackson's information would help me dodge a bullet I hadn't seen coming. I should be grateful for it.

But why did it feel like I was losing the love of my life?

Chapter Thirty-Two

Greg

I slammed the back door to my house with more force than necessary. Jackson jumped up off the couch.

"No luck?" he asked.

I shook my head. "His car was parked in the Oak Meadow neighborhood. Ran straight through the woods and peeled out when I got there. Put out a BOLO for a silver compact, no tags. Dented right bumper. From the look I got, he appeared to be alone. Same guy we've been talking about."

"Got it." Jackson pulled out his laptop and started entering in the info.

"Where's Janet?" I asked.

Jackson looked up momentarily. "I think she went to her room. Said she needed a minute."

I bit back the scolding I wanted to let loose. His job had been to protect her. He shouldn't have let her out of his sight while I was gone.

I knocked gently on her door.

"Yes?" Her voice was quiet. Too quiet. Something was wrong.

"Can I come in?" I asked.

"Yes." Even more quiet this time.

I opened the door and found her sitting stiffly on the bed, as white as a ghost.

"Oh, honey," I said, moving toward her. I pulled her into my arms, but she turned her head away. "What's wrong?" I asked, pulling back to look at her.

She stared at me a long minute before letting out a choked laugh. "What's wrong? Someone just threatened us and you went after him and..."

"Everything's okay," I soothed. "The guy is a coward. Hasn't done anything except break some windows. I saw his car. We'll get him. It's only a matter of time."

"I need you to catch him quickly," she said. But her voice sounded strained, and it felt like it was from more than just the situation—like there was something she wasn't telling me. And even though I stood there, still rubbing her arms and trying to reassure her, she wasn't touching me back. Just stood as stiff as a board, with that awful look on her face.

"Listen," I said, not sure how to break the bad news. "We shouldn't stay here tonight, not with this threat. I've got a place nobody knows about, a cabin up on the mountain. It's my own little getaway when I need a break from it all. It's not much. Just one room and it's pretty rustic. But it's safe. There's not a soul in this town that knows about it. I've never even told Emerson about it, if that tells you anything."

She just stared at me. "A one-room cabin?"

I nodded. "Used to be a hunting cabin. It's off the beaten path. We'll pack up some food and head out. I don't want you here tonight."

"But you said he was a coward, and you have a security system," she protested.

"I know." How could I possibly explain this to her? Whether or not it was logical, every sense in my body was telling me to get her out of here. Maybe I was overreacting. But a lifetime in law enforcement had taught me to never ignore those warning pulses, and the thought of something happening to Janet... It was unthinkable. "Look, if it was just me, I'd stay here. But I don't want to take any chances. Not with you."

She sat back and closed her eyes, a pained look on her face. "How many days should I pack for?"

"Just two or three. I doubt we even need that long. We'll get him, I promise. I won't let him hurt you."

She nodded but didn't meet my eyes. "I need some privacy to pack," she said.

I stepped back. "Of course. Yeah. I'll pack up too. Can you be ready in twenty minutes? Is that enough time?"

"Sure."

"Okay."

I STEPPED OUT AND CLOSED THE DOOR, COMPLETELY confused. The woman was a wreck. But she hadn't fallen apart or pulled away when I had gone after the guy in the field. Maybe she hadn't believed it was him that time. Maybe she'd thought it was just an animal and was trying to humor me. Now, it was possible the reality of the situation had sunk in and she couldn't handle it.

Either way, the man's threats had affected her in a big way this time.

So help me, he would pay for terrorizing the woman I loved.

Chapter Thirty-Three

Janet

I felt numb as I packed my things into one of the smaller bags tucked into my large suitcase. It was a bag I had slipped in there at the last minute, in case I bought any souvenirs or clothing on my travels. I had never expected to pack it with clothes to go on the run from someone intent on not leaving us alone.

And I had certainly never expected to be heading to a cabin with Greg Morrison.

A *one-room* cabin.

Oh, how quickly things could change. An hour ago, I would have felt a little thrill at the idea. We were both adults, it was clear we wanted each other, and I had decided to stay and see where things were going between us.

But now?

Now I needed to get away from him more than ever.

My things were packed in less than five minutes, but I stalled in the room anyway. I didn't want to face him. Was I being irrational? The way he looked at me... It wasn't the way someone looked at a consolation prize.

No, even now, he looked at me like I was all he wanted.

But I had fallen for that once, only to waste the best years of my life with a man who grew to hate me for not being Eileen Sullivan. Greg might have thought he was falling for me, but how long would it take for him to grow to hate me too? To realize I wasn't what he wanted after all?

I was terrible at relationships. Demanding. Stubborn. Ridiculous.

All the things Lonnie had told me for years.

I couldn't bear to watch Greg grow disinterested or to feel him compare me to an angelic late wife. I couldn't go through that again. It felt like such a cruel joke. Everything I had ever wanted had felt within reach for just a brief moment.

I would just have to find a way to let him down gently, to make him see now that I wasn't what he wanted. I just had to get through a couple of days. If he was right and they caught the guy quickly, then I could leave and go to Daphne's cottage. Greg would be okay. His feelings couldn't be that deep. After all, he barely knew me. He would get over me.

But somehow I knew I would never get over him.

Twenty minutes on the dot passed before Greg knocked.

"You ready?" he called.

"Yes." I stood up and grabbed my bag with both hands as he swung open the door. He immediately reached for it. "I've got it," I said.

He grabbed it anyway and tipped up my chin, forcing me to look at him. "When are you going to realize I like taking care of you?" he said before planting a firm kiss on my mouth.

I tried desperately not to respond, to pull away, but I couldn't—I was lost in it, lost in him. When his hand reached around my back and pulled me close, I sank into the embrace. It might be the last time I was held by him. I needed it, selfish as it might be.

When he finally broke the kiss, he wiped away the tears I hadn't been able to stop.

"Oh, honey," he said. "I'm sorry. I promise I'll get this guy."

"It's not that," I said.

"Then what is it?"

But my courage failed. I couldn't say it, not yet. I needed some time to gather myself.

"We'll talk later," I said. "We need to go, don't we?"

He looked worried, but he nodded and took my hand. "Come on. I've already loaded up the ATV."

"ATV?" I asked blankly. I had assumed we would take his truck.

"This place is a little off-grid," he said, chuckling. "Don't worry. It's not a bad ride."

Great. Just great. Not only was I going to spend the night with Greg in a one-room cabin, but we were going to drive there on an ATV.

He led me out to where he did, indeed, have an ATV ready to go. A small cart was attached to the back, with a cooler and some crates, including a carrier for Thor, who was practically grinning in anticipation. Greg added my bag and strapped it on, then climbed onto the seat.

"Hop on," he said, grinning. "And hold on tight."

I bit my lip and climbed on behind him, thinking I would do my best to sit back away from him. But that wasn't possible, especially as we started moving. My whole body was pressed up against his, with my arms around his waist and my chin resting on his shoulder.

He smelled of oranges and cloves, a sweet and spicy combination I couldn't get enough of now that I associated it with him.

This was not ideal for preparing to end things.

Greg was laser focused on our goal as he zipped the ATV through the path we had cut earlier, past the pond and meadow, into a sparse treeline far beyond. We started slowly climbing in elevation, forcing me to grip him tighter as he wound through the trees, cutting a snakelike path up the mountain on a trail only he could possibly recognize. I quickly lost my orientation, knowing I would be hopelessly lost in these woods if we were somehow separated. That, too, made me cling to him more closely.

It had nothing to do with that scent of orange and spice that was already starting to smell like home.

And it certainly had nothing to do with how incredible those abs felt underneath his light shirt, muscles that told the story of hours spent doing so much more than sitting at a desk.

"Is this all your land?" I asked, practically yelling over the sound of the ATV. I needed the distraction of conversation.

He chuckled and turned his head slightly so I could hear him better. "No way. We're way past the boundaries of my valley acreage. I own the land the cabin's on too, but that's just a couple of acres. We aren't there yet."

I nodded and sank back into silence, both wanting the time to go by quickly so I could get some space and also never wanting it to end.

The sun cut a low angled path through the trees by the time we pulled up in front of a tiny cabin practically hidden in the trees on the side of the mountain. I had lost track of time on our journey, too lost in my own internal war to pay attention to the passing minutes. But it was clearly growing late in the day, and the forest was lit by the magical golden glow that only came just before the sunset. Daphne had called it the "golden hour" once when she was talking to me about her photography. I hadn't quite understood it until now. But there was no other way to describe the way this world was glowing.

Greg reached back and squeezed my thigh, sending a thrill of pleasure I tried to ignore as I climbed off the ATV and surveyed the cabin in front of me.

"It's not much," he said, coming up behind me and wrapping his arms around my waist. "But I know you'll be safe out here, and that's all that matters."

"It's kind of beautiful," I whispered, unable to stop myself.

"It is, isn't it?" He nuzzled my neck, and I closed my eyes, wondering how on earth I was going to have the strength to end this when he had the power to make me feel the things he did. He was a drug I didn't want to give up but would destroy me in the end.

So I had to.

"What's wrong?" he asked quietly, like he could read me like a book.

"Let's talk later," I said. "We need to get everything inside first."

He let out a breath and pulled away slowly, his fingers holding on until the last second like he could sense what was coming and wasn't ready for it. I avoided his eyes as I waited for him to unlock the cabin and unstrap my bag for me. I grabbed it and headed straight inside, needing to get away from him for just a moment, to get my head back on straight.

The inside of the cabin was rustic like he had said, but I couldn't help feeling like it was almost as magical as the golden light outside. It was simple but clean, a one-room cabin Greg clearly loved and took care to furnish well for his getaways. It wasn't set up well for two platonic friends though. There was a single bed, a rocking chair by the fireplace, and a tiny table with two chairs close to the kitchenette.

Not so much as a loveseat for me to curl up and sleep on.

Thor lumbered in, followed by Greg, who carried in the supplies he had brought. When he was finished, he gave me an unsure smile. "Want to talk now?" he asked, clearly nervous about what I was going to say.

"We probably should," I said, anxious too.

He gestured for me to sit down at the table. "Look," he said, starting before I could. "If it's the bed situation freaking you out, don't worry about that, okay? It's yours. I'll throw a sleeping bag on the floor. I know things between us are new, and under normal circumstances, we wouldn't be living together yet, much less camping out together in a cabin." He gave me a faint smile. "I just want you to know if that's what's worrying you, there are absolutely no expectations here."

"It's not that. Not exactly." I took in a deep breath and blew it out, gathering strength. "Greg, I got caught up in things earlier and said things I shouldn't have. It was a mistake to suggest I might consider staying here in Rosemary Mountain." I went into business mode, drawing on all my experience in navigating difficult conversations with clients. "As I shared earlier, I've already signed a contract to go to Paris. I apologize for allowing myself to get swept up, thinking things could be different than they are. But the reality is that I'm leaving soon, and it would be a terrible idea for us to let things go further than they already have."

He stilled as he listened to me. "You got swept up," he repeated.

"Exactly. I apologize for leading you on. It was unintentional. We're both adults, and I hope we can remain friends. But that's all we can be."

"I see." His voice indicated that he didn't see at all.

Frankly, neither did I, but I had to hold to it anyway.

CHAPTER THIRTY-FOUR

Greg

I STARED AT THE WOMAN ACROSS FROM ME, FLABBERGASTED. Hours earlier, she had kissed me like a woman on fire and told me she wanted me to convince her to stay. Now, her mask was back in place. That layer of ice she kept on to protect herself had returned.

Now that I knew the real her, the mask was so obvious I couldn't miss it for the world. This wasn't Janet. This wasn't her heart.

This was her locking her heart up because she didn't trust me with it.

It was wrong to speak ill of the dead, but the whole thing made me want to punch Lonnie Sullivan in the face. The way he had wrecked this woman's heart made me angrier than I could possibly express in words.

I took a deep breath, calculating how to play it. Arguing with her wouldn't get me anywhere—I knew that much for sure. Calling her out wouldn't get me anywhere, either. She would just retreat further into that shell of ice, convincing herself that what was happening between us wasn't worth risking her heart for.

But she was wrong.

What was happening between us was worth *everything*.

And I'd be damned if I just stepped aside and let her walk out of my life without making her see it.

"Okay," I said simply, deciding to play it cool. For now.

"Okay?" she repeated like she was afraid she hadn't heard me correctly.

I nodded. "I already told you I would never ask you to give up your dreams for me."

"Right," she said, confusion on her face. She had obviously expected me to put up a fight.

I wasn't at all sure I was making the right move here by playing it cool, but I had to go with my gut.

It had gotten me this far with her.

"I've got to take care of a few things outside," I said. "You like fish? I think I'll catch some fish for dinner."

"Catch some fish?" she repeated again, still completely off guard.

"Yeah. There's a great fishing stream just a short walk from here. I keep some gear out back. Fresh trout sounds good, huh? I've got a little charcoal grill out back too. We can grill it up and have a nice dinner."

"Sure," she said.

I almost laughed at the look on her face.

Yeah, my reaction had totally caught her off guard, and I was good with that.

I had absolutely no intention of losing this woman I had fallen head-over-heels in love with. I was still fully committed to convincing her to stay. But if I knew one thing about Janet, it was that she would have to think it was her idea.

The woman was damn stubborn. But hell, I kind of liked it.

Chapter Thirty-Five

Janet

I was steaming by the time Greg walked out to go fishing. Fishing! I had thought telling him I was leaving would hurt him at least a little. But it was clear I had vastly overestimated his feelings for me. He was as cool as a cucumber, like I had done nothing more than tell him I was heading out shopping.

Damn Greg Morrison.

And damn that orange clove cologne that seemed to permeate this whole damn cabin.

I went to work scrubbing the cabin's kitchen even though it didn't really need it. I just needed something to do with my hands, some way to take out my frustration.

I shut down the little voice inside that told me this wouldn't do a thing to help the kind of frustration I was feeling.

At least two hours passed before Greg returned, during which time I scrubbed the entire cabin and somehow felt more irritated than ever. The irritation only grew when he walked into the cabin whistling, clearly not upset at all.

"Caught two trout. Got them cleaned up and on the grill out there.

I'm going to wash my hands, then find something in the cooler to go with them." He glanced around the cabin, apparently noticing my hard work. "Wow, it looks great in here."

"Thought I would give the place a good cleaning," I said.

"Appreciate it." He kept whistling as he washed his hands.

It was driving me crazy.

"Well, obviously, you're fine," I said before I could stop myself.

"What?" He turned the water off and looked my way, drying his hands on a paper towel.

"I was worried I would be hurting you somehow by telling you I'm still leaving, but you're obviously fine."

He gave me a long look, mulling something over. "Do you not want me to be fine?"

"That's not what I mean," I stammered.

He cocked his head. "I think that's exactly what you mean."

"I just... I—"

"Janet. Come here."

"What?"

"You heard me." His voice was calm, but even here, it carried a quiet authority in it.

I walked toward him even as I wanted to snap out that he didn't get to tell me what to do.

When I was right in front of him, he reached out and took my hands. "Janet. My feelings haven't changed at all. I'm yours if you want me. But I told you I don't want you to resent me. I mean that. This is your life, and you're going to have to decide what you want to do with it. Even if that means you run away to Paris."

I bit my lip. "I'm not running away."

"Yes, you are," he said, dropping a hand so he could run it through my hair, tucking it gently behind my ear. "You're running away from me, from us. You're scared. It's plain to see. But I don't see how me getting upset and throwing a fit about it is going to make you any less afraid."

"I'm not afraid," I insisted.

"You are. I don't know why. I don't know why everything was great, then suddenly it wasn't. But I see you, remember? I see the mask you put up. In the end though, you're gonna have to be the one who decides how this goes."

I was tempted to spill it, to tell him what Jackson had told me and explain all my fears. But what would it matter? It wouldn't change anything. I would still always be a runner up, a second-place prize.

I would still always live in the shadow of the one he'd chosen first, the one he would still be with if he had the choice.

He sighed and dropped my other hand. "Gotta go check the fish. Listen, I put a bottle of wine in the cooler. I don't know about you, but I could use a drink. Why don't you pour us a couple of glasses?"

"You have wine glasses out here?"

He grinned. "No. But there's a couple of coffee mugs in the cabinet. We can drink from those."

"Okay." I gave him a weak smile as he gave me one last look, then headed back out of the cabin. It felt like we had a truce for now, and maybe that was all I could ask for.

But it wasn't what I wanted.

Chapter Thirty-Six

Greg

Janet pouted all through dinner. I had to fight to keep from grinning about it. It felt like confirmation of everything I had thought earlier. She was just scared. And I felt sure that if I had made a fuss, she would have run even faster in the direction of Paris.

The woman didn't know her own mind.

She obviously wanted me to fight for her. She just didn't realize that was exactly what I was doing.

"Want to take our wine out front?" I asked after we had finished eating. "Stars are awfully pretty out here."

She nodded. "Okay."

I opened the door for her, letting myself slip a hand on the small of her back as she walked through it.

"Your turn," I told Thor, who was snoozing in the corner, having enjoyed his own portion of trout.

He got up and lumbered outside to do his business while I took my place beside Janet, sitting next to her on the tiny porch of the cabin. No chairs out here, but that suited me just fine. Gave me an excuse to sit close enough to her that our bodies made contact—and to notice she didn't pull away from it, either.

I heard her take a deep breath in and out as she gazed up at the sky.

"You're right," she said quietly. "The stars are pretty. I didn't realize how much we would be able to see them here in the woods."

"There's a big enough opening in the tree cover here to get a little window into the heavens," I said. "The stars feel even farther away here for some reason. You'd think it would be the opposite, seeing as how we're closer to them up here on the mountain. But either way, they're beautiful."

"Yeah." Her tone was uncertain, like she wasn't really paying attention to the stars. No, that mind of hers was going crazy, probably turning over everything from a million different angles.

More than anything, I wanted to reach out and slip an arm around her, pull her back over onto my lap like earlier today. I wanted to kiss that sweet mouth again. She tasted like vanilla, and I didn't think I would ever get enough of it.

But I knew better than that. I had to just keep treating her like the scared creature she was. Because deep down, she was exactly like a cat. Back her up in a corner and she'd get the claws out. Ignore her a bit, let her know you were safe, and she'd come around.

I had to hope I was right, anyway.

We sat in silence for a long time, letting the night grow darker as the stars moved above us. I didn't mind. I was comfortable with silence. It was one of the tools of my trade, using silence to get someone to open up. But it was also just plain nice to sit quietly with someone under the stars, to not have to fill the space with mindless jabber.

Janet was the kind of woman I liked sitting in the quiet with—and the kind of woman I liked sparring in the kitchen with. She was it for me. I knew that. And just like when I was dialed in on a case, I felt confident I would win in the end.

"What are you thinking about over there?" she asked, finally breaking the silence.

"You," I replied, my voice lazy. No sense in being dishonest about it.

She turned her head to look at me. "What are you thinking about me?"

I chuckled in a low tone. "I don't know that it would be gentlemanly to tell you."

"Greg." She slapped my leg softly, but I saw the little smile cross her face before she forced it away.

I also saw the way her hand lingered for just a second before lifting off my thigh.

"It's getting late," I said. "We should probably turn in."

She stilled beside me, unnerved by the comment. "Yes. Probably."

But I just smiled easily at her and jumped to my feet, offering a hand to pull her up. If I took the chance to slide that hand around her waist for a moment, well, that didn't make me any less of a gentleman.

I opened the door, letting her and Thor go in before me. Took one more opportunity to brush a hand across her back, watching the way it made her blush.

"You can have the first turn in the bathroom," I said, locking the door behind us. "I'll take a minute to set up my bed out here."

I turned, whistling, and pulled a sleeping bag from my pack. It was an ultralight bag, the kind of thing that rolled up small for long-distance backpacking. When I unrolled it on the ground, I couldn't miss the look on Janet's face as she stood in front of the bathroom door with PJs in hand, looking uncertain.

"Greg," she said timidly. "That looks terribly uncomfortable. There's no way you'll be okay sleeping on the ground like that."

I grinned up at her. "Janet, I've slept in far worse places. I'll be fine."

The struggle was obvious on her face. I ignored it and kept on making my bed. It really wouldn't bother me at all to sleep on the floor. A flat floor surface was a thousand times better than some of the rocky places I had backpacked. But her concern for me was cute, and I didn't mind it.

She disappeared into the bathroom. I took the opportunity to go ahead and change, slipping out of my jeans and into a pair of sweatpants. I had just pulled off my shirt when she came out and stopped suddenly, nearly dropping the neat pile of clothes in her hands.

"Sorry," I said, grinning easily again as I pulled a fresh t-shirt over my head. But I wasn't. How could I have been when the sight of me shirtless had sent such a look of desire flitting across her face? Nope, I couldn't be sorry about that at all.

She just kept standing there, fiddling with the clothes in her hand while I grabbed my toothbrush.

"I've been thinking," she said finally, keeping her eyes trained on her clothes. "We're both adults, and there's no reason you should have to sleep on the floor. After all, it's my fault you're out here. We both know you would have stayed at your home if you didn't feel a responsibility to protect me."

"What are you saying? Are you offering to sleep on the floor?" I chuckled. "Because that's not going to happen. There's no way I'm taking the bed and making you take the ground."

I knew that wasn't at all what she had in mind, but I was going to make her say it.

"No," she said, "of course not. No. We're both adults. We can both sleep in the bed. It's fine. You're a gentleman, and I know you'll behave as such."

I grinned again. I loved when the prim and proper Janet came out. It wasn't the real her—no, the real her was the one who had straddled me in the meadow, kissing me like I was a sailor back from sea. That was Janet when she felt free, happy, able to take what she wanted without worrying about all the what-ifs. But this version was part of her too, and I loved all of her sides.

"I'll keep my hands to myself," I said. *The question is, will you?* My eyes might have issued the challenge, but my lips stayed silent. The ball was in her court, and that was exactly as it should be.

I was hers if she wanted, but it was going to have to be her choice.

"I appreciate the offer," I said. "And I don't mind taking you up on it. I'll just go brush my teeth. Take whichever side of the bed you want. Put up a pillow barrier if you need." I couldn't help but grin again.

"That won't be necessary, I'm sure," she said, again in that exceedingly prim voice I had come to realize was Janet out of her depth, feeling nervous and unsure.

And man did I love every minute of it.

So I gave her a quick nod, brushed my teeth, and came out to find her under the covers, lying as straight as a board on the very edge of the bed. I climbed in on the other side, taking up a little more than my fair share.

"Goodnight, Janet," I said, my voice low. "Sweet dreams."

"Goodnight, Greg." Her voice was small and timid.

I closed my eyes but knew I wasn't going to get a wink of sleep with her lying beside me.

Chapter Thirty-Seven

Janet

I LAY AWAKE, STARING AT THE CEILING IN THE DARK, MY heart pounding. What had I been thinking, inviting Greg to share my bed?

He wasn't touching me, but I could feel him there just the same. Could feel his warmth, his strength.

How could one person make me feel so safe and so terrified at the same time?

I liked him. No, I loved him. That was terrifying. Love had never worked out well for me before.

A new thought hit. What if I took love out of the equation? What if I knew, going into it, how second marriages worked? Not that he had asked me to marry him. But he seemed like an old-fashioned sort of guy. I felt certain that's the outcome he expected from a serious relationship.

What if I went into a relationship with Greg with my eyes open? No expectation of being his "one true love." No childish fantasies about being his soulmate or of us being meant for each other. Just an understanding of companionship and, perhaps, a little fun.

There was something to be said for companionship, after all. Nobody wanted to get to the end of their life and find themselves alone. What if that was where I was headed? I knew myself. If I moved to Paris, I would make my job my entire world, and there wouldn't be room for anything—or anyone—else.

Was that really what I wanted?

No. I knew, in my soul, that Greg had been right. Paris *was* me running away from everything. It was an escape, a chance to start fresh where nobody knew me.

But it wasn't what I really wanted.

I wanted to be known. I wanted to be loved. I wanted to have a relationship with Daphne and be there when she had babies of her own. The thought of missing out on all that made me ache inside.

As crazy as it was, I even wanted Rosemary Mountain. I wanted to be friends with Fiona and share lemonade with her on the deck as we talked about all the truly important things in life. I wanted to embrace the town I had once written off and learn to live a slower life full of friendship, warmth, and community. I wanted Greg's valley and the peace I had found there.

And if I was being totally honest with myself, I wanted Greg. Oh, how I wanted Greg Morrison to be in my life.

As I thought it over, I realized it wasn't fair to compare him to Lonnie. They were two completely different people, and we were in a different life stage than I had been during my first marriage. Our friendship would only grow. I felt sure of that. Even if he never loved me like he did his first wife, we could have a healthy partnership.

Maybe I could stop wanting to be someone's everything and be okay with just being a life partner. Maybe that was the mature thing to do. Stop wishing for a fairy tale and settle for a good match with someone kind and interesting.

Yes, it was a good plan.

With those thoughts in mind, I slipped my hand out from under the covers and into Greg's. I didn't even think about it.

And with my hand in his, I finally slept peacefully.

•   •   •

I woke up the next morning with my head on Greg's chest. I jumped, realizing I had somehow rolled over and snuggled into him during the night.

"Morning," he said with that low, easy tone of his.

"Um. Good morning. Sorry."

"About what?"

I sat straight up. "You know. Cuddling up to you. I'm sorry. I didn't mean to."

His voice was low and gravelly. "Janet, you never have to apologize for rolling over to touch me in the middle of the night."

He looked up at me from the pillow, his eyes sparkling with flirtation as he said the words, and I blushed, unable to help myself.

"Breakfast," I said, not knowing what else to say. "We should eat. Yes. We need food."

I got out of bed, feeling unbelievably awkward, and went to the kitchen to rummage through the supplies he had brought. I stopped suddenly when I opened a tub and saw my teacup and a box of Darjeeling sitting on top.

"You brought my tea," I said, pulling the teacup out and holding it in my hands like it was the most precious thing in the world. In some ways, it was. It was one of the most precious, thoughtful gifts I had ever been given.

And it was even more precious because he was the one who had given it.

"Of course I brought your tea." He rolled out of bed and stretched lazily.

I couldn't turn my eyes away from the way his sweats hung low on his hips.

"I wouldn't survive a camping trip without my coffee. Sure don't expect you to survive without your tea." He grinned at me, catching me staring at the line of skin where his t-shirt had ridden up as he stretched.

I blushed and looked back at the teacup, cursing myself for being so obvious. "That was very thoughtful, especially considering how quickly we packed up. Thank you."

"There's a pot in that lower cabinet for heating up some water," he said, pointing. "Add enough for me to make some coffee in the French press, if you don't mind."

"Sure," I said, grateful to have something to do. I busied myself getting the water going, then jumped out of my skin when he came up behind me and planted a kiss on my cheek like it was nothing.

"Hope you don't mind granola bars for breakfast," he said.

"No, that's fine," I answered.

"There are a couple boxes in that tub. Take your pick. I'm going to let the dog outside."

"Okay." I kept myself busy, getting my tea ready to go, glad to have a minute to gather my thoughts. I wanted to talk to him today about everything I had thought about last night. I just needed to be mature, I reminded myself. The choice didn't have to be between being alone or being miserable in a marriage where I loved more than I was loved. I could be sensible. We could come to a mutually beneficial arrangement and I could simply keep my feelings out of the whole thing.

I wasn't a nineteen-year-old girl anymore, swept away by ridiculous notions of romance. This was completely reasonable. Sure, I lost my head every time I saw him. But that would fade in time, surely, and in the meantime, it would just make some of the benefits of our partnership more fun. It didn't have to be more complicated than that.

It didn't have to be love.

I felt stronger when he came back in, ready to have this discussion with him. It was like being business partners, really, and I understood business partnerships.

Frankly, had I taken this mentality while married to Lonnie, we might have had a successful marriage.

"Greg, I'd like to talk to you about something," I said, feeling quite proud of my sudden maturity.

"Oh yeah?"

"Yes. Have a seat."

He raised an eyebrow but did as I'd asked, sitting at the tiny table where we had eaten the night before. I took my teacup and sat down across from him, very aware of how our knees touched under the table. There was just nowhere to get any real space in this tiny cabin.

But that was okay. I could be mature.

"I've been thinking," I began. "I may have been too hasty yesterday about going to Paris."

"Go on," he said with an unreadable look on his face.

"Yes. Well, I did some thinking last night about my priorities."

"Your...priorities?" he asked, that single eyebrow rising again.

"Exactly." I took a sip of my tea, drawing again on my experience in negotiating contracts. Remain professional and unemotional. Make an offer, expect negotiation. Don't show how important it is to you.

"Go on," he said again.

"Well, it's important to me to follow through with what I've agreed to do. So of course, I feel obligated to go to Paris. However, in thinking about my priorities, I realize that accepting that job may have been a hasty decision. Paris is very far away..." My professional mask slipped as an unexpected wave of emotion hit me. "Well, I'm just now building a relationship with my daughter, and I don't want to give that up. I want to be here for her. I don't know anyone in Paris, and..."

"What are you trying to say, Janet?" he asked quietly, his face still unreadable.

"Well, I was just thinking. I don't want to move. Not really. And I also got to thinking about how, at our ages, we need to start thinking about companionship."

Those eyebrows shot up again. "At our ages?"

"Yes. You know, nobody wants to get to the end of their life alone. People make pacts all the time, you know. To be together if neither of them is married by a certain point..." I trailed off, feeling less sure of myself than I had a few minutes ago. Maybe this whole thing was presumptuous.

His eyes narrowed. "Marriage?"

"No. Well, yes. I don't know." I took a deep breath, feeling like this wasn't at all going the way I had planned. "Let me explain. What I mean is that, in thinking about things last night, I realized that you and I are really very good companions, and maybe that's enough. You said you wanted me to stay, and I realized that's what I want too. And I thought, perhaps, we might come to some sort of mutually beneficial arrangement. A partnership, if you will."

"Let me get this straight. You're proposing marriage for the sake of companionship in our old age?"

"Yes. I mean, no. I'm not proposing. But it makes sense, doesn't it?"

Greg just scowled. "Companionship," he repeated.

"Yes," I said, nodding, trying to shut down all other feelings, all other...imaginings. "We're both adults. I think we're both aware of what really matters. There would be benefits to both of us, having an agreement of easy companionship. There's no need to be unrealistic or put any other expectations on our arrangement. We get along, we enjoy each other's company. We're"—I swallowed hard—"attracted to each other and, of course, could enjoy the benefits of a marital relationship. But I don't expect more than that."

I looked at him, trying to read his face. He was still scowling. Before I knew what was happening, his hand reached out and snaked around my waist, pulling me onto his lap. His other hand reached up into the back of my hair, tugging it so I had to look up into his eyes—those piercing gray eyes that nearly made my heart stop.

"Maybe I haven't made myself clear," he said, his voice low and dangerous. "Companionship is a lovely thing, yes. And I'm offering that to you, too. I want to be your best friend. I want to come home to you every day and sit in those porch rockers with you. I want to talk to you about my day and hear about yours. I want to grow old together, yes. But we're not old yet, Janet. We're in our damn forties. That's barely midlife these days. Doesn't change the fact that I want to grow old with you, but I have no intention of growing 'old' anytime soon. And the way I see it, you're in the very prime of life." His eyes darkened, raking over my body, making me shiver. "I'll give you companionship. But if you think that's all I want, then you don't understand half of what I feel for you."

With that, he crushed his mouth against mine, teasing me with his tongue. My whole body came alive, feeling a rush of warmth like I was on fire from within. His hands roamed my body, taking new liberties for the first time, as he showed me exactly how much he wanted me.

And, oh, did I want him too. I wanted to devour and be devoured, to take and be taken.

I felt like a phoenix, burning, dying, and coming alive again all at the same time.

Chapter Thirty-Eight

Greg

I RAN MY HANDS UP JANET'S BODY, SLIPPING A PALM underneath that silky pajama top that had been driving me crazy since the first time I saw it. She gasped as I pushed aside the flimsy fabric, allowing my fingers to explore as they pleased.

Let her gasp.

Companionship my ass. I was in the prime of my life, not some decrepit old man with one foot in the grave, and I had every intention of proving that to Janet here and now.

But when she pulled away, crying out "I can't" in a voice that sounded so damn broken, I stopped immediately.

"Why can't you?" I asked, my voice coming out gruffer than I had intended. I shook my head, pulling it back. "Janet, if you don't want me, just say so."

"It's not that," she said, looking away. A tear dripped from her cheek, giving me instant remorse.

I picked her up and set her gently back on her chair, giving her some space. "What is it?" I asked.

She sat silent for so long I was starting to think she wasn't going to answer. Finally, she spoke, saying words that shocked me. "Jackson told me you were married before."

I was confused. "Well, yes, I was. But so were you. I don't understand what the problem is."

"It's not that I don't want you, Greg. I do. I wish I didn't, but I do. But I can't do this with you. I can't love you."

"Because I was married before?" I was flabbergasted. "Janet, I don't understand."

"Not just married," she said, shaking her head. "You're a *widow*. Your wife died."

"Yes." I still didn't see.

She looked me straight in the eye. "Just like Lonnie."

I took a deep breath, realizing what she was getting at. "I see."

"Greg, I just... I feel things for you. But I've already been a second-choice wife. I've already been someone's plan B. It was awful. Living in Eileen's shadow meant Lonnie compared me to her every day. I could never live up to it. How could I? When someone dies, all the bad memories fade away. That person becomes perfect somehow, canonized in memory. I couldn't live up to a saint then, and I can't now." She shook her head, sadness written all over her face.

Oh how wrong she was.

I reached for her hand, unable to help myself. "But you already knew that when you practically proposed marriage to me. I don't get it."

She shook her head. "A business arrangement. Companionship. I thought if I kept my emotions out of it, kept my head on straight, maybe we could make things work. That if I went into it with my eyes open, not expecting anything more, then maybe I could be okay. But when you kiss me... Greg, I don't know how to keep my emotions out of it when it comes to you." She looked at me with pleading in her eyes. "You make me feel things I've never felt. And I just realized I can't. I can't be your consolation prize. As much as that hurt me before, I think it might kill me with you. I don't want to go to Paris. But I can't stay here with you."

"I see," I said, finally understanding. Pain of my own rose up, things

I hadn't put into words for years. I knew I had a choice. I could keep burying those things, keep it all bottled up nice and safe where no one had to know of my failures. But if I did, I'd likely lose this woman I loved.

Or I could tell her what I had never told a soul and maybe get to keep her.

I pushed away from my chair. "I need a minute," I said, my voice still more harsh than I wanted.

Janet was fragile. But right now, I felt damn fragile too. I needed some fresh air, some space, a minute to prepare myself to say aloud the things I'd never wanted anyone to know.

So I did the only thing I could in that moment and walked away, heading outside where the breeze and sunshine could clear away the cobwebs in my soul.

WHEN I RETURNED, JANET HAD CHANGED INTO FRESH clothes and was packing her things away in her bag.

"I need to go," she said quietly, her eyes focused on the zipper of her bag like it was the most fascinating thing in the world. "Can you take me back? I'll head to the airport today. Tell Daphne and Emerson that I'm sorry I didn't wait for them. I just can't."

"Janet."

"Yes?" she answered, but didn't look up.

"Janet. Look at me."

She looked up and I saw the pain on her face, pain I wanted to wash away. Even if it meant walking through pain of my own.

"I want to tell you about my marriage," I said, forcing the words past the rock in my throat.

"I don't think—" she began, but I cut her off.

"Please. This isn't easy for me. I don't talk about it with anyone. But I want to tell you. When I'm finished, if you still want to go, I'll take you wherever you want to be. Okay?"

She nodded once, then dropped her bag and walked to the table.

"Let's go outside," I suggested. I needed the companionship of the outdoors to give me strength.

She nodded again, still quiet. Still broken.

Well, I was broken too, and it was time to share that with someone.

We walked outside and sat on the porch, just like we had the night before. I felt her small body beside mine and found that it gave me even more strength than the trees and sunshine did. That was one reason I didn't want to lose her. She didn't understand what her quiet strength meant to me, what her faith in me meant.

What her desire meant.

"I got married young," I said before clearing my throat. "I was young and stupid too, believe it or not. Fell in love, at least I thought. I was wrong."

She startled, obviously surprised by the confession, but she said nothing.

"Vanessa was a couple of years older than me. I was in the military at the time. I fell hard and fast. She convinced me we should get married quickly. Everyone told me it was a terrible idea. They could see what I was blind to: that we were too young, that she was in it for the wrong reasons, and that I was thinking with the wrong part of my body. But like I said, I thought I was in love. Plus, getting married meant an increase in pay and private living quarters instead of being in the barracks."

Janet gave a small laugh. "I didn't realize the military was so invested in getting their youth married off."

"Right? Anyway, we ran off and got married and I thought I was the happiest man on earth. I was crazy about her. Tried to be a good husband. I was so proud to have such a beautiful woman on my arm, a woman who adored me and wanted to wait for me when I was off serving my country. Or so I thought. Things went sour pretty quickly. My parents had offered us some money to get started, but I refused it. Probably stupid, but I wanted to make my own way in the world."

Janet patted my arm. "I understand that. You wanted to earn what you have."

I nodded. "Yeah. But Vanessa was furious, and it was just the start of it. Pretty soon, we were fighting about everything. I kept trying to connect with her, even asked her to go to marriage counseling, but she didn't want to."

"I'm sorry," Janet said with sincere empathy in her voice. I knew she could understand better than most what it was like to be the only one fighting for a marriage.

I squeezed her hand, gathering that strength again before continuing the story. "Things got worse the first time I deployed. When I came back, she almost seemed like a stranger. At first, I thought it was just the time apart. You're told there will be a transition period—you know, a readjustment as you get used to living together again. Reintegration they call it. We'd get through it, I thought. But we didn't. It felt like we were living separate lives. She was always running around with 'the girls,' or so she said."

"Was she cheating on you?" Janet whispered like she was half afraid to ask.

"I suspect so, yeah. Once again, I asked her to go to counseling. Once again, she said no. I should have seen the writing on the wall then, and maybe if I'd had enough time at home, I would have. But I deployed again, too quickly. This time was different right from the start. First time I deployed, she sent letters, care packages. You know. The whole 'supportive military wife' thing. They slowed down as time went on, but still. This time, nothing. I would write to her, call her, email her. She was always busy. I barely heard from her the whole time I was away, despite my reaching out every chance I could. You need someone while you're over there, you know? You need that lifeline, that connection to home. Plus, I was worried about her. Worried it was too hard on her, worried she was having to carry too much with me gone."

"That's horrible," Janet said, rubbing my arm. "I'm so sorry."

"Yep." I drew in a deep breath, preparing to admit the secret I had carried all these years. "She finally called me a few weeks before I was supposed to return. Told me she was leaving me. Had met someone else, a 'real man' according to her. Someone who could provide for her better than I could. She was angry about living solely on an enlisted salary, thought my need to prove I could make it on my own was stupid and selfish. Said she was done with that life and was moving up to better, along with a lot of other hateful things. Tried to make me feel small, and, boy, she succeeded."

Janet just sighed and laid her head on my shoulder, rubbing my arm.

Her empathy soothed me somehow, made it feel good to finally get all this out.

"Next day," I continued, "my commander comes in and tells me he has bad news. She had been killed in a car accident. Was out late at night, partying at some club. Got hit by a drunk driver on her way home. Killed instantly."

"Oh my goodness. That's...a lot. All at once."

"Oh, it gets worse," I said, shaking my head.

"Worse?"

"Oh yeah. What my commander told me was there was an officer in the car, a young captain. She had apparently found herself a new boyfriend with a much higher rank than me—better rank, better salary, and a better house."

"Ouch."

"Ouch is right. She was what we all called a 'tag chaser.' Wanted to marry someone in the military for the benefits. At my low rank, she probably wouldn't have given me a second look except that the friend who introduced us had told her about my parents' money. I guess she thought she had what she wanted either way—either she'd get their money or she could use me as a stepping stone to meet someone better. I felt like the biggest idiot in the world for not listening to everyone who tried to warn me."

"I can relate," she said softly.

"Yeah." I got quiet for a minute, then admitted the rest to her. "I didn't tell anyone."

"What do you mean?"

"Her family and friends. I never told them what she did. Never told them she was leaving me or that she was having an affair. Vanessa's parents had just lost their daughter. It seemed better to just let the truth die with her."

She stared at me, her eyes unreadable. "So you just, what, had to play the part of a grieving widow?"

"I *was* grieving," I said, nodding. "I was devastated. Just for more complicated reasons than anyone realized. But yeah, I went home and comforted her family and dealt with things on my own."

"That had to have been horrible," she said, shaking her head. "I went to Lonnie's funeral with Daphne. That was hard, but at least I was there as an ex. Nobody expected me to grieve his death. But you. To be going through so much and not say a word to anyone." She just shook her head. "I'm really sorry she put you through all of that. It was selfless of you to protect her reputation."

"It wasn't all selfless." The truth was bitter and made me feel small. But I wanted to tell Janet everything. "Truth is, I was humiliated. I didn't just keep the secret for her sake. I didn't want to admit I had been wrong about her, and I sure didn't want anyone to know I hadn't been man enough to keep her happy. Maybe she was right. Maybe it *was* selfish to not take the money and give her a better life from the start. Right or wrong, I was a failure as a husband, and I didn't want anyone to know."

"Oh, Greg," she said, turning my face to look at her.

I didn't want to. I felt naked, exposed, and like she might finally realize I wasn't the man she thought I was. I was afraid if I looked at her, I would just see pity.

But when she forced me to meet her eyes, they weren't full of pity at all. They were full of understanding.

"Greg, you weren't the problem. I didn't know you then, but it doesn't matter. I know the man you are now. It's not that you weren't good enough for her or man enough to keep her happy. She just couldn't see your worth."

I stared back at her, seeing myself in new eyes—hers. "Just like Lonnie couldn't see yours," I said.

She stared back at me as the realization dawned on her.

I kissed the top of her head, then wrapped an arm around her. "Well, aren't we a pair?" I asked.

She laughed softly. "I suppose we are."

I swallowed hard. Despite seeing the acceptance in her eyes, I still felt afraid somehow. Afraid that, now she knew what a failure I had been at marriage, she might have second thoughts.

"Now that I've told you my past, do you still want to leave? Is there any part of you that would ever worry again about being a consolation prize? Because, Janet, you're not a consolation at all. You're everything."

She kissed me in answer, soft and slow. It told me everything I needed to know.

Then she stood up, took my hand, and led me back into the cabin to tell me again.

Chapter Thirty-Nine

Janet

My heart was racing. I wasn't sure what I was doing, but all I knew was that I didn't want to hold anything back from Greg. Not anymore. All my fears seemed senseless now that I knew the truth.

How that woman had never seen his worth was beyond me, but hearing his story had done more than reassure me of the way he felt about me. It had healed me somehow from the belief I had never fully let go—the thought that Lonnie would have eventually loved me had I just been better somehow. That the reason he didn't see my worth was because I didn't really have much.

That belief had taken root in my soul and had never really gone away, no matter how much work I did to try to disprove it. No matter how good I was at my job, how much money I earned, or how high my social standing grew. None of that had changed the core fear that I simply wasn't enough.

But knowing Greg had been with someone who hadn't seen his worth either changed everything. Because his worth was as clear as day no matter what that woman had been unable to see. And he seemed to think the same thing about me.

We had both been wounded by our marriages. The difference was that Greg was brave enough to want to try again anyway.

And now I wanted to be brave too.

I led him into the cabin, toward the bed we had shared the night before, and turned to him. It was different now—not the breathless craze from earlier, when he had been angry and had something to prove. No, the man standing before me now looked uncertain, maybe for the first time.

So I kissed him softly, then slipped my fingers underneath his t-shirt, allowing myself to run my hands over his body. I still felt surprised at how firm his chest was, how tight his muscles were. He had mastered such an approachable, good-guy kind of vibe, but his body felt like a warrior's.

My warrior.

I pulled his t-shirt over his head and traced kisses down his neck.

"Janet," he growled as his own hands began to explore. "Are you sure this is what you want?"

"Yes," I whispered, breathless again. "I've never been more sure."

Everything was clear now.

We belonged together. I had been fooling myself, even thinking I could walk away from him—or, worse, having anything less than this, less than what we felt for each other.

He lowered me to the bed, gentle and slow.

"You're so beautiful," he said. "So perfect." He ran a hand down my thigh as the other one cradled the back of my head.

I felt myself flush pink at his adoration. It all felt so wild. Being here, in this cabin, in the woods... It was so unlike me, yet it felt so very right. And I never wanted to forget the look of pure pleasure on his face as his eyes raked over me, taking in everything.

I felt beautiful, wanted, and loved.

"You're not so bad yourself," I whispered, teasing him.

His eyes sparkled as he turned them back toward mine. "Glad to hear it."

Then his mouth was on mine as his hands explored the same path his eyes had just taken. Everything went hazy as I was lost to it, lost to him.

And when we finally came together, I knew I would never be the same.

I RAN MY HAND THROUGH GREG'S HAIR, SAVORING THIS TIME together. Everything felt different now. My heart felt at peace, as I knew exactly where I belonged. Right here, with him.

He put his forehead to mine. "I love you," he said.

My heart nearly burst. "I love you too."

"Hey, Janet?"

"Yeah?"

"I've decided to accept your offer of marriage. I think we'll make excellent—what was that word you used? Oh yeah. Companions."

I dissolved into giggles. "Sorry, I've changed my mind."

"Oh yeah?" His face turned serious.

"I take back my offer. I've decided I want more than just a companion. If you want to marry me, you'll have to do the old-fashioned thing and ask me yourself." I was teasing, but he wasn't laughing.

"Okay," he said, nodding, his eyebrows furrowed deep in thought. "That's fair."

I stilled. "I'm just playing with you," I said. "There's no pressure here."

He grinned suddenly. "I don't feel you playing with me at all, but if you're offering..." His hand slipped off of my hip and grabbed mine, pulling it where he wanted it.

"Oh," I said, my eyes widening. "So soon, Sheriff Morrison?"

He nipped my neck lightly with his teeth. "Yes, future Mrs. Morrison. Only this time, I want to take things slow. Savor every last moment. Kiss every square inch of your beautiful body. Watch you blush and squirm and go wild again."

"Oh?" I asked, already breathless again, as his hands—and lips— began doing just exactly that.

WHEN LUNCHTIME ROLLED AROUND AND WE FINALLY LEFT the bed and moved back to the table, it was hard to believe how different things felt from just that morning. I blushed, just thinking about how a few hours before I had thought myself so mature, so stable, for offering Greg elderly companionship.

Now, I knew that neither of us would be satisfied with anything less than a real marriage. And already, my thoughts on what a real marriage was had completely turned around.

Marriage to Greg Morrison would be a completely different story than being married to Lonnie Sullivan, even if I was a second wife to both of them. I knew that now. Greg was a completely different man, with a completely different past.

But more than that, I could see that he loved me with a completely different love.

The kind of love I had always wanted.

WE HAD LEFTOVER TROUT FOR LUNCH, HEATED OVER THE grill so it tasted nearly as good as the night before. We were both ravenous and polished off every last bit of it.

"Unless you want trout again for supper, I'll need to go get supplies," Greg said. "I'm afraid I didn't pack up much before we left."

"What do you usually eat when you come out here?" I asked, curious.

"Trout." Greg grinned. "And I've got some canned soups and dehydrated goods in the pantry, just in case I don't catch anything."

"Canned soup is fine with me," I said, smiling. "Stay here."

I didn't mind canned soup and fish at all if it meant we got to spend another day out here completely undisturbed.

I was exactly where I wanted to be.

Chapter Forty

Greg

I STARED AT THE WOMAN ACROSS THE TABLE FROM ME IN wonder. Damn was she beautiful. It didn't matter if she was decked out in silk, jewels, and those ridiculous high heels that most women would never be able to walk in; or if, like now, she was bare faced, with her hair a mess, wearing nothing but one of my old flannel shirts.

In fact, I liked her even better this way.

She glowed with a kind of beauty that was way out of my league, and I knew it. But she was here, and for some reason I still didn't understand, she was mine.

When I caught the man that had started all of this, I wasn't sure whether to punch him or thank him.

We'd been holed up at the cabin for three days—the best three days of my life. Being here with Janet was heaven. Didn't even matter that we were living on granola bars, canned soup, and trout. It was still more fun than the best vacation I had ever been on.

But we couldn't hide out here forever. Truth was, it had been an impulse to bring her here—one that had paid off in spades. Despite being officially off this particular case, I had a duty to the people of

Rosemary Mountain. I had a job to do, and I couldn't do it here. I just couldn't stand the thought of Janet being alone at the house when this man knew where she was and what she meant to me. If he wanted to hurt me, he had a clear target.

Hurting her would devastate me like nothing else could.

"What are you thinking about?" she asked me, looking at me with those big brown eyes.

I drummed my fingers on the table. No reason not to be completely honest with her. "About how I need to check in. See if they found the guy yet. And how, either way, I'm going to have to go back into town today, much as I hate to. Also, how leaving you is going to be the hardest thing I've ever done."

"Well, I can make that easy for you, because there is no way you are leaving me here," she said flatly.

"And why not?"

"First," she said, holding up a finger, "if something happened to me out here in the middle of nowhere, what would I do? Second, if something happens to you, nobody will know where to find me. I'll just starve out here, lost in the woods. I don't have your fishing skills, Greg, and we're almost out of soup. Besides, haven't you ever watched a horror movie? If you leave me alone out here, I'll be killed for sure."

I grinned at her. "You have a point there. But I don't feel safe leaving you at the house if this guy is still on the loose. Not when he knows you're there."

"So stash me at Fiona's. Or even at Daphne's. He won't expect me to be there anymore, right? Or take me to work with you, where you can keep an eye on me."

"If I took you to work with me, I wouldn't get any work done," I said, giving her a wink. "Seeing you sitting in my office might give me all sorts of interesting ideas."

She gave me a devilish smile. "I really think I would be safest if I come with you to your office, Greg."

"Uh huh." I picked her up and pulled her back into my lap, just like before. Only this time, she was mine and I was hers.

And I intended on keeping it that way forever.

"I don't know yet what the best plan will be for going back," I said, switching my tone to a serious one as I stroked her hair away from her face. "Let me think about that for a while. I'll call Jackson and check in, and we can go from there. But you're right. Too many things could go wrong leaving you out here alone. We'll go back together in a few hours. Figure out a plan from there."

"Good." She lowered her mouth to mine, kissing me softly. "I know you'll take care of everything. You make me feel safe."

"You are safe. I'll do whatever it takes to keep you that way. Can't have my future wife in danger, now can I?"

She laughed. It reminded me of a bubbling brook in the sunshine. "You haven't asked me to marry you yet."

"Haven't I?" I nuzzled her neck, playing dumb. "Well, don't worry. It's coming."

Chapter Forty-One

Janet

Greg stepped outside to call Jackson after lunch while I put on some real clothes. I wasn't ready to leave our little cabin, but I knew Greg was right. We couldn't hide out here forever. He was the sheriff. He had a job to do, and he couldn't very well do it from here.

But, oh, the things he could do here.

I had never felt so happy, so sexy, so content and needy all at the same time. It felt the way I had always imagined a honeymoon should. All golden, soft, and fun.

And we were just getting started.

He teased me about asking me to marry him. But I knew, as soon as the time was right, he really would.

There was no longer any doubt in my mind what my answer would be. In fact, as soon as we got back to town, I planned on canceling my flight and emailing Philip to tell him the bad news.

My future was right here in Rosemary Mountain.

. . .

GREG CAME BACK IN, A DARK LOOK ON HIS FACE. I KNEW immediately that Jackson hadn't caught the guy.

"Bad news?" I asked.

"A little bit of good news, and a whole lot of bad. In good news, Jackson got the repairs made to the window. At least that's taken care of. But no, they haven't caught the guy, and there have been new threats every day. More local businesses are getting messages about paying for protection. Nobody has paid up yet. Apparently the local business association had a meeting and decided to stand firm against it. No one pays. But he's escalating things, trying to force it. More broken windows. A break-in where a bunch of merchandise was destroyed. A fire—put out, thankfully, before the whole business burned."

He shook his head, and I realized there was more. "Thomas, the guy who owns the little art gallery on the square, caught him leaving a threat. Apparently confronted him. It turned ugly. The guy pulled a knife and stabbed Thomas multiple times. He's in the hospital right now and might not make it."

"Oh my goodness," I said. It sent chills down my spine, knowing that this guy was so reckless and aggressive and he wasn't letting up.

"He's terrorizing the town, Janet, and now there are whispers about some businesses caving and paying up."

I just shook my head. "I don't like the sound of that."

"I don't, either." He sank down on the bed and let out a sigh. "I hate this, Janet. And I hate that I've been hiding out here, away from it all, while someone causes fear and chaos in my town."

I climbed onto the bed behind him and rubbed his shoulders. "You haven't been hiding," I soothed. "You've been protecting me. And you're not supposed to be working this case anyway, not when you're a target. You're doing exactly what you're supposed to be doing. And you know that. But I know that doesn't make it any easier."

"You understand." He looked at me with gratitude on his face.

I just kissed him in reply.

WE PACKED UP THE LITTLE CART BEHIND GREG'S ATV. THE process seemed to take a lot more time than when we had packed up to come here. It felt like neither of us really wanted to leave. As the sun started sinking, lighting up the mountain in that golden glow, my heart ached. Who would have thought? This tiny, rustic cabin in the woods had become my favorite place on earth.

I stood looking at it as Greg put Thor in his crate. When he was finished, he came over and put his arms around me, pulling me into his chest. Leaning against him felt like finding an anchor in the middle of a raging sea.

"What's wrong?" he asked, kissing my hair.

"I don't know." I sighed. "I just worry that, when we go back to the real world, it might not be the same. *We* might not be the same. Everything feels so simple out here."

He tipped my chin up and kissed my lips this time. "Everything *is* simple out here. That's why I love it. And we'll come back, honey. We can come back a hundred times if you want. It's ours."

Ours.

"I'd like to come back soon," I said.

"We will. You're right. Things are more complicated back home. Jobs, responsibilities—"

"Bad guys," I said, interrupting him.

He chuckled. "Yeah, bad guys every now and then. But you know what's not complicated? You know what won't change?"

"What?"

He made sure I was looking at him before he answered. "The fact that I love you. That I think you're the most beautiful, incredible, sophisticated, elegant woman I've ever met. That I can't keep my eyes off you. Can't keep my hands off you. That I want to spend every day of my life with you. Those things? Those won't change."

"You promise?"

"I promise."

THE RIDE BACK WENT WAY TOO QUICKLY. WHEN WE reached Greg's ranch, he told me he had been thinking and felt the best thing would be to take me to Fiona's. No one would expect me to be there, and she had proven she knew how to take care of herself. It wasn't ideal, but it was the best he could come up with under the circumstances.

I reassured him it was a good plan. I could see the worry on his face and knew he hated leaving me at all. But he had a job to do, and we couldn't move forward with our lives until he had done it. So we dropped off our bags, got Thor settled, then loaded up Greg's truck—also repaired, thanks to Jackson—and headed up the mountain toward Fiona's cottage.

Greg reached across the console for my hand as we drove, making me smile. It was such a small thing, but it meant the world. I wasn't sure I would ever get used to how wonderful it felt to simply be loved.

Fiona's antique truck wasn't in her driveway when we pulled in, but Greg got out and knocked anyway. He was frowning when he came back to the truck. "No answer," he said. "Wonder where she could be."

"I can call her cell phone if you want," I offered.

He gave me a strange look. "Fiona Flanagan has a cell phone?"

"Of course." I was puzzled by his expression. "Why wouldn't she?"

He just chuckled and shook his head. "You're right. She's just so old and, um, eccentric. I guess I think of her as living in a different world entirely."

"She does," I said, laughing. "But she keeps a foot in this one, too." I was already pulling her number up on my phone.

She answered on the third ring. "Janet! Is everything okay?" She sounded out of breath, which was a first for her.

"Everything's fine. Greg and I are at your house right now. I was hoping to hang out with you for a few hours. Greg needs to go into the office and doesn't feel comfortable leaving me at his house alone. The threats have escalated."

"So I've heard," she breathed out. "Town's going crazy. I'm awfully sorry, Janet. Remember how I told you Laura Kistler was about to pop? Well, she's popping. I'm here with her now. Full labor. But she's going awfully slow for baby number three. I expect to be tied up here for a few hours at least. Want me to text you the address? Sheriff can bring you here."

"Oh, no," I said, immediately protesting. I couldn't imagine invading a stranger's home while she was delivering a baby. "We'll figure something else out. It's fine."

"If you're sure. Keep me posted, you hear?"

"I will."

I hung up and explained the situation to Greg. "Laura Kistler is having her baby right now. Fiona's the midwife, of course. She'll be tied up for hours. We'll have to think of something else."

A look of shock passed across Greg's face. "Laura Kistler? Matthew's wife?"

"Yes. Why?"

He closed his eyes and breathed out, shaking his head. "The man I've been seeing. I told you he reminded me of someone. I don't know why I didn't put it together before. He looks like Matthew Kistler. They have the same dark hair and face shape. And that skulking walk of his? It reminds me of Luke. It's so obvious."

It was my turn to frown. "Luke Kistler, as in the Luke who tried to kill my daughter?"

"One and the same." His face was grim as he put the car in reverse and backed out the driveway.

"But Luke's in jail, right?"

"He is. Besides that, the guy walks like Luke, but he looks like Matthew. I'd recognize Luke anywhere. It's not him, but..." Greg shook his head again.

I bit my lip, fearing now for Fiona. "Are you saying you think Matthew is behind all this?"

He shook his head firmly. "Not a chance. Matthew Kistler was cut from a different cloth entirely. He's a good man, solid as a rock. I trust him as much as I trust anyone in this town. Besides that, he's too short and stocky to be the guy I saw. Walks different too. He holds his head up high, because unlike Luke, he doesn't have anything to hide. But who knows? Maybe they have a cousin or something."

"Or a brother," I mused.

He gave me an odd look. "There's just the two of them. Matthew and Luke."

"That's odd though, isn't it? You'd think, if they were naming their boys after the gospels, they would have gone in order. Matthew, Mark, Luke..."

Greg was staring at me now. "Dammit." He scrubbed a hand over his face, then pulled a U-turn.

"Where are we going?"

"To see Patricia Kistler and find out if she has another son no one thought to tell me about."

CHAPTER FORTY-TWO

Greg

I LEFT JANET IN THE CAR WHILE I POUNDED ON PATRICIA Kistler's door. I had no idea if this hypothetical Mark existed, but I needed to find out.

A sour-looking Patricia answered the door.

"What are you doing here?" she asked, practically spitting at me.

"I need to ask you some questions," I said, keeping my voice kind. Truth was, I felt sorry for the lady. She had married a man who cheated on her, humiliated her, and put her in danger she still didn't fully understand. With his crimes and connections, the only reason she wasn't in jail herself was because we hadn't found a bit of proof she had known a thing about it. Personally, I thought she had kept herself deliberately blind, and I couldn't fully blame her for that.

"Am I under arrest?"

"No, ma'am."

"Then I don't have to answer your questions, now do I?" She started to close the door in my face.

"Please," I said, putting my hand up to stop the door. "You're not in any trouble, and I'm not here in any kind of official capacity. I was just wondering. Are Matthew and Luke your only children, or do you have another son?"

All the color drained from her face instantly. "Go away," she said before slamming the door in my face.

I climbed back into my truck, debating how to handle it. Her face had given me all the confirmation I was looking for. Now I needed information.

"You think Fiona would know about this Mark?" I asked Janet.

She grinned. "I think Fiona knows everything."

"Call her again. See if she can step outside, away from Matthew and Laura, to answer some questions real quick."

Janet spoke to Fiona briefly, then hung up. "She said give her five minutes. Then she'll call you back."

"Okay."

I decided to use that five minutes to call Jackson and give him the rundown of our theory.

"Give me a minute to look some things up," he said, keyboard clattering in the background. He was silent for a moment, then spoke up, excitement in his voice. "Looks like Janet was right. Birth records show that Patricia gave birth to a Mark Kistler about a year after Matthew was born."

"So what happened to him?" I barked out, putting the truck in reverse and heading back down the mountain.

"Hmm..." Jackson went quiet.

"What is it?"

"All the official records are clean. But I don't know if that means anything."

"Me either," I agreed. Mark's father, Don Kistler, had been blackmailing the former sheriff. "Remember all those paper files we pulled from Joe's house?"

"Yeah."

"Check those," I said. "If Mark did get into trouble, Joe would have kept something in those files to use as leverage against Don."

"I will."

"Call me back if you find something." I hung up the phone, feeling in my gut he would.

It didn't take long for Jackson to get back with me.

"Found him. There was a photo. He was a teenager when it was taken, but I'd bet money it's the same guy. Looks like he did get into some trouble—frequent trouble, in fact—and Joe kept it out of the official records. No surprise there. The kid's got one angry face," Jackson said, whistling.

"Any information on where he is now?"

"Nope. No mention of him after the early two thousands. It's like he just disappeared. But I'll do some more digging."

"Thanks."

I hung up the phone just in time to take Fiona's call, reaching across the console to squeeze Janet's hand before I did. She was incredibly patient, just sitting quietly as I dealt with all this, showing that strength and grace I had loved from day one. Having her by my side felt like the best gift in the world.

"How can I help you, Sheriff?" Fiona asked when I answered her call.

"Tell me everything you know about Mark Kistler," I said.

"Oh, my, my." She clucked her tongue. "So that ghost has come back from the dead, has he?"

According to Fiona, Mark had been a problem child from the beginning. Angry. Mean. Always getting into trouble in school, starting fights, and harassing young women. He had been a real embarrassment to Don and Patricia. Don had kept his own sins well hidden from the church he pastored.

Hard to hide a kid who kept getting into trouble.

Fiona said they sent him away a few times to "camps." Called them mission trips, said he was helping people. She always suspected they were some sort of reformation program, an attempt to rehabilitate him and put him in line.

He came back angrier every time.

Things had escalated after his last return. He apparently found a girlfriend, and that gave him the confidence to get bold—too much testosterone, Fiona said, like that explained everything. He was determined to be the biggest bully in school. After a few kids had been beaten to a pulp, people at the church threatened to leave and take their tithe money elsewhere, saying Don wasn't even able to control his own children. And all of a sudden, Mark was gone.

"The official story," Fiona said with an edge of disgust in her voice, "was that he had been called to the ministry. Supposedly went overseas to serve in missions. There was a letter that Don read to the church, supposedly from Mark, apologizing for all his wrong-doing. I never believed he wrote it, and more than one or two church members didn't believe it, either. We figured Mark got tired of it all and ran away somewhere he could live life on his own terms. Thought it might be all the better for him, honestly. I always felt his biggest problem was his parents."

"So no one ever heard from him again?" I asked, surprised. "How long ago was that?"

"Oh, goodness. Early two thousands, I'd say, but don't quote me on that. He was a teenager. And no, nobody ever heard from him again, not really. I think once or twice Don read aloud a letter in church, supposedly a ministry update. Took up a collection plate for him." Fiona snorted at that. "But he never showed his face in Rosemary Mountain again, that's for sure. No coming home for the holidays or anything like that. After a year or two, they just stopped mentioning him altogether. It was like he had never existed."

"And nobody ever questioned it?" I was flabbergasted. A child had gone missing and nobody had ever thought to look into it? It was practically criminal.

"There were rumors," Fiona said. "Conversations around dinner tables, I'm sure. But no, nobody ever did anything about it. Frankly, I think half the town was relieved. His school teachers were, that's for sure. Everything went a lot more smoothly without him stirring up trouble."

"What about the girlfriend? Do you know who she was or what happened to her?"

"I'm sorry, I don't," Fiona said. I could hear the regret in her voice. "They kept their relationship hidden in public, meaning it was someone his parents wouldn't approve of. You might have better luck talking to someone who was in school with that group."

"Thanks. Look, I know this is terrible timing, but do you think Matthew's in a place where he talk to me?"

Fiona's voice became firm. "It's not about Matthew. It's about Laura. And the last thing a woman in labor needs is a mess like this being brought up. It's not the time, Sheriff. I know you've got an investigation to handle, but there's no sense in bringing all this up now when it could endanger her life."

I grimaced, knowing she was right, no matter how annoying it was. Not to mention the fact that, technically speaking, this *wasn't* my investigation. "Keep me updated. I want to know as soon as you think it's safe for me to talk to Matthew."

"Will do." Fiona clicked off, signaling the end to the conversation.

I pulled my truck over in a parking lot, needing a minute to figure out my next move.

How could I track down a ghost?

I needed to work. Needed my desk and computer, needed Jackson to bounce ideas off of—needed the ritual of how I worked cases, more than anything. But I wasn't about to take Janet to the office—nor would I risk leaving her home alone without knowing where Mark Kistler was.

With a sigh, I turned the truck toward home and called Jackson, telling him to meet me there, along with whoever the TBI had sent. It wouldn't be the first time we had worked a case together from my kitchen table. Probably wouldn't be the last.

If I could convince them to let me quietly help at all.

Jackson had never been a stickler to the rules, but this was different and we both knew it. I was too close to the situation to be involved.

But there was no way I could stay away.

. . .

"We're going back to your place?" Janet murmured from her seat.

"Yeah. I need to think this through, do a little digging. Come up with a plan. Fiona doesn't want me talking to Matthew until after Laura delivers. I don't like it, but she's right."

"Why aren't you pressing the point with Patricia?" she asked. Her voice sounded curious but not judgmental. I knew she wasn't questioning my judgment. She just wanted to understand it.

I tightened my lips, frustrated by the whole thing. "I'm not officially on this case, remember? So I can't make her talk to me, not about this. I got the confirmation I needed anyway. We know he exists now." I fell silent, remembering the conversation with her. "Janet, that woman looked deathly afraid when I asked her if she had any more kids."

"Afraid of him, you think?"

"That, or of someone finding out what they did to him. If we're wrong and this isn't Mark at all? This might be a whole separate investigation, and she might be afraid of getting in trouble for the truth. I believe Mark's the one we're chasing. But if I'm wrong? That kid might not even be alive."

Janet shuddered visibly. "I hate even thinking about that."

"Me too. But I think he's alive, and I think that's why she's scared. And that makes me wonder if I underestimated him when I called him a coward."

CHAPTER FORTY-THREE

Janet

WE RACED BACK TOWARD GREG'S HOUSE. I COULD practically feel the energy radiating from his body. He was on the hunt, focused like a laser. I had no doubt he would find Mark.

It was exciting, seeing him like this. A thrill of anticipation rose in me as I thought of being with him again, wondering if I could help him find release for all this energy.

An awfully bold thought, but I liked it.

That would have to wait though. Greg was all business when we got back to his house, pulling out his laptop and setting up a workstation in the dining room. I put on a pot of tea, and on impulse, I started coffee as well. It felt surreal, like I was reclaiming that part of me in an even bigger way. It had been a statement to stop making coffee after the divorce. It felt like an even bigger one to make it again, a statement that the past no longer had a hold on me.

Greg was so wrapped up in whatever he was doing that he didn't seem to notice my movements until I put the cup of hot coffee in front of him. He stared at it a moment, then looked up at me, emotion all over his face. He clearly understood what a big deal it was to me.

"Oh, Janet," he said, reaching for my hand. "You don't ever have to make me coffee, baby."

"I know," I said, kissing him on his forehead. "That's exactly why I didn't mind doing it."

He pulled me to him, burying his head on my chest, and sighed. "I'm sorry I'm not going to be good company for a while."

"Don't worry about it. Do what you need to do." I kissed him again, then pulled away, leaving him to do his work. In the meantime, I quietly went to my laptop and sent an email to Philip, resigning from the position I hadn't even started.

I would tell Greg the good news after this mess was over.

Jackson arrived shortly, along with the TBI agent I had never met. Some of Greg's tension eased the minute he saw the man. They greeted each other like old friends.

"Agent Dawson," Greg said, clasping the man's hand in a firm handshake. "It's good to see you, man. I didn't know you were the one who got this gig."

"Good to see you too, Sheriff," Agent Dawson said, a grin lighting up his face. "I was sorry to hear about the troubles you guys were having here, but I admit I was happy for an excuse to come back to Rosemary Mountain. I'm sorry we haven't gotten him yet. The guy isn't smooth at all, yet he somehow keeps slipping through our fingers. He's always a step ahead, though for the life of me, I can't figure out how."

"I'm sure you're doing a fine job. Glad to have you here," Greg said, and I could tell he meant it.

I hadn't been sure what to expect, wondering if there might be some kind of turf war between the two of them. I knew that Greg liked to handle things himself. But it was obvious the two of them had worked together before and had equal respect for each other, and it didn't seem like Agent Dawson had any intention of cutting Greg out completely.

In fact, I got the distinct impression Agent Dawson was eager to get Greg's feedback on the investigation thus far.

The three men headed into Greg's dining room and immediately went to work, catching each other up on everything from the last few days. From my perspective, they seemed to work very well together, bouncing theories off each other, searching databases, and occasionally making phone calls. I kept my distance, not wanting to interfere, despite finding the process fascinating. I could feel their energy ramp up every time they found a possibility, until finally, Greg slammed down his phone and announced, "Got him!"

Jackson was immediately on his feet. "Where is he?"

"Holed up in a cabin on the east side. Owner listed it as a vacation rental. Mark didn't even bother using a false name. Mark Kistler checked in two weeks ago for an indefinite stay. Owner has one of those video doorbells. Checked. The car I saw leaving the neighborhood is there. Pulled up about an hour ago. Hasn't left since."

Agent Dawson grinned. "Fantastic. We'll head there now to bring him in. Want to go with?"

"Hell yeah I do," Greg said. He came over and planted a firm kiss on my lips, right in front of the other men. "We know where he is, so you should be safe. But don't take any chances. We still think he might have a female partner, and we don't know if she's with him or not or what she might be capable of. Lock up behind me. Turn on the security system as soon as we leave. Stay away from windows. Don't even let Thor out while I'm gone. Call me if anything—and I mean anything—feels weird. Okay?"

"I'm not the one about to arrest a guy," I said, smirking. "I'll be fine, Greg. *You* be safe. Call me as soon as it's done."

He kissed me again, then grabbed his gear. "Let's go," he said to the men.

Jackson gave me a nod, and they all headed out. I did as Greg had asked and set the security system, then paced the floors. I wasn't at all worried about something happening to me while he was gone.

But I was more terrified than I would ever show him that something was going to happen to him.

THE MINUTES TICKED BY SLOWLY AS I WAITED FOR HIM TO call. Minutes turned to hours as the sky grew dark and the moon rose in the sky.

Still, no call.

I wanted to call him, wanted to at least text to ask if he was okay. But distracting him could be a fatal mistake.

So I waited.

Shortly before the clock struck midnight, my phone finally rang. I felt a rush of relief until I saw it wasn't Greg's number on the screen—it was an unfamiliar number with the Rosemary Mountain area code. I hesitated, just for a moment, then answered.

"Hello?" I asked.

"Yes, is this Janet Sullivan?" A quiet woman's voice spoke.

"It is."

"I'm calling from Rosemary Mountain General Hospital. I'm so sorry to tell you this over the phone. Your friend, Sheriff Morrison, was badly injured tonight. He's mostly been unconscious, but he came to briefly. He was saying your name, crying out for us to call you. We got your number from his phone. I think you need to come up here."

My heart stopped in my chest.

"How...how bad is it?" I stammered, my voice shaking. I sank to the floor, right where I was standing.

"I'm afraid I can't discuss his condition," she said, continuing to speak in the quiet, unemotional tone of someone who was used to seeing tragedy everyday. "But I really do recommend that you get up here as quickly as possible."

"Of course," I said, letting out a shuddering breath. "I'll be there as soon as I can. What about Jackson? I mean, Deputy Ford. Is he up there too? Where is Agent Dawson?"

She paused for a moment. "I can't discuss the condition of any other patients, ma'am."

"Understood." I hung up the phone and held it to my chest like it could bring me comfort somehow. If I understood her correctly, Jackson was injured too, likely too badly to call me as well. I was certain he would have called me himself if it was only Greg who had gotten injured.

Something must have gone terribly wrong when they went to arrest Mark. My eyes swam with tears, picturing Greg lying in a hospital bed, calling for me.

I stood up and shook myself. I couldn't fall apart now, no matter how much I wanted to. Greg needed me. I had to pull it together and get to him.

I took a deep breath and gave myself thirty seconds to strategize. Clothes. Clothes and a toothbrush. When he recovered—because he *had* to recover—he would want a toothbrush and clean clothes to come home in. And since I had no intention of leaving his side until he did, I would need some things too.

I grabbed the same bag I had taken to the cabin and threw in the basics as quickly as possible. I let Thor outside to do his business—there was no avoiding it now; he couldn't wait any longer for Greg to come home—then locked up the house and headed out to the barn where Greg had stored my rental car.

Hold on, Greg. I'm coming.

CHAPTER FORTY-FOUR

Greg

MY BODY ACHED WITH FATIGUE. I WAS GETTING TOO OLD for this.

Although, who was I kidding? I still loved a good operation. I'd catch up on sleep later.

"Good work," I said, clapping Jackson on the back when he and Agent Dawson returned from dropping Mark off to be processed into the county jail for the night. "Thanks for your assistance, Agent Dawson."

"Same to you," he said, grinning back. "Now the fun part: paperwork."

I laughed. "Good thing that's all you guys. I'm not on the case, remember?"

Dawson snorted and shook his head. "Yeah. That's your story and you're sticking to it. Be safe driving home."

I smiled. *Home.* I had a beautiful woman waiting on me there, and the man who had threatened her was safely behind bars. It was only a matter of time before he gave up his partner. It was going to be a good night.

"Have you called her yet?" Jackson asked, pulling me out of my thoughts.

"What?"

"Janet," he said, rolling his eyes. "She told you to call her when this was over, to let her know you're safe."

"Oh, yeah." A stab of guilt hit. In the excitement, I had forgotten all about it. I always focused completely on an operation, forgetting about everything else until the smoke had cleared. "I'll call her right now."

The phone rang several times before she answered—but the woman who answered wasn't her. A too-familiar voice said hello, sending ice up my spine.

"Why do you have Janet's phone?" I barked out. Jackson immediately looked up from his desk and moved toward me.

"Because," said the smooth voice from the other line. "I also have her. And if you want to see your girlfriend again, you'll let my boyfriend go. Even trade. That's the only way this works."

"Your *boyfriend*?" I blanched. *No.* This could not be happening.

"That's right," she said with an edge to her voice. "Oh, I know what you thought. That nobody would ever want somebody like me. Poor, pitiful me. Alone and miserable, with only her cats to keep her comfort. I saw how quickly you always wanted to get away from me. How *boring* you found me. The joke's on you, Sheriff. You have no idea who I am or what I'm capable of. But you'll find out."

"Ms. Hall, I'm sorry if I hurt your feelings. Let's talk this out. Please, don't hurt Janet." My mind was racing a million miles an hour.

She laughed again. That laugh had made me cringe a million times, but it now sent ice straight to my gut. "Oh, I've already hurt her a bit. Oops. My bad. But she'll be fine. *If* I get Mark back. And while we're at it, we should discuss the way things are going to work from here on out."

"From here on out?"

"Yes. In case you hadn't figured it out yet, I was the brains behind our little operation. I decided I'm tired of being nothing more than an administrative assistant, handling schedules and making coffee for everyone more *important* than me." Her voice dripped with disdain. "I'm smarter than all of you, and I want a piece of the pie. I still plan on getting that piece, Sheriff. There's a vacuum in Rosemary Mountain, an empty seat at the head of the table since you took down the former king. That spot is mine. You can work for me, the way it's always been here. Or…"

Her voice trailed off, replaced by Janet's cry of pain.

My heart clenched. "Stop!" I commanded. "Don't hurt her. Don't lay a finger on her."

She laughed. "How adorable. The sheriff is in love." Her voice hardened. "But so am I, and you're not going to take that from me. He was already taken from me once before. I will not lose him again. I want Mark back."

"You know that's not possible," I said, trying to make my voice non-threatening. "TBI is involved. I can't just make that go away."

This time, she laughed even louder. "Sure you can. You're the *sheriff*. You can do whatever you want. Or at least you used to be able to. Now, you'll do whatever *I* want. You have one hour."

The phone went silent.

I stared at it until Dawson shook me, getting my attention.

"What the hell is going on?" he asked.

"We've gotta talk," I said.

CHAPTER FORTY-FIVE

Janet

I woke up groggy, with a sharp pain in my head. Opening my eyes felt like running a marathon. When I did, I was met with darkness.

What happened?

It took a few minutes to start coming back to me. The last thing I remembered was hurrying out to Greg's barn to get the rental car we still had stashed there. I hadn't been paying attention—all I could think about was getting to the hospital. Had I fallen?

I remembered fumbling with the barn lock, trying to get it open, then pain, then—nothing.

I forced my way up to a seated position, leaning against the wall at my back. My eyes were starting to adjust to the dimly lit room. Moonlight peeked through the broken blinds on a solitary window. This wasn't Greg's barn.

Slowly, my eyes adjusted, letting me take in more details. The room was small, with hard floors that felt like bare concrete. There was a twin-size bed in the corner. I shuddered, my mind instantly going to a thousand different true crime stories.

My heart pounded as I heard footsteps approaching. The door swung open and the lights came on, bathing the room in light that was now achingly harsh. I instantly closed my eyes, my head throbbing even more than before.

"Oh good. You're awake." The woman sounded amused.

"Where am I?" I asked, forcing my eyes open, blinking as I tried to adjust back to the blinding light.

"I'd be dumb to tell you that." She smirked. "And I'm not dumb. Listen up. We're about to call your boyfriend and tell him the terms of getting you back safely. "

"Greg's okay? How?" I grasped on to that one fact through my confusion.

"He's fine. I'm the one who called you, you idiot. Wow, you really are stupid."

"You're...you're the nurse?" Pieces started clicking into place. I had been tricked, and I had fallen for it hook, line, and sinker.

She laughed again, an ugly cackle that sent chills down my spine. "Now you're getting it. I could have taken you from his house, but this was easier. You're so gullible. You didn't even think twice before racing out to save him."

"You're a bitch," I said before I could stop myself.

She instantly crossed the room, slapping me so hard across the face that I fell over again, hitting my aching head on the concrete.

I stayed down. I wouldn't make that mistake again. I couldn't set her off because I still had hope to cling to—Greg was okay. He wasn't injured in the hospital. He would find me and save me.

I knew it.

Chapter Forty-Six

Greg

My world felt like it was crashing down around me. I never should have left Janet alone, especially when we had reason to believe that Mark had a female partner.

But I had underestimated her. Mark had done all the dirty work thus far, and I had assumed whoever he was working with was just a source of information. I had never expected his partner to actually go after Janet. Not really. Mark was the only threat in my eyes. I never would have left Janet alone otherwise, no matter how much I wanted in on the arrest.

Aubrey must have tricked Janet somehow, because the alarm hadn't gone off. I could see that Janet had disarmed it herself, had opened the door for some reason.

It was all my fault.

The mood turned serious as Agent Dawson, Jackson, and I all strategized. We couldn't involve anyone else from my office, just in case. I hoped beyond hope Aubrey was working alone. But until I knew for sure, I couldn't risk anyone else knowing.

Not with Janet's life on the line.

Aubrey had called back with specific instructions. I was to meet her at the wildlife refuge at two a.m., with Mark in hand. I had to come alone or Janet would die. I had to turn Mark over first or Janet would die.

Basically, if I screwed up in any way at all, Janet would die.

I knew she'd picked the wildlife refuge because it didn't have any cameras. And despite her annoyance that I didn't pay her enough attention, I also knew she was smarter than she looked—smarter than this unsuccessful takeover attempt showed. She had always been diligent in her work, detail oriented, with good ideas.

She had also been smart enough to ensure we couldn't get a location off the cell phones she was using to call in. Working with law enforcement for years had taught her a trick or two, and she was clearly intelligent enough to use them.

I was pretty sure her downfall was making Mark her partner. That at least meant she had a weakness, because she was willing to let him screw up and make stupid moves all for the sake of their partnership. She was in love and I would use that if I could.

But I knew better than to underestimate her again.

I PACED MY OFFICE WHILE AGENT DAWSON QUESTIONED Mark, trying to get any information about where Aubrey might be holding Janet. We didn't have much time, but if we could take her by surprise before she went to the refuge, we would have a better chance of getting Janet away safely.

The minutes crawled by until Dawson strode down the hall, looking confident.

"Well?" I asked, impatient for answers.

"Mark isn't talking. Thankfully, Ford is good with a computer. Aubrey Hall has a lake house over on the north side of the lake. It's not in her name. It technically belongs to her aunt, the one who used to work here. She could be there. We're also assuming she has a key to Mark's rental and may have gone there. That's easily checked. We know she owns a house here in town, and she has a storage building over on Eighth. Number forty-two."

I nodded. "Good. What are you thinking?"

"He's looking into those options more now. Then we'll make a plan." Dawson clapped me on my shoulder with a look of empathy on his face. "Hang in there. We'll get her."

I nodded, my lips tight, as the minutes continued to crawl by.

Jackson joined us relatively quickly, though it felt like forever. I was hoping desperately for good news. Three of the four options were minutes away. I just hoped she wasn't at the lake house. The lake was a forty-five minute drive at best. We'd have to leave now and drive like maniacs to get there and back before the two-a.m. deadline, and if she wasn't there, all our time would be wasted.

"What did you find out?" I asked, unable to keep the growl out of my voice.

"I think our best bet is the lake house," he said with a disappointed look on his face. He clearly knew that was bad news for us. "I woke the rental owner up. She wasn't happy, but she checked her cameras. Nobody's shown up since we grabbed Mark. Called the storage lockers too. Finally got someone. They checked their system. Nobody's been there, either. Aubrey's too smart to go to her own house. She knows it's the first place we would check. But we wouldn't know about the lake house if Mark hadn't told us. So that makes the most sense."

"Alright," I said. It was the worst-case scenario, but Jackson was right. It was our only real option. "Let's go."

Agent Dawson put a hand on my shoulder. "You know you can't go," he said. "Not this time. You're way too close to this. Besides, you've got to stay here in town. If we're wrong, you have to show up at the reserve at two. We can't risk you missing that meeting."

He was right, as much as I hated it.

"Janet, she—" My voice choked up.

"I know," he said, giving me a look like he really did. "We've got this. I've got backup coming in. I'll have some meet us at the lake house, and some will head here to back you up at the reserve. Hang tight."

"Call me the second you know something," I said.

"We will."

He clasped my hand again before heading out the door, with Jackson following him, leaving me alone to pace the floors and wait for answers.

EXACTLY FORTY-TWO MINUTES LATER, JACKSON CALLED. "She's not here," he said, the disappointment leaking through the phone. "I'm sorry. I got it wrong."

I closed my eyes, fighting back the waves of fear that hit, knowing we weren't any closer to finding her.

"It's alright," I said, my voice gruff. "We'll get her. Let me know what your next move is."

I clicked off the phone and headed straight to where Mark was being held.

It was time to take things into my own hands.

I HAD MARK PLACED BACK IN AN INTERVIEW ROOM AND GAVE him just a minute to acclimate before I joined him.

"I know what this is," said Mark, rolling his eyes. "Good cop, bad cop. You get that scary agent to put some fear in me about how bad all this is going to be, then you come in here all nice and friendly. Hometown sheriff just taking care of his people, right? Smooth me over, make me feel like I can trust you. Well, it won't work. I didn't talk to him, and I'm not going to talk to you."

Adrenaline coursed through me. "Good cop, bad cop. Sure, we can play that game. You just got one thing wrong."

"Oh yeah? What's that?"

I narrowed my eyes at him, making sure I had his full attention. "I'm the bad cop." I then proved my point by crossing the room and putting my fist through the wall behind his head.

Mark's eyes widened in shock. He raised his hands and backed away. "Look, I don't want any trouble."

"Then you shouldn't have started any," I said, my tone low and deadly as I stepped toward him again, throwing a chair across the room.

I had no intention of actually laying a hand on him. There were still lines I wouldn't cross. But he didn't need to know that.

"Stop!" he said, raising his hands, genuinely looking panicked. "Stop. I'll tell you everything. Just stop. Please."

Coward. Just like I thought.

"Sit," I said, crossing my arms. I planned to stand over him, keeping him in fear. It obviously worked.

I had to wonder if that's how Ms. Hall manipulated him.

"I don't know where she is," he said, shaking. He immediately put his hands up again when I cracked my knuckles. "But I have some ideas!"

"Start talking."

Chapter Forty-Seven

Janet

I heard the woman's directions to Greg on the phone. After that, she turned the light back off and left me without looking back. The sound of the lock turning on the door felt deafening. My chest tightened at the thought of being trapped in here.

Would she really let me go? That was doubtful.

Greg would find me.

I had to hold on to that hope.

Time passed slowly. I tried to get my bearings. The throbbing in my head was even worse after having been hit, but I forced myself to block out the pain and look around. I wasn't bound in any way, which honestly made me even more scared. It made me worry she simply never meant to come back for me.

I tried the door, just in case, despite having heard the lock click. It was locked tight, just as I'd feared. My chest constricted again. *Deep breaths, in and out. Breathe in for four, hold it, breathe out for four.* All the meditation and yoga classes I had attempted came back to me. It helped—a little. Enough to make me open my eyes and try again.

The window was small and high off the floor. I walked over to it, wondering if I could reach it. That was a definite no, even when I attempted jumping—a move I instantly regretted, as my head swam and the room spun when my feet hit the floor, forcing me to sit and rest again. *Deep breaths.*

If I moved the bed over, I could stand on it. From there, I thought I might be able to at least grab the bottom of the window. I was strong. My trainer made me do pull-ups every week in the gym. If I could grab it, I could—what? Try to open it? I wasn't sure I could keep myself up one-handed while the other hand tried to open the window. But I had to try. What else could I do?

I listened closely at the door, making sure I couldn't hear my captor. Everything was silent. I hoped she had left, hoped she was far, far away. If she heard me moving the bed across the concrete floor... But I couldn't think of that.

I had to try.

The sound of the bed scraping across the concrete floor was even worse than I had imagined. There were no rollers on the solid wood bed frame—just metal bottoms that scraped the concrete in a horrid way. Every inch was like nails on a chalkboard. After the first couple of inches, I stopped, listening again.

Nothing.

I breathed a sigh of relief and scooted it an inch at a time, needing to stop and rest in between movements. Was this all from the head wound, or had she drugged me? I didn't know, and I was scared to find out. Both scenarios felt terrifying.

But that was a future problem.

Right now, I took just one painful movement at a time. One inch, then another, and another, always stopping to listen for footsteps.

It took what felt like an eternity to move the bed, proving I was weaker than I had realized. A twin-size bed wasn't that heavy, even with the real wood frame. Whether it was drugs or the head injury, I had been significantly weakened. It would be even more important for me to be smart.

Because based on her slap, she wasn't weak at all. If she wanted to, she could tear me apart.

I gave myself some time to rest, holding my aching head in my hands, before attempting my exit.

But when footsteps echoed down the hall, I knew I didn't have another minute to wait.

Chapter Forty-Eight

Greg

I parked my truck at Emerson's cabin and jogged up toward Patricia Kistler's house.

Once Mark had started talking, I couldn't get him to shut up. Apparently, Aubrey had been his high school girlfriend. Most of the things he had gotten in trouble for were things she had talked him into doing. She was conniving and wanted to get back at everyone at school who had excluded her or slighted her in any way, but she didn't like to get her hands dirty. Mark had a lot of rage and needed an outlet for it.

The two were a perfect pair—in his mind at least.

Aubrey had been furious when the Kistlers sent Mark away. They had kept in touch through letters over the years, but Mark had always refused to return to Rosemary Mountain—until a few weeks ago, when Aubrey presented him with a plan to get revenge on everyone who had torn them apart. She wanted to take over Rosemary Mountain by building a new organization to replace the one I had just taken down. A romantic sentiment, in Mark's eyes. They would rule it together.

I didn't bother pointing out that extorting money from business owners didn't do a damn thing to change the past.

The most important piece of information he had given me was that part of their plan involved getting revenge on his mother. Aubrey had somehow managed to obtain a job as Patricia's weekly housekeeper, thus getting a key to her house. They had been tormenting Patricia ever since, leaving threats from the son she had abandoned. Mark admitted they planned on killing her at some point.

No wonder Patricia had been terrified when I'd asked about her having another son.

Mark had told me there was an outdoor entrance to the basement. Patricia never went down there anymore, he said. It was where he had hidden after placing the photographs on Janet's and Emerson's vehicles the night he seemed to disappear into thin air.

It was a perfect hideout, one I never would have suspected. It was also just minutes from the wildlife refuge where I was supposed to meet Aubrey. It fit the bill.

I just had to pray I was right because I was running out of time.

I PARKED NEARLY HALF A MILE DOWN FROM PATRICIA'S house, a calculated decision. The jog wasn't an easy one—gravel roads and mountain inclines required some exertion I would have rather saved in case I had a fight ahead of me. But I couldn't risk Aubrey seeing my truck approach.

I moved toward the house slowly, getting my bearings. I didn't want Patricia to spot me, either. I doubted she was involved with any of this, but either way, her spotting me could end in disaster.

Her porch lights were on, and I could see lights on in the house, but there was no movement in any of the windows.

I stayed in the treeline, slowly making my way around the house, grateful they hadn't cleared more land when they built. I had always thought it was crazy to leave so many tall trees where they could fall on your house during a storm, but right now, I was thankful for the cover as I scoped out the place.

At the back of the house, I spotted it—the almost hidden entrance tucked away behind the landscaping. It looked like an old-fashioned root cellar, which was interesting in and of itself since this house wasn't that old in the scheme of things.

I held my breath, scanning the yard and listening for movement, before sprinting from the trees to the entrance, crouching down quickly when I got there.

Locked.

Of course. I started to work on the lock when I heard a crash followed by a loud scream.

Janet.

I dropped my tools and ran toward the sound without a thought. As I turned the corner, I saw Janet halfway out of a storm window. She clawed her way forward, with blood dripping down the side of her face.

I raced to her and realized Aubrey had her legs and was attempting to pull her back in. Janet was putting up a fight but wasn't strong enough to break free.

"Let her go!" I yelled, dropping down where Aubrey could see me.

Her eyes were crazy. "Not until you give me Mark!"

"It's over," I barked out as Janet clung to me. I began to heave Janet out of the window but stopped when Aubrey pulled a large knife out of her pocket.

"I'll kill her!" she said, jabbing the tip of the knife into Janet's stomach. "I'll gut her like a fish!"

Janet's face turned white.

"Stop!" I said, releasing my grip, not wanting to put any pressure on that blade.

Aubrey immediately pulled her back through the window, away from my arms. I froze, scanning Janet's body. Blood seeped through her shirt but, thank God, the amount of blood suggested it was just a flesh wound.

Aubrey held the knife to Janet's neck, using her as a shield. "I swear, if you don't bring me Mark, this is the last time you'll ever see your girlfriend alive."

"How do you think I found you?" I asked, taking another calculated risk. I needed to get her off-balance, needed to distract her long enough to make a move.

"What?" she asked, confused.

"How do you think I found you?" I repeated patiently. "Mark told me where you were. He gave you up, Aubrey."

Now it was her turn to turn white. "He would never."

"But he did," I said. "I think he's scared of you. Doesn't like how far you pushed things."

"Scared of *me?*" She seemed genuinely confused. "I would never hurt Mark."

"His exact words about you were that you're mean and conniving. Maybe you've been bossing him around too much. Maybe he was afraid you would turn on him eventually, like those rabbits you killed and those fires you started. Maybe he was worried you'd slice him up like you did poor Thomas."

Now she looked truly shocked—and angry. I hoped with all my heart I hadn't screwed up, as I anxiously watched the knife she still held against Janet's throat.

"Is that what he told you?" she spit out. "I didn't kill those rabbits! He did that!"

"Oh," I said, drawing out the word like I was finally realizing the truth. "I get it. He did the dirty work but threw you under the bus for it."

"I had nothing to do with Thomas," she said with a look of disgust on her face. "That was all Mark. Thomas shouldn't have confronted him. Mark always wanted to get back at him for sticking his head in the toilet too many times in middle school. Thomas was stupid enough to give him a chance."

"Well, I guess it's your word against his," I said coolly. "But considering I'm watching you hold a knife to someone right now..."

"No, it's not just my word against his, I have proof!" Her face was triumphant.

"Proof?"

"Of course." She laughed now, relaxing a bit as she relished telling me just how smart she was. The knife inched away from Janet's neck, helping me relax a bit too.

"What proof do you have?" I knew she wanted to tell me. It was just a matter of keeping her talking.

"Video, of course. Lessons from Sheriff Joe 101. Keep receipts for everything. Sets you up well for blackmail later on."

"Interesting," I said, making my voice sound impressed. "You're very smart."

"Of course I am," she said, shaking her head. "It's a shame you didn't see that sooner." She glared at Janet and nudged the knife upward again.

My heart slammed into my chest.

"You and I could make a good team," Aubrey said, turning her eyes back to me. "Better than me and Mark. Mark's weak, obviously. I guess it took all of this for me to see how pathetic he really is. He couldn't do any of it right." She rolled her eyes. "I thought fate was bringing us together again, but maybe I was wrong. You're not weak though, are you?" Her eyes drifted toward mine, swimming with a lust for power. "You and I could *own* this town. And nobody would ever see it coming. Mark can take the fall for all of it, and we can go back to work tomorrow like nothing ever happened."

"That's not going to happen, Aubrey."

She turned her eyes to Janet and scowled. "What does she have that I don't have anyway?"

My heart.

"It's not about her," I said, keeping my tone easy. I didn't want to anger her, didn't want her to do anything else to Janet. I was calculating how quickly I could swing down into the room and if there was any way I could move fast enough to hit her before she saw it coming. I had my gun on me, but I was at an awkward angle and shooting would endanger Janet as well.

But if she kept nudging that knife into Janet's neck, I might not have another choice.

"Why don't you put the knife down?" I asked, keeping my voice calm like I was speaking to a child. "Let's talk this out without violence."

She immediately tensed, and I knew I had taken the wrong tack.

"I'm not going down for any of this," she warned. "I may not have killed before, but I'll kill both of you before I go to jail."

I shook my head. "It doesn't have to be like that. If you're right that Mark is the one who did everything, then nothing you've done is that serious according to the law. You don't have a record. You'll get off easy and you know it. Hell, if you cooperate with evidence against Mark, you may not even get any time at all."

Over my dead body.

Her eyes went crazy again. "I'm tired of people telling me what to do!" she shrieked.

I was losing her.

Janet's face went white as the knife pressed harder against her neck. I was calculating the shot, with my hand on the butt of my gun, out of sight, when the door to the room swung open.

"What in the—" Patricia's voice dropped off suddenly as she took stock of the situation.

Aubrey swung toward the door, pivoting her whole body, still keeping Janet in front of her as a shield. I acted in a split second, swinging through the window. Before Aubrey realized what was happening, I planted my fist into her face, knocking her out cold. The knife clattered to the ground, and Janet fell into my arms, sobbing.

"Sheriff Morrison, what on earth is going on here?" Patricia asked, her voice cold and reprimanding.

"Sit," I commanded, pointing toward the bed. I wasn't in the mood. "And be quiet."

I turned my attention back to Janet.

"It's okay, honey. I've got you. It's over now." I stroked her hair, trying to soothe it all away, holding her close enough to reassure my heart that she was safe.

"I knew you would come," she said, clinging to me. "I knew you would find me."

"Looks like I barely had to," I said, chuckling softly. "You were almost to freedom yourself."

"Almost. I just wasn't strong enough or fast enough."

I held her close until her breathing calmed, keeping my eyes trained on Aubrey—just in case.

"You know," I said to Janet, knowing it would make her laugh, "this is the first time I've ever hit a woman."

She did laugh, soft and sweet, easing my heart more than anything else could. "I won't count it against you."

Chapter Forty-Nine

Janet

I felt full of butterflies as Greg and I sat on the front porch of Daphne's cottage, waiting for the bride and groom to pull into the driveway. They were nearly here, and I couldn't wait to give them my good news. Philip had been incredibly understanding about my resignation. There was an endless line of people who would be overjoyed to take the position. I was replaceable.

To him, anyway.

I owed the company a bit of money for the relocation expenses they had incurred, and it would take some time to get my things back to me, but that was fine.

I had everything I needed right here.

Greg squeezed my hand as Emerson's truck pulled in. We hadn't told them about us, either, but I somehow doubted they would be surprised.

I was pretty certain that was part of why Daphne had insisted I stay with him in the first place.

Emerson went around to Daphne's side and opened the door, lifting her out of the truck and into his arms. "Gotta carry the bride across the threshold," he called out with a grin that lit up his whole face.

Greg moved to open the door for them, trailing his fingers down my back as he did.

Oh, how I loved when he did that.

We followed the couple in and poured the champagne we had waiting for them. They told us all about their honeymoon, two weeks holed up at a cabin Emerson's family owned on Lake Michigan. Two weeks ago, I would have cringed at the idea of a honeymoon taking place in a cabin instead of at a luxury resort. But after my time with Greg, I couldn't imagine a better way to honeymoon than to get away from the world in a private little paradise.

"Catch us up on what went down here," Emerson asked, obviously curious. "Are we in the clear?"

Greg nodded. "We're in the clear." He gave them the rundown on everything that had happened while they were gone.

Daphne shivered. "Man, the Kistlers just keep coming back to haunt us, don't they?"

"Probably feels that way," Greg agreed. "But I don't think we'll have any more trouble from them."

"So Patricia wasn't involved at all?" Emerson asked, clarifying.

"Nope." Greg shook his head. "She had no idea Mark and Aubrey were using her basement. They had just about convinced her Mark's ghost was haunting her. I guess it never crossed her mind that Mark would really come back. They were torturing her, with plans to eventually kill her as punishment for sending Mark away. In good news, Patricia is moving to California to be with her sister. I think she has a lot of healing to do from everything she's been through. She's just now starting to realize how screwed up her life has been. She really needs some help from victims' services, and I'm talking with her sister about how to make that happen."

Daphne leaned forward, curious. "So did you ever figure out what was going on with Sanderson?"

Greg cracked a grin. "Yeah. It wasn't about the threats. Turns out, his wife told him she thought she was pregnant. The man was near having a heart attack from anxiety about it all, especially since he had a vasectomy—without telling her—a year ago."

"Oh." Emerson's eyes got big. "Well, I suppose that did stress him out."

Greg nodded. "Yep. She wasn't pregnant after all, but at the time, he was worried sick thinking she was cheating on him. He couldn't very well confront her about it without telling her about his operation. They already have three kids and she wanted a fourth, but he didn't..." Greg shrugged. "Hopefully the stress taught him to be open and honest with his wife from now on."

"And Parker? I'm guessing she's not the Billy who nearly got sent to kill me?" Daphne asked.

Trouble passed over Greg's face. "I still don't know for sure who that Billy was. It's a loose end that's going to bother me until we finally tie it up. But I don't have any real reason to believe it's her. She has no known connections to any of that, and Agent Dawson dug deep in his investigation. For now, I'm trusting her."

"What about the rumors John told you about?" Emerson asked, still curious. "Who was saying you were about to be out of office?"

Greg rolled his eyes. "That was all Aubrey. I guess part of her plan to take power was spreading rumors and division throughout the office. She'd whisper in Miller's ear about how wrong it was for me to work with Jackson instead of him. She'd whisper in Tracy's and Parker's ears that I thought women weren't fit for law enforcement, and so on. I guess it was her way of trying to limit my influence and increase hers. She started a rumor that I was in trouble with the TBI and would be removed from office. Whispered it in Miller's ear, and he happily spread it to everyone else. All of it was complete bull."

"Sounds like you've got your work cut out for you still," Daphne commented.

"Things have been better, actually," Greg said.

I reached out and took his hand without thinking. Daphne's eye caught mine. She raised an eyebrow and smiled but didn't say anything.

"How have they been better?" Emerson asked, taking the last swig of his champagne.

Greg shrugged. "All this gave us the opportunity to really clear the air. Once we figured out where the root of all the anger and division was coming from, things started improving pretty quickly. I think Tracy and Miller both felt dumb for having been influenced so easily by Aubrey. They both apologized to me. Miller and I actually had some good conversations about how he can serve the community in a better way. I think we're going to be able to work together a lot better in the future."

He glanced over at me with a smile before putting an arm around me. "It didn't hurt that Janet cooked a feast for the entire office to celebrate our win. This woman can win anyone over with her food."

Daphne poured fresh champagne for all of us. "To love and new beginnings." She winked at me before raising her glass in a toast.

"To love and new beginnings," I echoed.

"Hear, hear," added Emerson as we clanked our glasses.

Greg cleared his throat. "Speaking of love and new beginnings..." He got down on one knee and pulled something from his pocket.

I gasped and covered my mouth with my hand. I couldn't believe this was happening.

Greg grinned at me. "Janet, you told me I needed to give you a real proposal."

"It's so soon though," I said, shaking my head. "Are you sure?" My heart pounded as I waited for him to answer.

He nodded. "I know we've both regretted moving too quickly in the past, and I understand if you want more time. I'll wait as long as you want. But I've never felt more certain about anything in my life. All I've been waiting for is for Daphne and Emerson to get back into town because I figured we'd like to celebrate with family. I love you. I'm so damn grateful your daughter came here stirring up trouble, forcing you to come here to bail her out of jail. I'm even more grateful you decided to stay this time. I want to wake up next to you every morning. I want to come home to you every evening. I want to sit in our porch rockers and grow old together—just not too fast." His eyes twinkled, and I knew exactly what he was thinking. "Janet, I love you. Will you marry me?"

"Yes," I said, unable to keep the grin from my face. "Of course I'll marry you."

"So you're staying?" Daphne asked, unable to wait. "You're not going to Paris?"

"Yes, I'm staying," I said, laughing. I turned back to Greg and stared into his beautiful gray eyes. "I found something much better than Paris right here."

Epilogue

Three Months Later

Janet

"It's perfect," I whispered, my eyes filling with tears as I surveyed my image in the mirror.

"Of course it is," Willa laughed. "I made it. Everything I make is perfect."

"It is," I agreed, flashing her a smile in the mirror. "I'm glad I convinced you to go into business with me. I'm excited to work with you."

She squeezed my arm. "I'm excited to work with you, too. This dress really is perfect. But it helps that you're a beautiful bride."

A bride. I couldn't believe it. I had once sworn I would never marry again, would never tie myself down in such a miserable institution.

But it was completely different with Greg. Today was just about celebrating what we already knew: that we loved each other, that we belonged together, and that we would spend the rest of our lives continuing to love each other well.

Very well, I thought, blushing.

Being with him was everything I had ever wanted.

It was as perfect as this creamy silk gown Willa had made for me.

"You look beautiful, Mom," Daphne said, joining me in front of the mirror. She was beautiful too—glowing, with the barely visible swell of her new bump peeking out from the burnt-orange silk dress Willa had made for her.

We were both starting new chapters of our lives, and I was more grateful than ever that I had found a home in Rosemary Mountain, where I could be part of hers.

"You know, I do have to ask you something though," she said, her voice suddenly serious.

"What's that?" I replied, turning toward her.

Her face stayed grave, but her eyes twinkled. "Don't you think we should postpone this for a while? After all, typical engagements last a year or more. It's only been three months! And a homemade dress? Really? What will people think?" She clucked her tongue and shook her head in mock judgment.

My cheeks turned red. "I'm sorry, Daphne. I was awful."

She smiled and shook her head. "I'm just teasing you," she said before kissing me on the cheek. "I'm so glad you're happy now."

She handed me my bouquet, one she and Fiona had made themselves with the most beautiful fall flowers from Fiona's garden. It was a gorgeous symphony of autumn tones. Fiona was magic in the garden as well.

The bouquet was perfect for today. No roses or equally stuffy flowers for me this time. I wanted sunflowers because they reminded me of Greg—tall, open, and full of sunshine. They also made me think of our time together in his cabin, how the world lit up with golden light, washing over all the wounds from our pasts and healing us in ways we hadn't known we needed.

Yes, sunflowers were perfect for walking toward him and pledging to be by his side for the rest of our days.

We said "I do" in that golden hour, underneath the tree by the pond in Greg's valley land. *Our* valley land. Our friends and family surrounded us, and as I looked around, all I could think was how overjoyed I was to have finally found this—to have found my home, my community, and my love.

As we walked down the aisle, hand in hand, finally husband and wife, Greg whispered in my ear. "I'm going to bring you back here later tonight, when everyone has gone home, to finish what you started the day of our first kiss."

I blushed furiously. "Greg, stop," I said, scolding him playfully.

He knew I didn't mean it.

We had already relived that afternoon more than once, and it felt like the perfect day to do it again.

Acknowledgments

My first thanks belongs to my incredible husband, Brandon. Thank you for all the ways in which you support my writing and encourage me to keep going. You're the reason I believe in love stories. You are my best friend and soulmate, and our life together means more to me than anything else in the world.

Thanks also to my sons, who light up my life and remind me to make time for fun. You both are amazing people, and I'm so grateful to be your mom!

Special thanks to my beta team members Jessica, Sarah, and Candice for your constant support and feedback. I appreciate you more than you know!

Thanks also to my editor, Mickey Reed, for your exceptional work on this book—and for never threatening to take away my many em dashes. You are a joy to work with!

This beautiful cover was created by Brooke Passmore of BY THE BROOKE DESIGNS. Thank you, Brooke, for continuing to create such perfect covers for the Rosemary Mountain books! I'm always in awe of how you nail the vibe so perfectly for each book.

Special thanks again to Juniper Tree Meadery and Weber's Book House, both in Paragould, Arkansas, for continuing to support this local author. I am truly grateful for your support! Readers, if you're ever traveling through Paragould, both places are worth a stop. They are incredible family-run businesses that truly embrace the local movement.

Finally, a big thank you to my friends, family, and community as a whole. I continue to be amazed by your support and encouragement. I hope you enjoy this romantic suspense spin-off series as much as you enjoyed Daphne's trilogy!

About the Author

Nicole Gardner lives in NE Arkansas with her husband, their two sons, and their two crazy dogs. If she's not at her desk, you'll likely find her either in the garden, or creating teas and tinctures in the kitchen.

Nicole's background is in psychology. This fascination with human behavior and relationship dynamics plays a significant role in her writing and the way she shapes her characters.

www.nicolegardnerbooks.com